THE SWEETEST MOMENT

A SWEET, SMALL TOWN ROMANCE

3 SISTERS CAFE
BOOK TWO

LAURA ANN

UNTITLED

"The Sweetest Moment"

Three Sisters Cafe #2

*To my father.
Your quiet support is everything
a daughter could wish for.*

ACKNOWLEDGMENTS

No author works alone. Thank you, Tami.
You make it Christmas every time
I get a new cover. And thank you to my Beta Team.
Truly, your help with my stories is immeasurable.

NEWSLETTER

You can get a FREE book by joining my Reading Family!
Every week we share stories, sales and good old fun.
Visit my website or facebook page to sign up!

PROLOGUE

FROM THE BACK OF "THE SWEETEST WORDS"

Harper pushed a piece of hair out of her face and studied her newest painting. It wasn't quite the type of work she normally did, but this one was special. She had been commissioned to paint a series of pictures that featured The Three Sisters Cafe signature desserts.

She was running a little behind…Austin was picking them up this morning, but Harper hadn't been able to stop herself from adding just a little more color.

Just as she finished cleaning her brushes, there was a knock at the door. "Perfect timing," she murmured to herself as she went to answer. "Austin! Come on in." Harper opened her door wider. "I've got your pictures back in the studio."

He rubbed his hands together, grinning wildly. "I can't wait to see them."

Harper led the way to the back. It was amazing how well Austin had settled into life here in small town USA. Especially after being such a big name and living in the city his whole life.

His brother, Tye, had moved down to Seagull Cove and almost immediately began to take online college classes. Last she'd heard, Tye was planning to go to college in person next fall. From her chats with

Aspen, Harper knew this was a big step for the young man who struggled in large, public settings.

He'd continued his writing, however, and apparently, had been hired for several guest blog gigs, which was doing a lot to boost his confidence after people realized he was the snarky voice behind the "Eat It Austin" posts.

As for Austin, he had also found a niche which fit him well. With his experience in building a brand, he had opened an online marketing business, building websites and promoting certain brands. It still required reading and writing, but not so much that he couldn't manage it with a little help.

He was now doing all the marketing for The Three Sisters Cafe, leaving Estelle more time to focus on decorating the treats and more wedding cake work, which had made her happy as well. The situation gave Austin the start he needed to get his business off the ground and Estelle had gratefully shifted her position after arriving home from Italy. Her father had been on the mend when she'd finally come home and the Harrison women were awaiting word that their parents were ready to come home.

The only downside to the story had been Austin's mom. She had been taken back to the rehab center in Portland, only to disappear once again. This time, however, she hadn't resurfaced. Aspen had confided in Harper that Austin had hired a private investigator to find her, but so far, she was staying out of the limelight.

For all they knew, she could have passed away on the street, marked as a Jane Doe, but Harper knew that Austin would keep looking until he had answers.

"Here we are," she announced, opening her studio door and breaking her line of thoughts. The winter had been busy and crazy as everyone had settled into their new roles and their little group of friends had welcomed Austin into their midst. But, Harper was getting anxious for the beauty of spring and the outside markets that would help her get into the sunshine and enjoy interacting with the public again.

Being an artist was a solitary life, which she didn't mind most of the time, but the last couple of years, she had found herself growing restless. It more than likely had to do with the fact that she couldn't seem to shake a crush on one stoic and as equally solitary lumberjack.

At least at the festivals, I can watch him do his live carving.

Other than when their friends gathered for game nights or to try one of Aspen's new desserts, she rarely had occasion to see the handsome Mason. But during the spring and summer, their schedules ran very similarly since he did log carving at live demonstrations at many of the markets.

Not that she should be looking forward to it. Trying to build her art into a full-time income took precedence right now and Harper knew she didn't have time for a relationship if she was ever going to prove herself to her mother and stop relying on a trust fund to pay the bills.

"Harper, they're perfect," Austin said with a smile.

He really had a nice smile. Aspen was so lucky. She was loved and adored by a great guy. Jealousy tried to rear its ugly head, but Harper pushed it back. It was no one's fault that the art world was a difficult one, or that her secret crush had to stay secret. It wasn't worth being upset at her friend's happiness because of it. Not to mention, it wasn't like Aspen and Austin's road to love had been easy.

"Do you have your part ready?" Harper asked.

Austin nodded. "It's in the car." He scrunched his nose. "Tye helped me write it, but it's ready."

"Awesome." She gathered up her canvases. "Let's get going."

It took no time at all for them to arrive at the cafe. Estelle let them inside. It was a Sunday afternoon, which meant they were closed to the public and it was the perfect time to set up a surprise for Aspen.

A half hour later, everything was in place and Austin was calling Aspen. "Hey, babe. Can you come down to the shop for a minute? I have an idea."

Harper held her breath, then relaxed when Austin gave them all the thumbs up.

"We don't have to leave completely, do we?" Estelle asked, raising her shoulders to her ears. "I was hoping to record this for Mom and Dad."

Austin pinched his lips between his teeth. "Do you mind doing it from the back corner, maybe? I'd like to keep her focus out here."

"Of course!" Estelle grabbed Harper's hand and with Maeve trailing behind, the girls made themselves as unobtrusive as possible in the back.

It only took a few minutes for Aspen to arrive. Short commutes was one of the perks of living in a small town and Harper's heart leapt to her throat. She was so excited for her best friend. All little girls dreamed of this day and it was wonderful that it was finally happening.

"Austin?" Aspen called as she pushed open the front door. She gasped and came to a halt when she saw the wall. "What's this?"

Austin stood in front of the latest decorations. They had displayed them on the wall around the leopard print sofa, which everyone referred to as "The A's Place". He held out his hands and Aspen slowly walked his way, taking in the pictures.

"Did Harper paint those?" Aspen asked. "They're beautiful."

Austin still didn't speak, instead guiding her to sit down. Once Aspen was seated, Austin knelt down on one knee, eliciting another gasp.

Harper clasped Estelle's hand, then forced herself to let go, so she wouldn't ruin the video. This was so exciting!

"Aspen Marguerite Harrison," Austin said carefully. "We both know I'm not much of a reader or writer, but I've spent my life hiding behind other people's words and I wanted to present myself to you with nothing between us. No fans, no internet, no ghost writers…just you, me and a proposal."

Aspen covered her mouth with her hands, tears beginning to trickle down her cheeks. Harper found her own eyes filling with similar emotions.

"I love you," Austin continued. "I love you more than I can express with or without help," he said with a smirk. "You're my rock. You're the reason I've survived the blowback from my job, you're the reason

I have a new job, you're the reason I wake up with a smile on my face and a bounce in my step."

Aspen reached out and cupped his cheek and Harper began to feel like she was intruding on an intimate moment. She glanced at Maeve, who pumped her eyebrows. Apparently, the sisters didn't have any trouble with it.

"I know what it's like to lose that light in my life and I never want to go through it again. I know that everyone refers to this corner as ours and I'm happy to keep going with that, which is why I had Harper paint your cakes. Those cakes are yours. They symbolize everything you are." He reached under the couch and pulled out a framed piece of paper. "And this is so we can put me up there with you."

Aspen took the frame and began to laugh through her tears. "I love you more than peanut butter, marshmallow surprise cake," she read the words with a laugh, then sniffed. "That's our cake," she rasped. "I made it with you in mind."

He nodded and cupped her face. "Which is why I'm going to ask you to keep making peanut butter, marshmallow surprise cake with me forever. Aspen, will you marry me? Will you help keep my days full of joy and my evenings full of sugary sweets?" He nodded to the frame. "Will you hang that on the wall and be my partner for the rest of my life?"

Harper put her clasped hands over her heart. What would it be like to have that kind of adoration aimed at her instead of listening to it spoken to someone else? Harper's heart ached with the desire for Mason to say those things to her, then immediately scolded herself for it. She needed to think of her career. Her mother would never let Harper live it down if she didn't prove once and for all that art was an actual career choice.

Clapping brought her out of her thoughts and she realized she had missed Aspen saying yes. At least, Harper assumed it was a yes, if the kiss Aspen and Austin were engaged in was anything to go by.

"Woo hoo!" Maeve hollered, followed by a very loud whistle.

Harper jerked to the side. "Whoa."

Maeve grinned. "Yeah. I've been practicing."

"I can't believe you guys were there the whole time!" Aspen said, wiping at her eyes and standing up.

"You were a little preoccupied," Estelle said wryly.

Harper held out her arms and hurried over. "Congrats," she whispered in her best friend's ear. "I'm so happy for you."

They pulled apart and Aspen positively glowed. "Thank you." She gave Harper another squeeze. "And thank you for the paintings. I LOVE them."

Harper smiled. "It was nothing."

"Of course, it wasn't." Aspen rolled her eyes. "Because you're amazing."

Harper just smiled and stepped back, letting everyone else squeal and celebrate the occasion. *If I was that amazing, I wouldn't be looking at another spring spent ogling a lumberjack from afar. I'd figure out how to have my cake and eat it too.* She shook her head. Now was not the time. This was a call to celebrate. Harper's nonexistent love life wasn't important. She clapped her hands loudly, getting everyone's attention. "Who wants cake?"

Laughter followed her call and slowly, they all worked their way to the kitchen. Harper was last as she wrestled with herself, but she was determined to stay focused. Aspen, Austin and cake were the subject of the moment. Nothing else. There would be time to sulk later. Right now, she had best friend duties to attend to and they were far more important.

CHAPTER 1

Harper carefully wrapped another canvas in brown paper. Finally, *finally,* after what seemed forever, spring was here, the sky was clearing from its perpetual gray and the humans were venturing into outdoor activities again.

As an artist who captured landscapes with her brush and paints, Harper always had a hard time staying put during the cold weather. Living on the Oregon Coast meant that she rarely saw snow, or sub zero temperatures, but the whole coastline seemed to lose its color and life during those few months. Brown and gray dominated the horizon and the bite of the ocean wind was enough to have anyone running for a cup of hot cocoa and the warmth of a crackling fire.

Her favorite time of year was filled with color and the opportunity to socialize with friends and customers in the outdoor art exhibits or open air markets found up and down the Pacific coastline. She loved chatting with the adults and children alike as they admired her work and asked questions about her technique.

Harper's cheeks flooded with warmth as she considered the other reason she was looking forward to the warm season.

Mason Turley.

While his day job consisted of working in the lumber industry, during the warm months, he could often be found at Harper's art festivals, doing live wood carvings. His skill with a chainsaw was awe inspiring, but Harper found herself staring at more than just the art.

Who could resist a man as tall and broad as a linebacker with the most mesmerizing golden eyes she had ever seen?

She shook her head. Apparently, she wasn't more immune than any of the other women who tried to swarm him at the festivals. The difference was that she couldn't let herself melt like a fangirl. Handsome or not, Harper was still in the middle of building her professional life and trying to break into the art world took *a lot* of time and persistence. She simply didn't have time for anything else. Not that her hormones were willing to listen to her logic.

She had known Mason for nearly five years, after she moved to the coast in order to make a career of her artistic talents. Her crush had come on slowly, though she'd thought him handsome from the beginning. A chat here…a laugh there…a moment when their eyes caught… his quiet willingness to help every person he came in contact with… Ugh!

The paper Harper was wrapping with tore at a corner and she grit her teeth to keep from saying a word her mother would definitely *not* approve of. She dropped the paper to the ground and began again, forcing her breathing to slow as she turned her mind to something other than her unrequited feelings for a handsome lumberjack.

It wasn't even fair to call them unrequited. Harper had never bothered to try and see if Mason could ever see her as more than a friend. She couldn't. For years, her mother had been breathing down her neck to try and force Harper into a mold that her artistic brain just didn't want to comply with. Sharon Woodson wanted her daughter to be a lawyer…just like her.

As a single mother, Sharon had learned that not all jobs paid the bills and Harper was more grateful than she could say that her mom worked two jobs, went back to school and managed to pass the bar exam, all while raising a little girl. Their life had gone from difficult to luxurious, all because of Sharon's dedication.

But Harper didn't have the same ideals. She saw how hard her mother worked, and admired her for it, but she wanted something different. Harper didn't want premature age lines. She didn't want to try to keep up with "The Good Old Boys" at work. She didn't want to create arguments or try to find holes in other people's stories.

Harper wanted to create. She loved color and nature and her mind often wandered to how she could capture the beauty around her. Sharon said it came from Harper's father's mother. A woman Harper had never met before her death. Sharon and her husband hadn't been together long, but it was enough that Harper's grandmother had left Harper a small trust fund that she'd been able to use to pay for art school and now help her live independently, despite her mother's complaints.

"There." Harper put the last canvas down, admiring her work. Everything was neat as a pin, just as it should be. She even had a few new paintings this time around in order to catch new eyes. After Austin, Aspen's husband, had asked her to paint some pictures of cake for their bakery, Harper had discovered she enjoyed the bright whimsy of the product and spent some time creating cute, food-centric pictures that would be darling in a little girl's room, or liven up a brightly colored kitchen.

With a deep breath and a practiced force of determination, she began hauling everything to her car. The crossover vehicle had a large back, which allowed her to drive her paintings around without worry of them being squished or broken during transport, and had been her first big splurge after arriving in Oregon.

After depositing the last canvas in the back, Harper shut the hatch and grabbed her buzzing phone from her back pocket. "Hey, Aspen!" Harper cried, recognizing her friend's number. "How goes the baking today?"

Aspen's laughter came through the tiny speaker. "We're almost sold out of the red velvet whoopie pies already," she replied. "So I'm busy whipping up another batch. Apparently, people are really into hand held desserts today."

"Who wouldn't be with that marshmallow filling you use," Harper teased. She could practically feel her pants getting tighter as she imagined eating more of Aspen's delicious treats. The whole town loved them, but Harper loved them a little too much.

"Let's just hope the trend continues," Aspen retorted. "It never seems to fail that I replenish something, only for people to decide they want mint instead of red velvet."

Harper grinned, but didn't respond. She completely understood the sentiment.

"Anyway…" Aspen continued. "I was calling to ask about the market today. Wait… It is today, right?"

"Yep."

"Oh, good." Aspen huffed. "For a second there, I thought maybe my brain was going crazy."

We call that newlywed brain, Harper thought, though she didn't bother saying it out loud. She was beyond happy for her friend. The road to Aspen and Austin's marriage had been a difficult one, and a very public one. There was no way to be anything but ecstatic that the two had finally gotten together and their marriage last month had been just as sweet as a bakery display case. "Nope. You're right on. I just finished packing the pictures and now I'm gonna shower."

Aspen laughed softly. "Sounds about right. The paintings always were the priority."

Harper shrugged even though Aspen couldn't see it. "People don't buy them based on how I look."

"True enough…mostly. So…what are the hours? And remind me what park you're in?"

"Haven Park. Eleven to seven." Harper had it memorized. She had been a little eager when the schedule had begun to emerge.

"Perfect," Aspen responded. "I don't have to leave early in order to make it."

"And if you showed up with leftovers…I certainly wouldn't be upset…" Harper hedged. Who needed slim hips? A couple of Aspen's cookies would definitely be worth the extra speed walk on the beach or another session of yoga.

"I'll see what I can do," Aspen said, her smile heard in her tone. "But I gotta run. See you later! And good luck!"

"Thanks!" Harper shut down the call and headed to her bathroom. Her cottage was tiny but cozy and it only took seconds to reach her destination, but she didn't mind.

Aspen's call had reminded Harper that she wasn't alone. She might live by herself and her work might be slightly isolating, but with friends and future customers on the horizon, Harper knew everything would be alright. Unrequited crush or not, she had everything she needed in order to be healthy and happy.

"Will these work for you?" Mr. Davidson asked Mason, waving his arms at a couple of logs.

Mason studied the wood. He already had plans in his head for what he wanted to do with them, but his designs had been in mathematical terms only. Now that the wood had actually been delivered, he needed to see it from all sides to make sure it would work. After walking a circle, Mason nodded. "Looks great." He stuck out his hand, shaking the festival director's hand. "Thanks for having them brought here."

Mr. Davidson beamed. "We're thrilled to have you doing a live exhibition," he said, pumping Mason's arm. "It always brings in more people to have a demonstration going on."

Mason smiled and nodded, then turned back to the logs. They were in great shape and he knew the wolf and bear he had planned would turn out great. Chainsaw carving was a creative outlet he loved, but didn't do as often as he would like. During most of the year he was too busy with his work in the lumberyard office, but he always itched to get outside, and this was his opportunity to do it.

Mason worked in sales for a large lumber mill, which allowed him to work from home. That was a definite perk since the main office was several hours away from the coast he enjoyed. But the best part of his job was that Maynard Lumber acted as a sponsor whenever Mason had a live carving session. It was the best of both worlds. He had permission from his boss to let loose his creative side, and the lumber company got free publicity.

Really, Mason knew he couldn't ask for a better set up. Yet, lately... he'd found himself feeling like something was missing. He couldn't quite find a word for his emotions, though he knew most people would say he was lonely. If he wanted to be brutally honest with himself, he probably was, but that didn't mean he had to like it.

A flash of blonde hair caught his attention and Mason jerked to look before catching himself. The woman didn't even notice his reaction and continued walking across the park, oblivious to his inner turmoil.

"Get yourself under control," Mason grumbled to himself. He shook his head. How stupid was it to react so strongly to blonde hair? Even if it had been Harper, jerking like an idiot would only have frightened her or made her believe Mason was having some kind of seizure.

As soon as he thought of her name, a picture of the petite woman flashed through his mind. Compared to his six-foot-three-inch frame, Harper was the size of a child. She was probably a full foot shorter than him, yet despite her height, her curves meant no one would ever mistake her for anything but a woman.

Clear, blue eyes that always seemed to see too much, and long, straight golden hair that looked like silk were her best features. Though soft pink lips and a dainty sprinkle of freckles across her nose didn't hurt either.

Mason shoved one of the logs over and began rolling it into a better position, his mind still stuck on the woman who had been invading his dreams lately. He had known her for several years, but it had only been recently that he'd noticed his feelings changing. They were part of the same large friend group in Seagull Cove and saw each other often, though at first Mason had only chatted with her occasionally. Now, however, he found himself looking for her whenever he entered a room. Her laughter drew him in like a bee to honey and if there was an open seat anywhere near her, he took it without hesitation.

Somehow, slowly, she had wiggled herself under his skin, though Mason couldn't exactly pinpoint the exact cause or moment. He was certainly attracted to her physically, but there was more. She was unerringly kind, something Mason thought a dying art in today's world. She was loyal and had a good sense of humor. She was creative and had always made him feel like a giant among men whenever she spoke of one of his creations, though her own artistic skills far surpassed his own. Being around her simply felt…good. And the more Mason did it, the more he wanted to.

This last winter had been a hubbub with Aspen and Austin's dating and eventual marriage, and Mason was truly happy for them both, though he wanted nothing to do with such a big spotlight himself. Now, however, things had calmed down and he was wishing he could make his move. If only he was in a position to do so.

Despite his wishes, his time, money and attention were already spoken for and until there was a change in the case…Mason knew he would only be able to give any woman half of himself, and he wanted more for someone like Harper.

"Mason!"

His entire body stiffened. *Speak of the angel.* He forced himself to move slowly as he turned around. "Harper! Hey." He waved his hand, knowing immediately he looked like an idiot. Perhaps the ground would swallow him up and he could try again another time?

No such luck.

Harper's smile was wide and stunning. Her even, white teeth were on full display. "I was hoping to see you here."

Mason blinked a couple of times. Was she…?

Harper's smile dropped a notch. "I just knew you'd be anxious to get out and get moving now that the weather's warming up." She looked up at him expectantly.

His burgeoning hope splattered like a broken egg on a sidewalk. Mentally face-palming himself for his over eagerness, he opened his mouth and prayed something intelligent came out. "Yeah…it's always nice to get outside." *Absolutely brilliant. Friends, idiot, just friends! She knows that, why can't you remember?*

"I'm excited to see what you create with the logs this time."

Mason looked at the wood and nodded. "Yeah. Should be fun."

Harper nodded with him, as if waiting for more, but Mason was tongue tied. She glanced over her shoulder. "Well…I better get unloaded and set up. The festival's opening soon." She took a few steps away, paused, then smiled and left.

Mason opened his mouth, but nothing came out and he snapped it shut again. *Can I help you unload? Did you paint a lot over the holidays? Anything new in your collection?* He growled low. What was wrong with him? How hard was it to carry on a conversation with someone he was *friends* with! She wasn't a stranger and she definitely wasn't going to bite his head off for speaking to her. In fact, *she* had started their chat in the first place!

Mason pushed a hand through his hair and rubbed down his beard. If his brother Crew saw him acting like such an idiot, there would never be an end to the teasing. Forcing his stupidity out of his head, Mason went back to putting the log in place. He might not be good with women, but darned if he couldn't handle wood.

This daydreaming of something he couldn't have was killing him. Every time he got close to Harper, he realized just how strong his crush was, but every time she walked away, his rational brain reminded him that he had a mission, and it didn't include getting cozy with a beautiful woman.

He finished setting the log upright and stepped back, breathing heavily. This was ridiculous. If he could handle dealing with whirling blades at fifty miles an hour, he could stay friends with a woman he was attracted to.

He glanced in the direction she had disappeared. He could do this. He *had* to do this, if only to try and salvage his pride. As soon as his first live demonstration was over, Mason determined that he was going to walk by her booth and strike up a conversation. He couldn't ask her on a date, but he could talk with a buddy.

And say more than two words to her.

He nodded firmly, committing the decision to memory. Harper had never treated him with anything but kindness and Mason could do the same. He was positive that by the time he wrapped up his family drama and was able to focus on dating, she would already be taken. And it'd be fine. He would just find another blonde…who was beautiful…and kind…had adorable freckles…and painted stunning coastal pictures…

He rubbed his forehead. This might be harder than he thought.

CHAPTER 2

"Thank you so much," Harper gushed to a customer who bought her biggest canvas of the day. "Enjoy!"

"Oh, we will!" the older woman said with a smile. "It'll look just perfect on the wall above our bed."

Harper gave a little wave as the adorable couple walked away, the husband holding the wrapped artwork under his arm. She was always so grateful when people saw value in her work. It gave her hope that her plan to be full time might eventually come to fruition. With the launch of her online store last year, Harper had seen an increase in orders, but it still wasn't enough to live on. *Someday...*

A loud cheer rang through the air and Harper couldn't help but look over. She could hear the roar of the chainsaw as sawdust filled the air, but otherwise the only visible details of Mason's demonstration were the crowds' backs. Her mind went to their short conversation earlier that morning. She had nearly told him exactly how she felt about him, before managing to cover it with a lame excuse.

Harper rolled her eyes at herself. Luckily, Mason had bought it, or at least seemed to. As usual, however, he had barely spoken two words to her. She had tried to leave herself open for him to join her in unloading her paintings or coming to see her booth, but he hadn't taken her up on any of it, just reaffirming the fact that her stupid crush was one sided.

She shook her head and turned back to her booth. She shouldn't complain. She really had had a good day so far. It seemed other people were just as happy to see the winter end as she was.

Tilting her head to the side, Harper took a quiet moment to assess her booth. Some of the paintings were now gone, so she set about trying to move her inventory around until it looked more even. "There," she murmured, squinting to make sure it all felt perfect.

"Looks good," a gruff voice said from behind her.

Harper spun, a gasp escaping her lips. "Mason!" she scolded. She put a hand to her racing heart. "How in the world did you sneak up on me like that? I thought you were carving."

Mason grinned. Pieces of sawdust were stuck to the front of his shirt as he shrugged his massive shoulders. "I wasn't trying to be quiet. You were too caught up in making things pretty around here."

"I guess so," Harper murmured. She hoped the bright pink on her cheeks could be mistaken for time spent in the sun. She glanced up, but the sun was currently behind a cloud. *Crud.*

"I, uh, just wanted to…" Mason scratched the back of his head, looking decidedly uncomfortable.

Harper held back a sigh. Was she really that scary to talk to? She could tell Mason was trying to be nice, but really!

"How's the selling been going?" he asked, his arms folding over his large chest.

Harper nodded politely, praying her face didn't show her sadness. A pinching sensation sat in her sternum. Why did life have to be so hard? Why did the art world have to take all her time and concentration? Mason was such a good guy and it was so hard to let that go when she wasn't sure she'd ever find someone like him again.

"Good," she responded, forcing a bit of cheer into her tone. "I sold my biggest canvas just a few minutes ago, when you were still carving." She furrowed her brow and leaned closer. "Hold on." Without stopping to think of her actions, Harper stepped forward and reached up to grab a small piece of wood that had lodged itself in Mason's beard.

His beard felt coarse, but was well groomed, she realized as she brushed her fingers along it to grab the piece. Holding it up triumphantly, she grinned. "Got it!" Her eyes went to the piece. "Hazard of the job, I suppose." When she looked back at Mason, she froze. She hadn't realized how close she had gotten in order to pick up the shaving.

His golden eyes bore into hers and for the first time, Harper didn't feel like he was anxious to get away from her.

"Thank you," he said in a gruff tone.

"You're welcome," she said, backing away quickly. Dang it. Why couldn't she be better aware of others' boundaries? People didn't just go around plucking wood from handsome men's beards.

She sucked in a deep breath, trying to cool her embarrassment, and noticed the enticing scent of freshly cut wood immediately, followed by a softer smell of fresh pine. It fit Mason. Even if he hadn't been carving a log, the smell would have been perfect for him. There was something distinctly manly about the outdoor scents that only made Harper's attraction grow even stronger.

"Miss?"

Harper blinked, her brain scrambling to catch up. "Y-yes?" she asked, forcing herself to look away from Mason. She smiled tightly when a middle aged woman glanced between her and Mason.

"Are you the artist?" the woman asked hesitantly, as if she knew she had interrupted something.

Harper nodded. "Yes!" She cleared her throat. "Would you like to look at anything in particular?"

"I…" The woman still hesitated.

"I'll stop by later," he said in a low tone. "We both need to eat, right?"

Harper's heart fluttered. Dinner with Mason sounded great, but could her heart handle it? "That sounds wonderful," she responded.

Mason's smile was as charming as always and he nodded at the woman as he left.

Harper turned back and brought her mind back down to earth. "I'm sorry about that. Did you say if there was anything particular you wanted to see?"

The woman smiled understandingly. "More of that handsome young man would be fine."

Harper laughed softly. "You and me both," she admitted.

"Well, if that's not on the menu, how about that picture with the seagull flying through the sunset?"

Harper nodded. "That I can do." The next hour passed quickly as Harper chatted and made a few sales along the way. She was just finishing up talking to a little girl about her painting when she noticed someone come up to her side. "Aspen!" Harper cried. She held up a finger. "Hang on a sec." After finishing with the child, Harper stood and hugged her friend. Aspen had been simply glowing ever since she and Austin had gotten married and it turned her already beautiful looks into something stunning. "I'm so glad you made it!"

"Me too," Aspen agreed. She looked around. "It's nice to see so many people getting outside."

"Yeah...nothing like being stuck in the kitchen all day," Harper teased.

Aspen laughed and set down the box she had brought with her. "Do you have time for a treat?"

"Actually..." Harper hedged. "I think I might save them for a little later."

Aspen's eyebrows shot up. "Is there something I should know?"

Harper snorted. "I wish." She couldn't seem to stop herself from thinking about sharing them with Mason. They were friends. Just friends. But a girl needed a dream, right? And if hers included a particularly handsome lumberjack who sent butterflies through her stomach, well...no one could blame her.

* * *

MASON WASN'T sure why he was bothering to bring Harper dinner. He was positive that at any moment, he was going to throw up and it didn't make sense to be eating when his stomach was doing flip flops like an Olympic gymnast.

It was amazing to him how one tiny woman had the power to make him quake. It frustrated him and intrigued him all at the same time. But the fact that he didn't have the freedom to pursue the feeling made it extra difficult.

Ever since his younger sister graduated from high school four years ago, Mason had been on a mission. Aimee had dropped off the radar within weeks and no one had found her since. Crew, Mason's younger brother, had also been working to find their wayward sibling, but all roads had been dead ends.

Now he stayed glued to his phone, desperate for any news from the private investigator he'd hired. When his thoughts weren't full of tempting blondes, Mason was online searching for his sister or trying to contact her friends to see if she'd made contact. He knew she was out there somewhere, and until he knew where, he just couldn't let himself get distracted with anything else. Starting a relationship with Harper, no matter how exciting and good it might be, felt like a direct betrayal to his family.

But when Harper had stepped into his personal bubble to pull a sliver of wood from his beard, Mason was sure he'd died and gone to heaven. He hadn't even touched her, but having her warmth close and the sweet smell of flowers wafting to his nose was enough to make him roll his eyes in contentment. And then her slim fingers had brushed his face and he'd had to clench his fists to keep from grabbing her and kissing the dickens out of her.

Dinner, he reminded himself. *Dinner is the plan, not assaulting her.*

He marched her way, trying to pretend he wasn't shaking in his boots as he carried two plates with fish and chips in them. It was the essential food of a coastal town and he assumed it was a safe bet as to something Harper would eat. If he'd been thinking clearly earlier, he would have asked her what she wanted, but he didn't want to come over empty handed and look like an idiot, only to have to leave again.

She spotted him as he drew closer and her smile grew wide.

Anyone could see she looked happy to see him and his stomach did another little flip. *Easy, man. Easy... Remember Aimee.*

"I hope fish is okay," Mason said, handing her the cardboard square.

"I love fish and chips," Harper replied, her smile never wavering. She jutted her chin to a chair. "Aspen brought me leftover goodies from the bakery today, so I have dessert!"

"Sounds perfect." He followed her to the side of her display where she had chairs and a small table set up. Water bottles were already waiting and Mason couldn't stop his goofy smile at the evidence that she'd been waiting for him.

A quick blessing preceded them both biting into the crispy filets. "Mmm..." Harper moaned, closing her eyes for a moment. "There's nothing like deep fried fish to really finish off a long day."

Mason grinned. "Long day? Has it been a hard one?"

Harper shook her head and dipped her fish heavily into the tartar sauce, making Mason snort quietly in amusement. "It's been a great first day. Lots of sales and lots of smiling faces."

Mason nodded.

"How about you?" Harper finished chewing before continuing. "Did you sell the wolf?"

Mason's eyebrows rose up. "You saw what I was carving?"

Harper's cheeks turned pink and she dropped her eyes to her food. "Several people were talking about it, so I walked over for a few seconds between customers." She looked up from under her lashes.

Mason swallowed hard. "Did you...did you like it?" Truth was, he had fashioned the wolf after one he'd seen in a painting she'd done last year. He had no idea if she would recognize it, nor was he sure how he'd feel if she did. He had assumed she would be too busy to see what he'd done, but he couldn't deny that her good opinion sent a little thrill through him.

"It's stunning," Harper said easily. She shrugged. "Your work always is. I can't imagine turning a log into something so realistic."

Mason nodded to her pictures. "I can't imagine taking a brush and something resembling toothpaste and turning it into that." He pointed to a nearby canvas. "So I guess we're even."

Harper laughed before setting her food aside to jump up and help a customer.

Mason continued eating, but watched her interact with the people. Now that he was closer he could hear their conversations and understood even better why people were always smiling. Harper was amazing at making people feel special and worthwhile. No one arrived without receiving some kind of compliment and when she sold a painting, he realized the way she said thank you was so sincere that no one could mistake it for anything but truth.

Finally, she sat back down and grabbed her food. It had to be cold by now, but Harper didn't complain at all.

With each piece of her he uncovered, Mason knew more and more that if he spent too much time around her, he wouldn't be able to keep from making a move. She checked off every quality on his list of what he was looking for in a woman and there'd be no way to keep from pursuing his attraction if he stuck around too long. This little dinner would have to be it. When they ran into each other again, he'd have to make sure to keep some distance between them.

Guess that means I should make the most of tonight.

"So..." he started, then cleared his throat. "Tell me how you got started in painting."

Harper laughed softly. "That's funny. I was just going to ask you the same about carving." She kicked at his foot playfully. "Painting is a common enough hobby, but wood carving? Particularly chainsaw wood carving?" She shook her head. "That's definitely unusual."

Mason shrugged. "What can I say? I like to work with my hands and my mom was desperate for something that kept me from breaking everything in the house." His grin grew sheepish. "As you can imagine, I was a bit like a bull in a china shop as I grew up. Being outside and breaking down wood instead of my mom's crystal was a good distraction."

"Oh, come on," Harper pressed. "There has to be more to it than that."

Mason shook his head. He wasn't keeping anything from her. It really had just been a weird thing that fell into his lap and he discovered he liked it and had a knack for it. "Honest. It was just one of those things I played around with and discovered it was fun." He nodded toward the area he'd been working in today. "Enough hours later and it's what I do in my spare time."

"About that..." Harper leaned forward. "How is this a spare time thing? When we first met, you told me you work for a lumber mill."

Mason nodded. "I do. I'm head of sales for one over in Eugene."

"But you work here?"

"Yeah. It's mostly a phone and desk job, so I'm able to live on the coast and work from home. I travel to Eugene about once a quarter to meet with the head honcho, but otherwise I just make sure I have a good internet connection."

"Ah..." Harper nodded. "That makes sense." She smiled. "And it's really awesome that you can live wherever you want. I'd much prefer our quaint little Seagull Cove to a place like Eugene."

"That makes two of us," Mason agreed. "It's peaceful and quiet, but if I want something bigger, it doesn't take long in either direction to hit more elaborate entertainment options."

Harper's smile was wide. "You know, Mason, I'm starting to think you and I are two peas in a pod."

Hope soared, followed quickly by dismay. *And this is why I need to keep my distance.* He was starting to realize the chemistry he was feeling wasn't one sided, or at least he didn't think so. It was hard to tell with someone who was so sweet to everyone they met, but Harper seemed a little more...eager with him than the others.

The pull he felt was strong and if Harper felt any of it, then he knew he'd fall hook, line and sinker.

The french fries turned to ash in his mouth, but he forced a tight smile and swallowed. This wasn't actually a date, but in his memories, he would count it as their first...and also their last.

CHAPTER 3

Harper shivered slightly, holding her brush up so the movement didn't affect her stroke. It was still a little chilly in the evenings, and she should have brought a jacket with her, but the sun had been out when Harper had left her house and she stubbornly refused to act as if it was still winter.

"Idiot," she mumbled to herself as she stiffened her hand and continued adding another layer of color to her canvas. She was going to have to call it quits. Stupid weather.

With a soft sigh, she dipped her brush into the cleanser and began to get ready to pull everything down. She was sooo ready for summer. Even spring wasn't cutting it anymore, though she was grateful for the markets. They helped keep the winter blues away.

She smiled to herself as she packed up. The first market of the year had been a dream come true. The customers had been happy to buy and Mason had spent an entire meal at her side. It had been lovely, but she knew better than to try and encourage anything. She still had so far to go with her business and despite bringing her dinner, Mason hadn't spoken to her since that day last week.

For a bit she had thought that maybe her crush had been returned, but if that was the case, then why hadn't he spoken to her since? Why hadn't he texted? Or at least stopped by to say hi? It's not like she was a world traveler or something. It wasn't hard to get a hold of her.

"Maybe he's been busy?" she asked the evening air. The excuse sounded lame even to her. If Mason wanted to speak with her…he would.

She sighed. Apparently, their little connection had been completely in her head. Nothing had really changed and nothing *should* change. Imagined connection or not, Harper just wasn't in a position to date.

"It's a little chilly out here, don't you think?"

Harper jerked upright. She recognized the voice, but hadn't been expecting to hear it. Spinning, she put her hands on her hips and did her best to fight the flood of pleasure pouring into her system. "I do believe that's twice you nearly scared the living daylights out of me," she scolded, though there was no real bite in her tone.

Mason chuckled. The low rumbly sound was glorious to Harper's ears. "I'm sorry." He put his hands in the air. "I really don't know how you don't hear me coming. I'm huge."

Harper looked him up and down. "True enough, but geez." She shook her head. "You're going to give me a heart attack."

"I'll stomp extra loud next time," he teased.

Harper laughed. It was then she noticed that his hands were full. "Taking a walk?" she asked. He held two steaming cups and Harper realized he was probably meeting someone. She had parked herself at the beach today in order to paint in real time, but there were several walking paths along the wild grass border, and a little closer to town was the boardwalk, which couples strolled all the time.

The pain of the revelation hurt more than she would have expected it to, since she held no true expectations in regards to a relationship with him.

Mason held up one cup. "I happened to see your car parked along the boardwalk while I was heading home from dinner and a little birdie told me you like hot chocolate." He smirked. "Unless you're different from every woman I've ever met, then you're probably freezing right about now." He offered the drink.

It was amazing how the human body could go from the depths of despair to the soaring freedom of the sky in less than a second, and Harper was shocked she didn't have whiplash from the swift turnaround.

Slowly, she reached out to take the offering. The cup was warm and felt nice on her chilled digits, but it was the brush against his fingers against her own that sent enough heat to light a fire rushing through her veins. She just hoped that in the waning light, he couldn't see it on her face. "Thank you." She inhaled the scent of sweet chocolate and moaned. "Oh my gosh, I love hot chocolate." *Just friends, just friends...career, career, career.*

Mason chuckled again. His eyes went to her canvas. "Is it alright if I look?"

Harper nodded. She used to be shy about anyone seeing an unfinished project, but she'd gotten over that. She might not be Rembrandt, but she was proud of her work, even if that meant it had to look chaotic before it looked finished. As an artist himself, surely Mason understood that.

Mason tilted his head, studying the painting. "It's beautiful. Are you done?"

She shook her head. "No. I'd like to add a few waves in the water and some clouds over the moon."

He nodded. "It'll give it a deep and mysterious look. I like it."

Harper smiled, pleased with his kindness. "Thanks."

Mason sucked in a deep breath. "Can I help you carry things to your car? You looked like you were putting things away..." He trailed off as if unsure.

"That'd be great!" Harper chirped. Geez. She really needed to get a hold of her emotions. Just because Mason was being nice didn't mean he wanted more than friendship with her. Right? Even as she thought it, the words felt false. She wasn't the only one to feel this pull between them. What was she going to do?

Ten minutes later, they were trudging through the sand toward the parking lot, each holding something under one arm and a cup of cocoa in the other. "I'm starting to think I need to invest in a cart or wagon," Harper said breathlessly. The loose sand was difficult to walk in at best. When she'd arrived earlier, she had made three trips to get her stuff out into a good spot. Hauling it all at the same time was a much heavier load and she was one-handed this time around. *Oh well. This should help me have nice-looking calves, right? Maybe I'll burn off a few of the calories from the hot chocolate.*

"I'm not sure the wheels could handle the sand," Mason said as he waited for her at the top of a small hill. Now that they had reached the grassy areas, it was much easier going.

"True enough." Harper sighed. "I guess I'll just keep getting decent workouts, huh?"

Mason's smile could be seen even in the semi-dark. "Let's look on the bright side. By the time we get to your car, the hot chocolate will be cool enough to drink."

"Thank heaven for small mercies," Harper agreed. Mason was right. After loading everything in her trunk and backseat, the hot chocolate was at the perfect sipping temperature.

"Mmm…" she murmured, letting the sweet drink slide down her throat. "This was really thoughtful of you. Thank you."

Mason looked at the ground, shrugging. "It wasn't that big of a deal. Just being friendly."

The warm drink forgotten, the words were like a splash of cold ocean water to the face. *Why?* she scolded herself. *Why should that hurt? You CAN'T have him. It's as simple as that. A guy is a distraction that will only take you farther from your goals, not closer.* "Well, it was really nice of you. Thanks." Harper had the sudden desire to wash her own mouth out with soap to get rid of the bitter taste of the lies.

"Want to walk down the boardwalk?" Mason asked. He held up his cup. "So you don't have to drink and drive?"

MASON HELD his breath while he waited for Harper to answer. He wasn't the type to do anything rashly, but when he'd seen her car and realized she must have been on the beach, he hadn't even thought it through. Simply stopped, grabbed the drinks and hurried over the grassy rise.

He shouldn't have done it. It was stupid and reckless and was probably sending the exact message that he didn't want to send. The lack of information about his sister, however, was starting to drive him batty and Harper always helped him forget his worries. She was an angel and trying to avoid her pull was nearly impossible, as evidenced by his spending all his free time at last weekend's exhibit with her.

He'd gone home with a wide smile on his face, unable to wipe it off for a full twenty-four hours. Even speaking to the private investigator hadn't gotten rid of all his energy. It was utterly ridiculous.

"I'd like that," Harper said with a smile.

Mason tried to keep his chest from puffing up with pride, but it was harder than he would have expected. "Great." He tilted his head down the boardwalk and waited for her to start. The breeze was slightly chilly, but the drink helped keep him warm, though he worried about Harper. Maybe this wasn't the best idea after all. "Are you warm enough?" he asked.

Harper held up her cup. "This is keeping me perfect at the moment."

He let out a breath of relief. "Good." He cleared his throat and put his focus back on the boardwalk. Now what? He had a stunning woman by his side, a warm cup of cocoa, the sounds of the crashing waves... Could anything really be more romantic? *Or any worse of an idea?* He mentally smacked his forehead. This wasn't fair to Harper. Anybody could see that he had an interest in her, but only he knew that he wasn't going to act on it.

Harper deserves better than that.

He cleared his throat again, regretting his hasty decision. "It's getting colder. Maybe we ought to head back."

. . .

Harper gave him a sad smile, as if she knew exactly what was going on. "I think that's a good idea. I think the temperature is dropping a little too much for comfort."

They were silent as they walked the short distance back to the cars. Mason wasn't sure how Harper was feeling, but a sense of mourning had overtaken him. He was positive he and Harper could have had something beautiful. Something worth fighting for…but he just couldn't bring himself to do it.

In his gut, he knew something had happened to his sister. Something horrific. She reminded him of Harper, in a way. Both were bright, beautiful beacons of light, making everyone in their presence smile.

But Aimee's had been snuffed out when she'd run away after high school graduation. The day after the big celebration, she was gone. Only a small note, saying not to look for her and that she would be in touch when she was ready, had been left behind.

At first, Mason had honored her wishes. He'd been hurt, but had wanted to give his little sister her space. As time went on, however, he'd started to grow worried. Both Mason and Crew had started asking around, looking for her trail. It had been too long and she had been too quiet.

He hadn't blamed Aimee for leaving. Their mother wasn't the easiest person to get along with. Mason had survived by quietly going about his business, Crew had bulldozed his way through, ignoring their mother's proper Southern teachings, but Aimee…Aimee had taken the brunt of it. As the only daughter of Mrs. Patricia Turley, Aimee had been expected to become yet another woman in the long line of Southern belles.

And she'd wanted nothing to do with it.

Aimee was much more like Crew than Mason. She enjoyed life to the fullest and flung happiness around like confetti, but whenever their mother was near, it all faded. She became quiet, subdued and someone that Mason barely recognized. Her desire to escape had come from too many years of not living up to their mother's standards of perfection.

But it had been four years. There was no way she would stay away from her brothers this long unless something had happened. A year ago, Mason had finally given up on the idea that he could find her himself, and he'd hired a private investigator, but every lead had ended in disappointment.

She'd done a very good job of falling off the face of the Earth.

"Thanks for the cocoa," Harper said as she unlocked her car door.

Mason blinked. He hadn't realized they'd already gotten back. Heat crept beneath his beard as he understood he'd been stoically silent the entire walk. *Well, that probably sent her the right message.* He nodded and smiled. "We'll see ya around."

He waited until she had pulled out, then trudged to his truck. For the first time ever, he found himself angry. Truly angry. He didn't want to let this thing go with Harper. He was tired of going home to an empty cabin, of spending his Sundays pouring over internet articles of unidentified female victims, of scrolling through countless social media profiles... He wanted his life to begin, and he wanted it to begin with Harper and him going out to dinner.

His cabin was dark when he got home, just another visual example of how he felt on the inside. His growling stomach only emphasized his heavy thoughts. "Why did you do it, Aims?" he whispered. "Why didn't you tell Crew and me where you were going?"

He let his forehead fall to the steering wheel, his misery swallowing him whole. For just a few minutes tonight, he had basked in light and joy, but reality had quickly set in, forcing him to step away from the warmth of it.

"Where are you?"

No one answered him. *Of course not,* he mentally snorted. *Get a grip.*

Taking a fortifying breath, he went inside, turned on all the lights, flipped the switch to light the fireplace and headed to the kitchen. His place wasn't glamorous. It was slightly rustic, with wood beams across his ceiling and Western-style blankets draping his couches, but it was his, and it was warm and homey. And right now, it was all he had. His sister was still missing and Harper was nothing but a distant dream.

Not even his best friend, Ethan, knew about Aimee and it would have to stay that way. Nothing said *I'm crazy* like having a perfectionist mother who drove her daughter off the deep end. It wasn't exactly the type of conversation one shared over a warm bonfire.

Mason cracked a couple of eggs into a sizzling pan and began stirring them into scrambled eggs. They weren't much, but they'd at least take the edge off. Not to mention he didn't have the energy for anything else. Tonight he just needed to make it all go away. Aimee's silence, Harper's beauty, his mother's pride…Mason wanted it all gone.

A few bites of dinner and a soft bed. He'd face his demons again tomorrow, but at least by then he'd have the strength to do what needed to be done.

CHAPTER 4

*H*arper's heart skipped a beat when she pulled into the cafe's parking lot. There was an extra large truck parked in the back corner and she knew exactly whom it belonged to.

Pulling into a slot, she waited. Should she go inside? She loved this cafe and every year on her way to the farmer's market in Florence she stopped to get herself something sweet to start the day. But Mason was here and they'd left things off rather awkwardly last week.

Her thumbs beat an unsteady rhythm against the steering wheel. Would he think she was following him? He was more than likely going to the same market–their schedules were nearly identical this time of year–and it had never been a problem before.

"So why is it now?" she asked her empty car. "We're friends, right?" She pulled back on the key, shutting down the engine. "Friends can randomly run into each other without it being a big deal."

She ignored the fact that one side of her brain was flashing a red flag and the other was screaming with excitement at seeing the handsome giant again. How he could create two such contrasting emotions was truly remarkable, but she'd been nursing a slightly bruised heart during the last several days and she wasn't eager to go through it again.

Their uncomfortable walk down the boardwalk was purely her fault. She should have told him no. Should have said she had to get the paints home. Should have done *something*, other than agree to stroll with him. She knew she'd given him the wrong impression and from the silence that followed them and his retreating invitations, she also knew he understood her lack of interest.

She snorted. There was no such thing as a lack of interest on her part, but she had definitely had the body language of someone like that and Mason wasn't stupid. He'd taken her back to her car within a couple minutes of starting to walk. He'd clearly gotten the message.

Guilt had taken a long ride on her shoulders, along with a sadness that she'd struggled to shake. She felt guilty for leading Mason on and sad that she couldn't pursue whatever this *thing* was between them. Oh, how she wanted to explore it. Her week had been colorless and lonely, even with Aspen and Maeve showing up for a game night.

Their laughter and antics usually broke up the monotony of living alone, but this time it hadn't helped at all. When the women had left, Harper had gone to bed feeling worse than she had before they'd arrived. Not that any of that was Aspen or Maeve's fault. Harper was the sole person to blame here.

She stood next to her car, keys biting into her fist as she stared down the entrance. She could do this. She was an adult and ran her own business, even if family money helped keep her afloat. She had managed to get herself through art school and move to Oregon on her own. She could do this.

Harper thrust back her shoulders. No man was worth making her cower in the corner. Mason was wonderful, but she didn't need him in order to live a good life. When she made it as an artist, then she could look at opening up her heart. But until then, she could be professional and a friend. Two things that should be easy.

She grabbed the door handle and firmly jerked it open, hiding a wince when it practically crashed into the side of the building. *Perhaps a little less enthusiasm*, she scolded herself.

Refusing to look around, she headed straight to the counter, feigning an all-consuming interest in the glass display case, even though she knew exactly what she was going to get.

"Hi! How can I help you today?" a middle aged woman asked, wiping her hands on her apron.

"A cup of milk lemon loaf, and a chocolate croissant, please," Harper said politely. There was movement in her peripheral vision, but Harper studiously ignored it. *Real professional,* she thought wryly. Something red was headed her way and her heart began to beat in a crazy rhythm.

"We'll have that right out for you," the woman said, a teasing smile on her face as her eyes went over Harper's shoulder. "But I think you have a welcoming committee."

Harper finally turned, Mason's presence at her shoulder too much to be ignored now. "Oh. Hey, Mason." She ignored the quiet chuckle of the woman behind the counter. "Fancy meeting you here."

Mason gave her a half grin, which amazingly enough was even more attractive than his usual smile. "Hey, yourself. You headed down to Florence today?"

Harper nodded. "Yep. I have a booth there."

He nodded in return.

"Are you carving live? Or just selling?" she finally asked into the silence.

"I have a booth as well, but I'll be doing some carving." He shrugged. "They didn't hire me for that, but I booked two spaces so I could. It seems to gather a crowd and it's good for business."

"Right."

"Here you go."

Harper turned to see the woman behind the counter smirking and pushing forward a to-go cup of tea along with her wrapped pastry. "Thanks," Harper said softly. She could feel a blush creeping up her cheeks and quickly turned away, holding up her items as an excuse. "Looks like I'm all set."

Mason glanced at his watch. "We've got a couple minutes. Might as well sit down and enjoy it." He waved toward a table.

"Uh…" Red flags waved in her vision. She knew he was just being friendly, but this was exactly what had happened last week. She really needed to put some boundaries into place if she was ever going to get over this crush. "That's really nice of you, but I need to get there early," she said lamely. "It takes a bit to unload all the canvases and make the booth look pretty, you know?"

Mason rubbed the back of his neck. "Yep. I get it." He stepped back. "I'll see you there then."

Harper nodded a little too eagerly. "Yep. I'll see you there." She turned and headed back to the door. Guilt churned her stomach and she knew she'd never manage to get the croissant down.

Dropping her food and drink into the allotted slots in the car, Harper blew out a breath and bit her lip to keep the tears at bay. She'd done it. She'd turned him down in a polite and professional way, keeping their relationship from resembling anything but friendship.

Then why does it hurt so much?

She put a hand against her chest, trying to ease the sharp pain there. Why? WHY? She wanted to scream at the heavens. This wasn't fair. Why couldn't she have met him in a few years? Why did he have to be so nice? Why couldn't life be simple enough that she could have both at the same time?

The first time's always the hardest.

The words helped her calm down slightly. The thought was true. Stepping away from Mason would get easier. She just had to hold on until that time, then the tension between them would fade out and they could go back to enjoying each other's company in an easy, friendly way.

MASON SHRUGGED at the woman behind the counter, who shook her head.

"She's crazy, that one." She nodded toward Harper's car for emphasis.

Mason forced a tight grin through his embarrassment. "We're just friends," he said, though no one had asked.

The clerk looked skeptical. "Uh-huh." She turned her head away, mumbling under her breath.

Mason was glad he couldn't understand the words. He was pretty sure they weren't complimentary. He rubbed the back of his neck again. It felt hot, and though he shouldn't have been surprised by her rejection, it still stung. He'd been hot and cold, sending her mixed messages and Harper had just set down the boundary of not being willing to deal with that.

Good for her, he thought. *She deserves better.*

He gathered what was left of his breakfast and walked out the door to his parked truck, but his mind was still with Harper. She *did* deserve better. She deserved a man who would worship the ground she walked on. One who had the time and money to smother her with attention and bask in her presence.

Mason *wanted* to be that man, but he couldn't. "Which is exactly why you need to let her go," he snapped as he practically tore his truck door off. The hinges protested his rough treatment and Mason purposefully slowed down. An expensive repair right now wouldn't help his *Find Aimee* budget.

He pulled out onto the road, turning up the radio to keep his mind occupied, but after two minutes, he turned it back down. His head was beginning to pound and everything sounded like noise. He had about a half hour drive until he reached the market and Mason dreading every bit of it.

Normally these events were his creative outlet and chance to shake things up a little, but today he felt as if a dark cloud had settled over him. His brain and his heart were in a war and it was messing him up inside.

He liked Harper...a lot, but wasn't in a position to have her.

That was it. End of story. It shouldn't be this hard to get it settled in his mind. His time for a relationship would come, it just wasn't right now.

He sighed and pushed a hand through his hair. He had never been bitter toward his sister until the last few weeks and he didn't like it.

Aimee didn't deserve his disdain any more than Harper his preoccupation.

"Seems like you're just letting down all the women in your life," he muttered. A buzzing sound pulled him from his self inflicted misery and Mason pushed the speaker button. "Yeah?"

"You sound like you're driving, Sasquatch," Crew teased. "Don't tell me you're heading to another one of those artsy shows."

Mason rolled his eyes, but was grateful for his brother's interruption. He and his thoughts weren't getting along at the moment. "Whattya need, Shorty?" Mason asked. Crew wouldn't be considered short by anyone's standards, but when they were younger, Mason had needed something to respond to his own childhood nickname.

"Can't I just call my brother to say hello?"

"You could," Mason drawled. "But I know you better than that."

Crew chuckled. "Fair enough." He cleared his throat. "But seriously, did I catch you at a bad time? You really do sound like you're driving."

"I'm on my way to one of those artsy shows," Mason confirmed. "You know, the ones where I wield a chainsaw and turn wood into a cool animal?"

"Hmm…" Crew responded. "I thought those were the ones where you sprinkled yourself with man glitter."

Even Mason had to laugh at that one. "I've got a few minutes," he finally said. "What do you need?"

Crew's voice grew a little quieter. "Just wondering if you'd heard anything lately."

Mason's shoulders drooped. "I wouldn't keep something like that from you," he assured his brother. "If I find out something, you'll be the first person I call."

"I know, but I just…" Crew sighed. "Sorry. I know you wouldn't hide something from me, but sometimes I can't help but wonder what's going on. Why has she been so hard to find?"

Mason didn't answer. There was nothing to say. Nothing that would make them feel better. The only possible explanation was that she had somehow died, but even then, Mason felt sure that they should have been able to find the record. *Unless she was a Jane Doe.*

He shook his head, refusing to even consider the idea. If Aimee was dead, they would figure it out. Otherwise…well, she was just really good at keeping their mother at bay.

"Sorry," Crew muttered, taking Mason's silence as a scolding. "I guess it's just been a difficult couple of days and I'm letting it get my mind churning."

"What's the matter?" Mason asked, trying to lighten the mood. "A kid bite your finger off?" Crew was a dentist, specializing in pediatrics, though he saw all ages.

"You should see where they tried to sew it back on." Crew laughed. "It'll make a great scar. Maybe I'll catch up to you one of these days."

Mason chuckled at the reminder. He had quite a few scars from when he was first learning to carve wood, including one just like what Crew described after Mason nearly lost his finger.

His mother had fainted and eventually swore he would never be allowed to carve again, but Mason just made sure she wasn't around when he did it after that. Now as an adult, living in a state his mother called uncivilized, he did what he wanted and didn't worry about hiding it, but there had been a few close moments during his teenage years.

"I thought you told me chicks dig scars," Mason said without thinking. The comment immediately brought to mind the woman he would want to share those scars with. He cursed in his head. Those blue eyes were going to be the death of him.

"After this heals, I'll put it to the test," Crew replied, completely unaware of Mason's turmoil. "You haven't exactly been a shining example in the dating department."

"Yeah, well…" Mason didn't have a good comeback for that one. His mother constantly called him a hermit. She had no idea of his other activities. Crew might know what Mason spent his time and money on, but he didn't realize it was the very thing keeping Mason from moving forward with his own life.

Patience, he reminded himself. *Someday it'll all work out. And when it does, you'll find someone who makes you feel even better than Harper does.*

"Yeah, well…" Crew imitated in a sarcastic tone. "Fess up, Sasquatch. Your appetite just terrifies all the women in that tiny town of yours."

"You got me," Mason said, praying his brother bought the false cheer.

"Well…when you do find that special someone who finally makes enough money to keep you fed, be sure and let me know," Crew continued.

"Why's that?"

"Haven't you ever heard that the oldest has to fall first?" Crew said. "I'm not going anywhere until you test out this love thing and prove it won't kill me."

Mason grinned. His brother's sense of humor was helping. "We might both die bachelors if that's the case," Mason warned.

Crew snorted. "Tell me something I don't know."

CHAPTER 5

"Thank you so much!" Harper called to the woman who had just purchased a small set of canvases. They were part of the food theme she was testing out after painting some for Aspen's shop.

The customer smiled and rubbed her swollen stomach. She planned to put the pictures up in the nursery they were creating for their baby girl who was due in only six weeks.

Harper sighed. She couldn't think of a better situation for her artwork. That nursery was going to be bright and cheery and full of feminine colors. It would be lovely.

Her eyes drifted to the crowd that surrounded Mason's stall. She could hear his chainsaw roaring, and sawdust was flying. People came and went, most stopping for several minutes to watch his progress. The carvings that were displayed in the front showed off his already finished artwork.

Harper sighed. She still hadn't quite recovered from telling him no this morning. But it wouldn't work. Harper had seen firsthand what happened when a woman got married before going after her career and she was hoping to avoid the stress.

Harper wanted a family. She wanted a husband and children, but she also wanted a chance to let her wings soar. Not in her mother's courtroom, but in the studio. Once she had made it, then she could take the time to pursue love and, eventually, marriage and children.

And let's hope someone like Mason is available whenever that day finally gets here, she thought sourly.

Her mother was right about one thing. Harper wasn't getting any younger, though Sharon meant it as more of a timeline for becoming a lawyer. Law school as a middle-aged woman would be much harder than law school now. Which made sense, and Harper got it, but she herself felt the timeline choking her for different reasons.

She had thought she'd be making a full-time living by now. She wasn't aiming to be the best artist in the world. Or even famous throughout the United States. All she wanted was to make enough money to support herself. She *needed* to prove her capabilities to her mother and herself.

Having the trust to help her along had been a wonderful blessing, but Harper wanted to make it on her own. She didn't want to *need* her grandmother's money. Surely she was capable of doing this under her own merits.

Her phone buzzed and Harper grabbed it out of her back pocket, groaning when she realized who it was. "Hi, Mom," she said, forcing a smile so her tone didn't give away her feelings.

"I thought you had one of those…bizarre thingies today," Sharon snipped.

Harper closed her eyes and counted to three. She might be grateful to her mother, but that didn't mean she wanted to be like her. "I do," Harper said carefully. "I'm at it right now, but I was in between customers, so I went ahead and answered." She nodded and smiled at people as they walked by her booth. *And because I knew you'd just keep calling back until I gave in.*

Sharon sniffed. "You'll never make a living selling at farmers' markets, Harper."

"I realize that," Harper said, still carefully controlling her words. "But it's a good way to start. Lots of people are here to purchase decorations and other homemade goods for their homes and my artwork is perfect for that."

Her mother sighed long and loud. "How long are we going to play this game, Harper?"

"What game?"

"You know full well what," Sharon snapped. "This...thing with your art just isn't enough. You don't make money at it and at this point, the odds are you never will."

"You haven't given me enough time," Harper said through clenched teeth. "Being an artist can be slow, but this is what I want to do. Why can't you understand that?" She forced herself to close her mouth. How many times had they had this argument?

Sadness pooled in Harper's chest. It was her life. Why was her mother so dead set on making it a certain way? Harper didn't need a mansion or a marble bathtub. All she wanted was to pay her bills and keep hearing the ocean from the backyard of her home. And yes, she wanted to do it all on her own, but her trust was there for a reason and would last for a long time yet.

Harper tried not to let her internal clock put too much pressure on her and most days, she succeeded. It had been harder lately with Mason, since Harper knew someone as special as him wouldn't last long enough for her to get her career off the ground, but there were other fish in the sea. Right? Her heart would heal and she would find someone else when the time was right.

"I'm sorry," Harper said softly. "I don't want to fight, Mother, but I've told you before...this is what I want to do. Grandma's trust is enough to help me out until my art takes off, not to mention I would make the world's worst lawyer."

"You're certainly adept at arguing with me," Sharon shot back.

"I'm sorry," Harper said again. "I shouldn't have argued, but I'm not changing my mind."

Her mother sniffed again, a sure sign she was irritated. "Then I'm afraid you leave me no choice."

Harper's heart skipped a beat. "What do you mean?"

"I mean that you've been using your trust as an excuse to pursue a hobby that'll never turn into a career and I, as your mother, can't let you continue to waste your life."

Harper's grip on the phone tightened. "I don't understand."

"As trustee for your money, I have the ability to stop all payments, if I deem them unworthy. The rules your grandmother laid down gave me executive power to stop all payments if you chose to be frivolous with the money."

Harper's jaw dropped. Inside her head, she was screaming, but no sound came out.

"I've been generous, allowing you to go to art school and spend the last five years chasing this dream, but enough is enough."

"Mom," Harper croaked. "You can't do this."

"I can…and I will."

"You have to give me more time!" Harper cried. She rushed around the back of her booth, trying to keep her drama from any passersby, but she was sure some of them could hear her anyway. "I…" Her brain scrambled for something…anything…that would help her argument. "There's a competition in California for amateur painters. It's very prestigious," Harper hurried to say. "I'm working on a piece for it right now and, and…and if I win, it'll be the last real push I need to make it full time." She bit her lips between her teeth, stopping her rambling.

She wasn't lying, there really was a competition, but Harper hadn't planned to enter. There were always thousands of entries and the winner was almost always someone who favored an abstract style, which was nothing like Harper's realistic ocean sunsets. But if it kept her mother off her back and the trust money coming in for a little bit longer, then Harper would do anything.

Sharon let out another long sigh. She was very well practiced in those. "When is the winner announced?" she asked, sounding tired.

"The deadline is next month," Harper said. "I don't know the exact dates of the announcement."

There was a pause on the line and Harper squirmed when it drew on for too long. How her mother had the ability to reduce her to being ten years old again, Harper didn't understand, but she hated it.

"If you don't win, you go back to school," her mother said clearly. "The money will only continue if you move to a new career. One that means you'll never need another handout again."

Harper squeezed her eyes shut, trying to hold back tears. This was it. She had one month to make enough money as an artist to live on. She knew the competition probably wouldn't be the way, but if she could somehow get the money flowing through other means, then she'd survive. She could live without the trust. "The money will only continue if I take on a new career," Harper repeated. She wasn't going to agree to the school aspect. That was asking too much.

"Fine. I'll plan on hearing from you soon."

The line went dead and Harper collapsed in a chair. She leaned her elbows onto her knees and let the silent sobs wrack her body. This was exactly why she couldn't be with Mason. If there had ever been a stark reminder of why it wouldn't work, this was it. She had been right to turn him down. It hurt, but there was nothing for it. She had one month to build a career. One month to save her dreams. She couldn't let anything distract her or she'd end up losing it all.

MASON SIGHED as he sank into his couch later that night. He was exhausted. Traveling on days of the festivals always meant long hours and after doing two live demonstrations, his mind was mush and his arms were still shaking from holding onto the chainsaw. If he wanted to dig a little deeper, his pride and heart were also a little shaky today, after being rejected by Harper and still having to watch her smile and interact with customers all day long. She had been right to put some distance between them, but Mason's emotions didn't seem to be getting the memo.

A banging on his door had Mason scowling. Who in the world would be coming by at this time of night?

Grumbling, he climbed to his feet and shuffled over. "Ethan! What the heck are you doing here?"

Ethan grinned and sauntered inside when Mason stepped back to make room. "Just thought I'd come hang out with my buddy. Is there something wrong with that?"

Mason rubbed his forehead. "I've known you too long to fall for that."

Ethan laughed and plopped into a recliner, pressing the button to push it back all the way. "I was bored, okay? I was bored."

"I thought you were going surfing today." Mason came back to the couch and slouched into the cushions.

Ethan nodded. "I did. This morning." He glanced at his watch. "That was a long time ago."

"Have you opened the shop yet?"

Ethan shook his head. "No. Not enough tourists. Probably another two to three weeks."

Mason nodded and rubbed his beard, grimacing when he caught sawdust. "I need a shower."

Ethan smirked. "You always do. I can't figure out why you have that dead rodent on your face anyway. All it does is catch food and dust."

Mason gave his friend a look. "You just summed up the whole reason in a few words."

Ethan made a face. "Are you growing mold in there?"

"Some of us spend time outside in the winter," Mason shot back.

"Yeah…like those of us working construction. Not the ones spending time at a cushy desk job." Ethan was grinning widely, softening his dig.

Mason rolled his eyes. "If you don't like it, you can always change careers." Ethan had been raised on the coast and spent his summers surfing and running a rental and lessons shop. During the winter he worked on custom board jobs, when available, but otherwise worked construction to make ends meet during the downtimes. "I hear Aspen might be looking for a dishwasher."

"Would Maeve be there?" Ethan's eyes sparkled with mischief.

Mason paused. "Uh…I have no idea."

Ethan rubbed his chin. "It would probably be worth my time if she was hanging around. I think there's an office in the back of the bakery. She probably presses all those calculator buttons back there."

Mason stood up. "Want something?" He headed to the kitchen.

"Got a soda?"

"Sprite or root beer?"

"Do you really have to ask?"

Mason shook his head and smiled as he grabbed two bottles of root beer and brought one back to Ethan. He twisted off the lid and sat down again. "Why are you wondering about Maeve? I didn't think you two got along."

Ethan chuckled. "*She* doesn't get along with *me*. Not the other way around."

"Why?" Mason took a sip of the cold, bubbly liquid. It felt nice after such a long day working and he leaned back, trying to keep his eyes open.

"Long day?"

Mason totally caught the change of subject, but he ran with it. "I guess. The festival was two hours south."

"Ah..." Ethan took another long pull from his bottle. "What did you make this time?"

"A totem pole with a tree on the side and the usual bear. Those always sell best."

"And the tree? Is it gone?"

Mason nodded. "Yeah. It was sold before I finished."

Ethan snorted. "I think that's the norm at this point."

Mason shrugged. "I guess. It's nice that people are interested in it. I mean, what would I do with dozens of bears and wolves sitting around?"

"And trees," Ethan pointed out.

"And trees," Mason agreed. He grinned. "Don't think I didn't notice you didn't answer my question. I've never had any trouble with Maeve, though she's almost as quiet as I am, which makes for hard conversations."

Ethan's snort was less amused and more derisive this time. "She's not quiet. Believe me."

Mason paused with the bottle halfway to his mouth. "You really are fighting."

Ethan stared at the label, picking at its edge. "Fighting isn't the right word." He looked up, his usual mischief dimmed. "She won't forgive me for something that happened when we were kids."

Mason's eyebrows nearly hit his hairline. "That's...a long grudge."

Ethan shrugged and emptied his drink. "Yep." The men sat in silence for a moment. "Speaking of noticing things..." He narrowed his eyes at Mason. "To use your own words, don't think I didn't notice that you're wearing your nicest flannel shirt. Normally, you'd never wear that to carve. What gives?"

Mason looked down. How the heck did Ethan know this was one he usually saved for special occasions? "What are you? The wardrobe police?" Ethan and Mason had easily become friends when Mason had moved into town. The surfer reminded Mason a little too much of Crew and it had been a natural transition to begin hanging out together. They had enough in common to enjoy similar activities, but their introvert and extrovert personalities also kept them on their toes.

Ethan simply raised an eyebrow, not backing down.

Mason sighed and pushed a hand through his hair, knocking sawdust all over the couch. "I need to vacuum that," he muttered.

"You need to answer the question," Ethan retorted.

Mason groaned. "There might have been someone at the festival that I...wanted to see."

Ethan jerked forward. "You're joking. Right? The great lumberjack who takes two years to clear a chess board is after a woman?"

Mason growled lightly. If only Ethan really understood the situation, but there was no reason to hash it out. He couldn't have her. End of story. "Watch it. Just because I don't jump in feet first doesn't mean I can't knock your block off."

Ethan laughed and held up his hands. "Color me intrigued, but I'll let you keep your secrets." He smirked. "For now." He pressed his hands onto the arms of the chair and pushed upright. "You need sleep and I need to watch *Miami Vice* reruns. I'll catch ya later." He headed to the door. "Thanks for the drink!"

As quick as he came, Ethan was gone. Mason shook his head. He never knew what he was going to get with the guy, but the variety brought some laughter to his otherwise dreary life.

Standing with a groan, Mason stretched. Ethan was right. He needed sleep. "But first…a shower."

His phone buzzed before he could reach the bathroom and Mason hesitated. He didn't really want to get into a conversation right now, but if someone was calling this late…

He made a face, but lunged across the room to catch the call before it ended. "Hello?" he asked breathlessly, not having seen the ID before answering.

"Mr. Turley? This is Jason Clark."

Mason had to catch himself on the edge of the coffee table. "Yes?" he croaked.

"I think I might have found your sister."

CHAPTER 6

Harper pushed open her door with a groan, stumbling inside. Her purse plummeted to the floor but her keys managed to land on the small side table, though they did miss the dish she usually kept them in.

Making her way to the couch, she fell into it, burying her face in a pillow. This had to be the worst day in the history of her life. It might even top losing her grandmother too early or having her parents get divorced.

Being told she only had a month in order to sink or swim had caught Harper completely off guard. She had no idea how she was going to do it. Should she go ahead and enter the competition? Would that matter in the end? Maybe she needed to spend her time building up her online orders. Should she run ads? Who would she target?

A low groan slipped through her lips. How did her life get to be such a mess? She had worked so hard during school, keeping up a part-time job in order to pay for the things her trust didn't cover, and eventually leaving home to build a life here.

She had wonderful friends, had a crush on an amazing guy, even if he was only a dream at this point, and had built her art business up to about half of her monthly income. Neither her art, nor the trust were quite enough to live on, but combined, she had enough to be comfortable. And it was wonderful. Yes, she wanted to make a full-time living at her art, but she had faith she would get there.

"Just not in a month," Harper whispered to her dark home. For another fifteen minutes, her mind swam. What could she do in such a short amount of time? Her heart sped up and she felt sweat bead at her hairline when she realized she had no choice.

I'll have to win that competition.

Nothing else would be fast enough. Harper planned to do her best to build up her sales, but the odds of being able to double her income within just a few short weeks was almost impossible. Winning an award, however, could be a boost that could launch a career to the top.

She sat up, feeling three times her age, but forcing her stiff body to move. Walking down the hall, she opened her studio and turned on the light. Life would be a lot easier if Harper could find a painting she already had ready, rather than starting from scratch.

She began searching through the stacks of canvases piled along one wall. They were all so similar to each other that looking at one was like looking at the other. Harper had learned what people enjoyed in her area and had catered to it. Her first foray into something different was those food pictures, the very ones she had sold just this afternoon.

Disgusted, Harper let the canvases fall back into line and stomped out of the room, heading straight to the fridge. Half a slice of Aspen's mint chocolate cake was in there and if there had ever been a need for sugar, it was now.

Harper practically threw the door off the hinges when she jerked the door open. Grabbing the box, she slammed the door, snatched a fork out of the drawer and threw herself at a chair. The first bite that landed in her mouth was much bigger than anyone would consider polite, but Harper didn't care. She didn't need manners. She needed to figure out how to win a competition she had no chance of winning.

While trying to chew, she stabbed at the cake, turning it into broken little pieces. *Just like my life,* she thought bitterly.

Closing her eyes, Harper hung her head. This was stupid. "Stupid, stupid, stupid," she muttered through her bite. Everything was wrong and Harper found herself wanting to curl up in a ball and cry.

"It won't help," she whispered, shoving another bite in her mouth. "It won't help." She barely got the last word out, her emotions choking her and making the cake taste like dirt.

She hated this. She hated feeling lost and unable to fix anything. She hated feeling like she was at her mother's mercy. She hated the fact that her paintings were boring and all the same. She hated that her heart had chosen to yearn for someone she couldn't have. She hated…

"I hate that I'm not doing anything about it."

Harper shook her head. None of this would help. She wasn't a victim. She had spent years going against her mother's wishes in order to try and live her own life and Harper didn't want to give up all that progress now. She couldn't.

Her hand tightened on the fork to the point that the metal began to dig into her skin. She wasn't a quitter. She might be struggling tonight, but that didn't mean it had to stay that way. Slowly, Harper straightened her back. She took in a deep breath, expanding her chest as far as it would go before slowly letting it out. A month. She had a whole month. There was no need to panic. She would revamp her website. She would look into advertising. She would ask about putting her art in local shops and restaurants.

And I'll paint something new and amazing for the competition.

She nodded firmly. She hadn't come this far, to only come this far. Closing the container, Harper put the cake back in the fridge and grabbed a sketch pad and pencil. She was going to design something completely new. Something fresh and bright. Something that would catch the judge's eye and give her the very attention she needed to save her business.

Harper bit the eraser, her mind jumping back and forth as she tried to settle on a specific design, but it was all a muddled mess. She needed to move. Jumping to her feet, she grabbed her keys and headed out the door. It was a little late, but she lived in a quiet neighborhood and the fresh air would do her good.

Harper turned right from her driveway and marched down the street. She let her eyes wander across the dark asphalt, noting the outline of picturesque cottages and clean-cut landscaping. Nothing around her was fancy, but it always looked nice. She knew if she took another turn, she would hit the boardwalk after a while. The ocean would be roaring, going about its business as if the world wasn't falling apart at Harper's feet.

She paused at the end of the street. Maybe a walk wasn't exactly what she needed. Maybe it was sleep. She'd had a long day. She was emotionally spent and she was still frustrated with the situation. She needed her strength in order to handle the next four weeks.

Spinning on her heel, she went home. Her mailbox caught her attention as she arrived at her driveway and Harper stopped to check it. A pile of envelopes was inside and she grabbed them, closing the box and heading inside.

Once in the light, she flipped through, feeling a surge of excitement when she found a check from a small exhibit she had been a part of a few months ago. She hadn't sold much, but right now every bit would help.

Continuing through, she paused. One of the envelopes was addressed to Mason Turley. "What in the world?" Harper looked at the return address and realized it was from one of the outdoor vendor markets they had both been a part of. Somehow, they had mixed up hers and Mason's addresses. They were probably the only two people at the market from Seagull Cove.

Harper shook her head. Whatever. First thing in the morning, she'd deliver his mail, and then bury herself in the cottage and get straight to work. Her whole future depended on it.

* * *

Mason pushed himself away from his desk and pinched the bridge of his nose. He was exhausted. Today's work had been all consuming and every one of his contracts seemed to have concerns or business troubles. He'd talked two CEO's off the cliff and nearly had to renegotiate his terms with several others. This is why he liked to think things out before making a move. If the businesses he was working with would simply take the time to monitor their workers, they wouldn't have such internal turmoil right now and their contracts wouldn't be in danger.

He stood and walked to the kitchen to get a drink of water. Resting one hand against the sink, he stared out the dark window, wishing his life was as peaceful as the woods seemed to be in his backyard. He had another exhibition coming up in a few days and unless things calmed down, it wasn't going to be nearly as fun as normal.

His mind kept going back to his conversation last night with Jason. He had a lead on Aimee, but the details were fuzzy. He had promised to call back soon, but Mason couldn't seem to relax. Between work, Harper and now this…he felt as if he might explode at any moment.

Heading to the fridge, he grabbed the ingredients for making a sandwich. Maybe food would help him calm down. He had just finished building his third sandwich when his phone buzzed. At first, Mason ignored it and stood leaning against the counters, biting off half a sandwich with a single bite, but when the phone went off again, he yanked it out of his pocket. "Yeah?" he asked with peanut butter stuck to the roof of his mouth.

"Mason."

Mason paused. "Crew?"

"Yeah." Crew's voice was wrong. He sounded so serious, which was completely unlike Mason's upbeat brother

"What's going on? You don't seem yourself." What sounded like a sob broke through the line and Mason dropped his sandwich, clutching the phone with both hands. "What's going on?" he demanded again.

"It's…Aimee."

Mason froze. How had Crew heard anything before him? Why hadn't Jason called back? "Did they find her?" he whispered hoarsely. "Is she with Mom and Dad?"

Crew took in a shuddering breath. "She was killed in a car accident," he managed to get out.

Mason crumpled to his knees. The pain of hitting the hardwood should have jolted all the way to his shoulders, but he barely felt anything. "What?" The word was barely audible, but Crew must have heard because he responded immediately.

"She gave the first responders Mom and Dad's number," Crew explained. "But she died before they even got to the hospital." He coughed. "Internal bleeding."

Mason's hand was shaking so hard he could barely hold the phone to his ear. "Where was she?"

There was a long pause and he began to wonder if Crew had heard the question. "Seattle."

Mason closed his eyes. So close. She had been *so* close. A short plane ride would have gotten him to her side at any time, but he hadn't even known she was there. A black hole opened up in his chest and he was positive his heart would stop beating any moment. He had loved Aimee. As the older brother, he had taken care of both Crew and Aimee, looking out for their safety and keeping them in line. Aimee had been so much younger that she had required a lot more help than Crew had, but Mason had been glad to give it.

And now Crew was saying his baby sister was dead.

It didn't seem real. This had to be some kind of joke. Sweet, laughing, bright Aimee couldn't be dead.

"How did it happen?" Mason asked quietly. His mind couldn't seem to catch up with what he was hearing. How could such a brilliant star suddenly be gone? She had her problems, but Mason had been sure once her wild oats had been sown, she'd come back home as if nothing had ever happened. She would snort in amusement at dinner, mortifying their mother. She would punch Mason's arm and tease him about being bigger than the Jolly Green Giant. She would smile and throw her hair over her shoulder, making every guy in the vicinity take notice.

"I'm not sure," Crew admitted. "I was only given the bare details." He sniffed. "Mom wants us both home tomorrow."

Mason's head hung to his chest. "I'll have to find a flight."

"Yeah…me too," Crew said. "I called you before checking."

"I just…" Mason swallowed. His throat felt dry, and he felt like he should say something, but he didn't know what.

"I know," Crew assured him. "I feel the same way." He sighed. "Want me to fly by way of Portland? I'm sure I can find something that'll have a stop there."

"Nah. Head straight over, if you can. Mom will need you." Mason cleared his throat. "She's going to be catatonic."

"Alright. I'll text you my flight details."

"Sounds good." Mason closed his eyes. "I'll do the same. And Crew?"

"Yeah?"

"Thanks for calling."

Crew didn't answer right away and his voice was more fragile than before when he said, "Sure. See you tomorrow."

Mason hung up and let the phone fall to the floor. He didn't even care if the screen cracked. Falling onto his backside, he leaned against the stove. His entire world had just taken a nosedive and Mason wasn't sure what to do first. "The flight," he whispered. "I need to book a flight." Picking his phone back up, Mason used numb fingers to find and book the first one he could find. He'd arrive home tomorrow evening.

Home. He hadn't been home in years and never without Aimee there. Would the house feel empty without Aimee's presence? Would her essence be tangible? Would Mother be walking around as if nothing had happened or would she be willing to admit that the loss of her wayward child had hurt her deeply? His intensely Southern mother could be an Emmy-award-winning actress when her pride was at stake.

Mason scrubbed his face. He had been tired before, but now he was broken. His eyes swam with tears and he didn't bother to wipe them away. His sister had just died. He figured he had the right to cry for a bit before pulling himself together and packing.

No matter how tired he was, he knew there would be no sleeping.

On the plus side, that would give him plenty of time to shoot off some emails and make sure his boss knew he was taking a few personal days. He had no idea how long he'd be gone, but it would at least be through the funeral and after that, Mason would have to figure out what he was doing next.

    He sighed. Work. He needed to get to work. With a deep breath, he pushed himself up. Time to start closing the loose threads. He had a family to take care of.

CHAPTER 7

Harper took a deep breath. The check for Mason was heavy in her hand. Instead of coming the next morning like she'd planned, it had taken Harper three days to work up the courage to come deliver the envelope. Three days of knowing she would need to face the guy she liked and walk away for the last time.

Mason, of course, had no idea how significant this moment would be, but Harper did. And her heart was breaking over it.

But how else can I save my life?

She'd been trying to keep her focus on her painting and the marketing side of her business. Revamping her website, starting a small ad on social media. She was dipping her toe into new waters, praying desperately that something would help her see the progress she longed for.

But the envelope for Mason had been like an albatross around her neck. She was too scared to face him and yet too full of yearning to hand it off to someone else. Fortifying herself, she knocked firmly on his door.

She could do this. She *had* to do this.

She waited…her toes bouncing in her shoes, but no one came to the door. Frowning, Harper tried again. Mason worked from home.

Where could he be? She took a careful peek through one of the windows. The home was dark.

Huffing, Harper walked back to her car. "So much for choosing to be courageous," she grumbled. All that wasted time…for nothing.

She spent the rest of the afternoon trying to ignore the unfinished task, but after dinner, it ate at her again, pushing her to her feet and back to Mason's house.

Once again, she knocked. *This is it. It'll all be done soon.*

The porch light wasn't on and no lights glowed in the home either. Harper realized Mason was still away from the house. She walked back to her car, wondering where he could be. They all had the same friends… Surely one of them would know if he was out of town.

Punching in her Bluetooth, she called Aspen on her way home.

"Hey, Painter Extraordinaire, what's happening?"

"Hey, Aspen, do you know if Mason is out of town? Or does Austin know?" Harper made a turn and pulled out into traffic.

"Oh, ho!" Aspen crowed. "Just why do you need to know?" She dropped her voice dramatically. "Come on, Harp. Tell me everything."

Harper sighed. If only Aspen knew the big complicated mess that was her life. "It's nothing like that," she assured her friend. "I just got some mail for him by accident and tried to deliver it twice today, but his house is dark. I don't want to keep wasting my time if he's out of town."

"Ah, well, that's not nearly as exciting as I hoped it would be," Aspen grumbled. "Hang on." Shouting could be heard from the other side of the line and Harper pulled it away from her ear, wincing at the noise. Those Harrison sisters really knew how to be loud when necessary.

The line was quiet for a moment and Harper was beginning to think she'd lost the connection. "Aspen? Are you there?"

"Yep," Aspen said. "I'm just waiting for Maeve to work up the courage to ask Ethan if he knows where Mason is."

"Why does it have to be Maeve?" Harper asked. She knew as well as anyone else that Maeve couldn't stand Ethan. Something to do with a childhood situation gone wrong, though Maeve refused to share what it was. Ethan didn't appear to let the situation bother him, but he also didn't offer up any explanations.

"Because I think it's time she grew up and forgave him," Aspen said loudly, obviously wanting Maeve to hear her words. More shouting… this time followed by what sounded like shuffling and fighting.

"Oh, good grief." Harper groaned. She pulled into her garage and shut off the car. This wasn't getting her anywhere. "Aspen, I have to get back to work. If you hear anything, can you let me know?"

"Hang on, Harp. Maeve headed over." There was an unholy amount of glee in Aspen's voice.

Harper rubbed her forehead. All she wanted was to know when she could get rid of this envelope and therefore get rid of her crush. In her mind, they were one and the same at this point. Hand over the envelope, mentally and emotionally say goodbye, and viola! She was free and clear of any and all obligations. She'd only see him at friend gatherings from here on out.

Easy-peasy-lemon-squeasy.

"Ethan said Mason had a family emergency," Aspen said, her voice more subdued than before. "He should be back next week."

Harper's heart sank. "Is he okay?" she asked before she could think better of it. *No!* she scolded herself. *Don't get involved.* Harper shook her head. Friends cared, right? She'd care if Harper had a family emergency. Mason was still her friend, even if she was saying no to anything more. She could care and not get too involved…she hoped.

"He doesn't know," Aspen admitted. "But it sounds like he left in kind of a hurry."

"Okay, thanks," Harper said. She headed inside. "I'll chat with you later." Shutting off her phone, she dropped it and her keys on the side table and walked to the couch, falling into its softness. She studied the envelope. "Guess I'll just have to give you back later."

Once again, that weight sat on her shoulders. She wanted this done now. *Needed* it to be over. As long as she kept thinking about Mason, and now worrying about him, she wouldn't be able to give enough attention to her work, and she was desperate to finally make some headway on her road to independence.

Harper shook her head. "No. I'm in control here." She straightened and dropped the envelope on the coffee table. She refused to give it another thought until next week. Once Mason was home, the problem would be over. Until then, she would simply be a grown up. That's what women do.

If there was anything Harper retained from her mother's story, it was that she could handle anything life threw at her. She could fix her business. She could make it succeed. She could win against her mother's machinations, and she could definitely get one handsome lumberjack out of her head.

Walking to her art room, Harper turned on the light and went to her current work in progress. She tilted her head, trying to look at it objectively, but it was no use. She hated it.

Three days of work, three thrown away canvases. She had been trying to shift her style to be more like the past winners of the award, but it just wasn't working. Harper had certainly learned abstract painting during art school, but it had never resonated with her. It felt like trying to fit a square peg in a round hole.

Sighing, she threw the picture into the discard pile. Time to try again. She needed to be bold, to draw out emotion, and to really put together something eye-catching.

Pulling up another canvas, she grabbed her stool and prepped her tools. She could do this. There was no other option.

* * *

"I HAD no idea she would have a will," Mason whispered to Crew as they walked through the lawyer's office. He nodded to a few people as they walked, all dressed in business suits and looking like they were heading to important meetings. Mason tugged at his collar. His favorite flannel shirts had collars, but he always left the button undone and he almost never wore a tie. *Also known as a choking hazard*, he thought wryly to himself.

This whole funeral and reception had felt like a farce. Aimee had almost no friends left at her childhood home, but Mama had made sure the church had been packed. Afterwards, she hosted a luncheon dressed in her best black dress, her hair professionally styled and an unused handkerchief in her hand to signal her mourning.

More and more, Mason was coming to understand why Aimee had run off. After having a taste of his own freedom, his eyes were beginning to open to the prison his younger sister must have felt when she was growing up.

This morning his mother had redone his tie three times before they had been allowed to leave the house and it had irked Mason more than it should have. He had never really noticed when they were younger how much she was constantly…fixing them. Her words were often disguised as being helpful, and being the laid back guy he was, he had taken it all in stride as a parent loving their child enough to help.

Now he was seeing things differently. Since arriving home, he had been told his hair was too long. The beard needed to go. He was eating too much. Didn't they ever see the sun on that coastline? His skin was too pale. He didn't eat *enough*. His clothes were too casual.

Mason had tried to be understanding, but the more she had nitpicked on him, the more he had had trouble controlling himself. Crew had been smart enough to book a hotel. Apparently, he had caught on long before Mason that home wasn't the most uplifting place to be.

"I wish you would have shaved before we came," Mama murmured as they arrived at the lawyer's door.

Before Mason could reply, she continued.

"How unprofessional. Who brings their child to work?" Mama sniffed and stuck her chin in the air.

"Enough, Patricia," Mason's dad scolded under his breath. "People can hear you."

Mason's mom frowned, but didn't argue.

Small mercies, Mason thought, then felt bad for his impatience. His mother was doing the best she could. Her daughter leaving home and refusing to have any contact couldn't have been easy. A little compassion could go a long way right now.

He glanced sideways, noting the secretary his mother had been complaining about. She held a small girl on her lap. The child couldn't have been more than one or two years old. Her hair was dark and curled slightly at the edges. While Mason was watching, bright caramel colored eyes looked up to meet his.

Mason almost jerked back as a jolt of something hit him in the chest. He rubbed his sternum, unsure what was coming over him. He had no experience with little kids and had never been particularly drawn to them. They were fine and he hoped to be a father someday, but as a single man in his upper twenties, he hadn't found much of a need to spend time with any.

But there was something about the girl that tugged on his heart, not to mention…she looked slightly familiar.

Mason shook his head and turned away. He'd never seen that secretary or her little girl. His mind must still be going crazy.

"Mr. Musk will see you now," the secretary said, standing up and planting the little girl on her hip as she led the way to the other side of the room. With a wide, polite smile, the woman held the door open, allowing the whole family to enter.

Mason almost groaned when Crew gave the woman a wide smile. He elbowed his brother. "Now is not the time," he scolded.

Crew gave his brother a look. "It's always the right time to notice a beautiful woman," he whispered back.

"She has a child," Mason pointed out. "Which more than likely means she's married."

"Not always."

"Whatever," Mason conceded. "Just focus, huh? Mom needs us right now."

Crew scowled, but nodded.

"Mr. Musk," Timothy, Mason's dad said loudly. He walked forward to shake the man's hand. "We appreciate you doing this on such short notice."

Mr. Musk, a man who appeared in his fifties, shook Timothy's hand, but otherwise didn't appear moved. "It's my job," he said bluntly. "And Aimee asked me for a special favor."

"You saw her?" Mason blurted out without thinking.

Mr. Musk looked at Mason and his face softened. "She was friends with my youngest daughter. I heard from her now and again."

Fresh pain squeezed Mason's chest. He had always thought himself a conscientious person, one whose careful planning led to much more success than failures. But he was beginning to see how wrong he had been. Not only had his eyes been opened to his mother's issues, but to his own. When his sister had left, he had tried to contact her a few times and she hadn't responded. He'd tried to give her space, assuming she knew he would always be there to call on. She was an adult and she knew he loved her.

But maybe she hadn't. She hadn't turned to him when she was in trouble. She hadn't contacted him even though she had settled not very far away. She hadn't told him about the will or let him into any part of her adult life. Somehow…despite his best efforts, there had been a wedge between them and Mason had never seen it.

"Please have a seat," Mr. Musk instructed, sitting himself in his leather chair.

He nodded to someone behind Mason and Mason turned. The secretary closed the office door, but stayed inside, the child resting on her hip. Once again, those eyes were on Mason and he felt slightly uncomfortable with the little girl's attention. Turning around, Mason faced the desk, waiting for Mr. Musk to begin.

"Let me just say before we begin that Aimee was a lovely young woman and she will be dearly missed." Mr. Musk cleared his throat and put on a pair of reading glasses, ignoring Mrs. Turley's huffing.

It took a few minutes to get through the preliminary part of the will and Mason mostly tuned it out. It wasn't as if Aimee could have had much in the way of worldly possessions. Being here, for him, was merely a formality.

"I only have two things I would like to bequeath," Mr. Musk said. "To my brother Crew."

Crew straightened, showing his intent to listen.

"I would like you to take all of my assets and liquidate them as best you can, donating the money to charity."

Crew nodded immediately.

Mason joined him. It was a nice request. He was glad to see that Aimee wanted to help others.

"And to my oldest brother, Mason."

Mason jerked his head toward the front. He hadn't been expecting this.

"Even though you tend to favor Mother, needing to be in complete control—"

"Well, really!" Mama huffed.

"Patricia," Papa warned.

"She had no right to say that in her will, of all things," Mama argued.

"Mrs. Turley," Mr. Musk said plainly. "If you cannot quiet down, I'll have you removed."

The little girl began to whimper and Mason wondered why the secretary didn't just take her out. It was apparent the child didn't like it in here. Heck, he didn't like it in here!

Mr. Musk cleared his throat and went back to the will. "Even though you tend to favor Mother, needing to be in complete control, you've always been kind. I feel that my most valued possession would be best kept in your hands because you have the potential to provide her with the most solid foundation."

Mason leaned forward. "Her?" He had to have heard wrong. Did Aimee have a pet?

Mr. Musk tilted his head toward the door. "Mason, please meet Layla, your niece."

Slowly, Mason turned around. This had to be a dream. There was no way this was real.

"Layla, meet your Uncle Mason, and now, also your guardian."

CHAPTER 8

Harper had to give herself a pep talk over breakfast. Today was the day she would take that letter to Mason. The last week had been a disaster, to put it mildly. Her painting still wasn't coming together. Her ads weren't churning up any sales. Her mother seemed to take great joy in calling and checking up on her. *Every. Single. Day.*

And that stupid letter sitting on the coffee table was almost all Harper could think about. She knew it wasn't that important, but in her falling apart world, it seemed like one thing she could control. She was at the mercy of her skills when it came to her art. She had absolutely no control over her mother. She couldn't force patrons to buy her paintings, but she absolutely could take the mail down to Mason's and say her personal goodbye.

"Because you're an adult," she told herself in the bathroom mirror as she wadded her hair up in a bun on top of her head. "That's what adults do. They do hard things." She stared at the dark rings under her eyes and sighed. There was no makeup in the world that would be able to cover the fact that she wasn't sleeping well.

On the plus side, her pants were a little looser than they had been before. Apparently, going stark, raving mad was good for the waistline.

Closing her eyes, she shook her head. This was as good as it was going to get. She wasn't trying to impress Mason. She was simply giving him his check and walking out of his life. End of story.

A half hour later, she was driving down the street to Mason's house. Unlike last time, she could see the lights on and the garage was open, his large truck half in and half out. She frowned as she stepped out of the car, hearing loud screaming coming from inside.

It was so different than what she would have expected that Harper looked around, double checking she had pulled into the right driveway. It sounded like a pack of hyenas were loose inside and Harper almost climbed back into her car and left him to whatever chaos was going on. It didn't sound like a good time to knock on his door.

Before getting back in the car, Harper hesitated. She couldn't keep putting this off. She needed to get at least one weight off of her shoulders and this was the only one available to her. It had to be done.

Squaring her shoulders, she shut the door and headed up the front steps. Whatever was going on in there would have to wait for just a moment so Harper could say what she needed to say.

She knocked, loudly, then clasped her hands in front of her, squashing the envelope between her fingers.

"Hold on!" Mason bellowed, causing Harper to stumble back a step.

There was more shuffling inside and another loud scream before the door was yanked open. Mason stood in a T-shirt and jeans, looking worse than Harper had ever seen him. His eyes were red rimmed and bloodshot. His hair stood up on end and his beard looked like it hadn't been trimmed in several days. "Harper?" He blinked and scrubbed his face. "What are you doing here?"

Harper's eyes widened and those shaking hands went straight to her hips. "Um…" She had no idea what to say. What in the world had happened during the time he was gone?

Mason continued to stare as if he wasn't sure she was real.

Harper threw up her hands. "I came to give you some mail that was accidentally sent to my house. I wasn't expecting to have my head bitten off." *Though, maybe it's for the best,* she had to admit. It made it easier to think of leaving if he was being rude.

Mason deflated and he rubbed his forehead. "I'm sorry," he said hoarsely. "I didn't…" He sighed. "It wasn't…" He shook his head, seemingly unable to finish a full sentence.

Harper waited, but he didn't seem to have an explanation for her. "Whatever." She held out the envelope. "Here. See ya around."

"Harper…"

She paused, part of her hoping he would say more, but he didn't. She shouldn't want him to say anything else. This was the perfect way for her to leave without any leftover attachments.

Then why is this so hard?

She was fighting her nurturing instincts. Almost every part of her wanted to rush up and envelop Mason in a hug. He looked like he needed help, even more than she did. She wanted to listen and brainstorm and help him overcome whatever had him tied in knots, but it wasn't her place.

It'll never be my place.

With her heart in her throat, Harper began to walk away, but turned when she heard another scream. Looking over her shoulder, Harper almost stumbled to the ground when a toddler approached Mason with her arms up and tears pouring down her cheeks. She looked to Mason, who appeared so weary he was going to fall over.

He picked up the little girl and propped her on his hip. "I'm sorry, Harper," he said tightly. "It's not a good time."

"What in the world?" Harper's feet moved toward the house before she could stop herself. She stopped in front of Mason and put a hand on the child's back. "Whose baby is this?"

Mason closed his eyes. "This is my niece, Layla." When he opened them again, there was such a depth of sorrow that Harper almost burst into tears on his behalf. "My…sister was killed…in an accident."

Harper gasped, her hand covering her mouth. "No." It really was a family emergency.

"And I've been appointed Layla's guardian."

Harper froze. "You what?"

Mason sighed. "I know," he said, bouncing the little girl slightly. She laid her dark head down on Mason's shoulder and her eyelids drooped. It was definitely naptime.

"Look, why don't you go put her down and then you can tell me what happened," Harper suggested. Her thoughts of leaving and saying her own mental goodbyes were gone. This whole situation wasn't about her anymore. Mason didn't just need help, he needed an intervention. What was his sister thinking by handing the baby over to an unmarried brother who had no experience with children?

Mason shook his head. "I appreciate the thought, but I can't. She won't sleep unless I'm holding her."

Harper frowned. "You can't do that, Mason. You'll never get sleep yourself. Just put her in her crib. She's exhausted, she'll fall asleep."

"A crib? Is that what children her age sleep in?" He huffed. "I thought she would be too big for that."

Harper blinked, trying to process his words. "Mason…" she said carefully. "You do have a crib, right?"

He shook his head.

Harper looked around, noting the mess in the family room. Torn diapers, tipped over glasses, plates and cups, small broken toys, and shredded paper littered nearly every surface. It looked like a pack of monkeys had been let loose. She turned back to Mason. "Do you have *any* baby equipment?"

Mason shook his head. "Don't they only use special stuff for newborns? She's two. I thought…" He trailed off. "I'm guessing I was wrong."

Harper nodded and patted his arm, ignoring the thrill that gave her. "Listen. You're both exhausted. Lay down and take a nap…both of you." She gave him a tight smile. Looked like she wouldn't be doing any more painting today. "I'll be back soon."

* * *

MASON SHUT THE DOOR, not fully comprehending all that had just happened. He'd been home for less than forty eight hours and his life was in complete shambles. What in the world had Aimee been thinking?

She was thinking you were too demanding, but kind.

Those had been her words and they still sort of stung. He always thought of himself as fairly laid back, but his sister seemed to think otherwise. All those years he'd thought he was taking care of Aimee, trying to help, but apparently, she'd taken it as more control.

Although, who could blame her? Spending time with their mother for the first time in years had opened Mason's eyes to things he had never noticed before. And it wasn't pretty. All those times Aimee was upset and sneaking out of the house made much more sense. Mason had always just thought she was the wild child, and maybe it was partly true, but the other part surely had to do with their overly controlling mother.

The revelation that anyone thought he was similar had been a hard slap in the face and had given Mason a determination to make sure he never drifted that far off the direction he wanted for his life. Well, he'd be determined about it as soon as he had the energy. Right now, he needed sleep more than he needed air, but unless Layla was going to fall asleep, he wouldn't get any either.

He had no idea what to do with a child. He didn't know Layla, she didn't know him. She wouldn't sleep. Didn't eat anything he set in front of her. He couldn't keep up with her messes or keep her out of his stuff. In other words...he was slowly drowning. And he had very little hope that Harper's sudden appearance would change anything.

"It's just as well," he told himself as he took the crying child farther into the house. He winced as he stepped on a toy and had to physically stop himself from kicking it in anger. This was not supposed to be his life. Harper probably ran away and had no intention of coming back. He wouldn't blame her.

"Do you want something to drink? Some juice?" Mason carried Layla to the kitchen and offered her a small, plastic cup.

She grabbed it eagerly, only to dump almost all the contents down the front of her shirt and subsequently on him, since he was still holding her. The action set off another round of crying.

Mason bit back a curse and refilled the cup, then tried to hold it for her. He would have to wash off the stickiness before too long, but that could wait…maybe. The next ten minutes consisted of him fighting with her for him to hold the cup so she could actually drink the juice while Layla screamed to be the one in charge.

"I think your mom had the in control thing labeled on the wrong person," he muttered.

Finally, Mason walked to the couch and collapsed, Layla still sniffling against his shirt. He leaned his head back, wishing away the migraine that hadn't left since he'd heard his dead sister's words announce that he had become an instant father.

The sniffling quieted and Mason let out a slow breath. This seemed to be the only way that Layla slept. On him. In the middle of the day. He had always assumed he'd have nieces and nephews, even kids of his own, but Mason had had no idea that this was what it would be like. How did anyone survive to adulthood if it was this hard to deal with them? For that matter, why did anyone have more than one kid?

His mind wandered back to the shock on Harper's face. Yeah…he was positive any possible future chance for the two of them was gone. He'd held off for a long time, trying to find his sister, but now he was raising a little girl. What woman would want to take that on?

Layla shifted and squirmed, causing Mason to hold his breath until she quieted down again. Moving meant waking her up and he was going to avoid that at all costs. He rubbed his eyes. They were so gritty he could barely see. Keeping them closed, he blew out a couple of breaths.

As his body quieted, his mind began to wander and it instantly went back to the reading of the will and everyone's reactions. His parents had been just as shocked as Mason and Crew. Apparently, they hadn't known about their granddaughter either, and getting Layla out of Virginia and back to Oregon had taken a feat of Herculean proportions. Without Crew's interference, Mason was positive he would still be at his mom's home, fighting off his mother's demands to keep Layla there.

He might not like it, but Aimee had left Layla to him for a reason. And the more time Mason had spent with his mother, the more he realized just how difficult she was to live with. He didn't know Layla yet, but after hearing some of what his sister went through, Mason found himself determined to save her from that fate. He owed Aimee that much. He hadn't been there when she needed him most. She hadn't felt like she could turn to him when she was a lone teenager under their mother's unfairly strict rules and regulations. She had felt so alone that she had disappeared halfway across the country and never contacted a single one of them for fear their mother would find out.

His hand flexed on Layla's back. No…he couldn't save Aimee, but he could save her daughter. Or he could at least try. And if that cost him sleep, a clean house and…his love life…then that was a sacrifice he was willing to make.

His head flopped to the side. If Layla was sleeping, he might as well catch a couple of winks himself. It was his only shot. And maybe it would help ease the ache in his chest of losing something he'd never even had.

Harper would simply become the one who "got away".

CHAPTER 9

*H*arper paced the baby aisle. She was torn between worry, hurt, shock…actually, she wasn't sure what she was feeling. How often did a person just get handed a baby and told… good luck!

She snorted. Mason needed help and she was determined to give it. She had always had a natural instinct to help people. It helped Harper feel needed and important and she loved stepping back to see her hard earned results. But right now she was fighting an inner battle.

Mason needs help.

But I'm supposed to be walking away for good.

Helping him means less time for painting.

I wasn't having much luck anyway. One day won't be a big deal.

She checked her cart and counted through her list in her head. "Diaper bag, snacks, baby wipes, diapers…" Harper glanced up. "Oh, right. Sippy cups." She dumped a package in the cart. "Booster seat." She pushed the cart out into a larger area and grabbed a booster seat for the dining table and then picked out a few outfits that looked about right for Layla. Mason had said she was two, so Harper went with the corresponding size. After a few more things Harper thought might be helpful, including a lovely little teddy bear, she was done.

Heading up to the register, she pulled her heavy cart and continued to fight with herself. "Enough," she whispered, hoping no one caught her talking to herself. "They need help. You can't just walk away. Tomorrow you can go right back to work." With a firm nod, she began loading her purchases onto the conveyor belt.

"If you'll wait just a minute, we'll have someone come carry out the crib," the clerk said.

Harper nodded. "I appreciate it. Thank you." She stepped to the side and waited until a teenage boy brought out a larger cart to lift the heavy item. With a smile as her greeting, Harper guided him to her vehicle, praying everything would fit.

With a very stuffed and heavy car, Harper drove the hour back to Mason's house. By the time she pulled into his driveway, Harper had gone from frustration and despair to acceptance and resignation. She could be an adult about this. She could help him get his feet wet in the world of parenting and then walk away, just like she had planned before. It would all turn out just fine.

She grabbed a few bags and marched up to the door before she could chicken out. She set the bags down to knock and then waited… and waited… Harper knocked again before hearing a thud, a cry and a curse. She grimaced. *Oops.*

"Harper," Mason said, his jaw dropping in shock. "What are you doing here?"

Harper raised her eyebrows. "I told you I'd be coming back." She glanced at her watch. "Have you two been sleeping the whole time I was gone?" Slowly, Harper shook her head. "She'll never sleep tonight if you let her go this late in the day."

Mason rubbed the back of his neck. "I told you, she doesn't sleep at night anyway. She only sleeps when I'm holding her."

"Unless you don't want to sleep for the next ten years, then you need to set up a routine and schedule," Harper stated, trying to be kind about it, but he really did need to make some changes.

Mason sighed and nodded. "I know." He shrugged. "But how?"

She raised her eyebrows. "Can I come in? I brought a bunch of baby stuff with me. Maybe we can get it set up around the house and I'll try to give you some pointers?"

Mason hesitated, then stepped back. "You already saw that everything's a wreck," he said glumly. "But I haven't been able to keep up, not to mention I'm exhausted."

Harper gave him an encouraging smile. Exhausted Mason was actually quite adorable, but she could never say that out loud. *You're just helping a friend,* she reminded herself. *Your competition painting is waiting for you.* "Stick with the schedule and in a few days you'll be feeling better." She stepped inside. "Though I can't guarantee complete rest until Layla is out of the house," Harper teased. "I've heard parents never truly sleep again."

Mason groaned. "I didn't need to hear that."

Harper glanced over her shoulder as she set bags down on the coffee table. "Sorry!"

"No, you're not, but I can't blame you for laughing." Mason scrubbed his face. "I'd be doing the same if this happened to someone else."

Harper's shoulders drooped. "No, you wouldn't. You'd just dig in and help." She sucked in a deep breath and put her hands on her hips. "So I'll be quiet and do the same."

Mason gave her a grateful smile. "Thanks."

She returned to the bags. "I have bibs and sippy cups and plates and utensils in here. If you'll grab the crib out of the car, you can work on putting it together while I get Layla fed." While she was talking, the little girl shuffled into the room. Two fingers were in her mouth and she stared with wide eyes at Harper. She was a pretty little thing. Someday those eyes were going to have no trouble getting male attention. They were large and soulful… *Just like Mason's.*

Harper shook her head. Nope. Not going there. Her attraction wasn't welcome. "Are you hungry?" Harper asked the little girl, leaning back to see her face. A red, wet but hopeful set of eyes met

Harper's. Harper smiled, hoping the baby couldn't tell how strained it was. "Do you like macaroni and cheese?"

"You bought a crib?" Mason asked in shock.

Harper glanced over. "Of course."

"I…" Mason shook his head. "Right. A crib. I'll get right on that." Still shaking his head, he walked out the front door.

Layla watched him go, then turned to Harper again.

Harper nodded. "Macaroni and cheese? Let's go get it." Searching at her feet, Harper grabbed the bag she wanted and headed to the kitchen. She would get the little one settled with a plate of food, then start guiding Mason through everything he would need.

Layla followed, but Harper was surprised to find the girl was silent as a stone. Didn't two year olds babble like crazy? Harper tried to remember her babysitting days, but it was a little difficult to completely break down who had been what age. She was pretty sure, however, that as soon as they *could* talk, all little children never stopped talking.

"It's fine," she whispered to herself. Harper picked up Layla and propped her on her hip, then began to work around the kitchen one handed, quickly settling into a rhythm. Tonight wasn't going to be the most nutritious meal, but it was a start. If Harper could help Layla find something familiar, hopefully getting her settled into a routine with Mason would be a little easier.

After all, Harper only had tonight to do this. Tomorrow she was right back to work and lumberjacks and cute kids were no longer her responsibility.

* * *

Mason watched from the doorway, the heavy bags dangling from his arms as Harper spoke to Layla. The toddler had two fingers stuck in her mouth and her head on Harper's shoulder as the wonder woman stirred a pot of boiling pasta. If he'd been in a better frame of mind, the scene would have been quite touching, but as it was, Mason was too tired for it to be anything but shocking. "How do you know so much about kids?" he blurted out before he could think better of it.

Harper looked over her shoulder, looking entirely at ease. "I babysat, just like most teenage girls."

Mason grunted and set the bags on the small kitchen table. His house was a complete and utter mess and he should probably be embarrassed for Harper to see it, but he couldn't muster the energy. It wasn't like anything was going to happen between them anyway. He'd already made that clear. *So why is she here?* The question begged an answer, but Mason was afraid if he asked, she'd leave, and this was the first true sign of hope he'd had since Layla arrived.

Harper hummed and swayed from side to side. "Layla," Harper crooned. She kissed the tiny girl's head with a smile. "Such a pretty name for such a pretty girl." Harper wrinkled her nose. "Who needs a diaper change." Harper looked to Mason and he groaned.

"I, uh…would you mind…" He scratched the back of his head. How could a grown man who worked a full time, successful job and played with chainsaws for fun be so incompetent?

Harper rolled her eyes. "What is it with men and dirty diapers?" She started toward the bags.

"No…I mean…I can't quite figure out how to make them work."

Harper paused. "You don't know how to put on a diaper?"

Mason shrugged. "We've been getting by, but they always seem to sag and I'm pretty sure I go through more wipes than is necessary. Could you teach me?"

To her credit, Harper looked like she tried to stop her smile, but Mason couldn't exactly blame her for finding humor in the situation. It was utterly ridiculous how something so small had taken him to his knees.

"Didn't you ever change her diaper when she was smaller? When you visited your sister?"

Mason shook his head. "My sister ran off after high school. I haven't heard from her in four years."

Harper's jaw dropped. "Did you even know you had a niece?"

Mason shook his head slowly, the shame slithering through his gut once again. What kind of an uncle was he?

Harper sighed and squeezed Layla a little tighter. "No wonder this is all such a mess. You guys are having to get to know each other on top of adjusting to living together. Good grief."

Mason would have chosen other words, but he couldn't say them in front of Layla or Harper. "So, uh…the diaper?"

Harper nodded. "Okay. I brought diapers with me, but why don't you show me your setup?"

Mason led her to what used to be his spare bedroom. He had used it for storage, but all the boxes were now against the wall and a blow up mattress covered in blankets sat on the floor. It was all he had. Buying anything at the store had been impossible as of yet since he hadn't managed to make it out of the house since getting home.

Those perfectly shaped eyebrows went up again. "Okay…" She turned to Mason. "Mason, you're a great guy. But as your friend, I'd like to say something."

As your friend. Why did that sentence hurt? He'd already decided that's all they'd ever be. He couldn't ask someone like her to wait for him to get his life together. "Go ahead." He braced himself.

"You might need more help than I can give you. I have a project I'm working on and won't be able to help after tonight, but it's clear you're starting from square one."

Mason nodded wearily. "I know. I was completely caught off guard by all this and I'm just…not sure how to fix it."

Harper laughed lightly. "Men and their need to fix things," she teased. "Layla isn't something that can be fixed. She just needs to be taken care of and loved."

Mason didn't know what to say to that. Well, he had some ideas, but none of them were appropriate. Did Harper also need love? Did she want someone to take care of her? Would she ever consider being with a guy who was a father?

Harper stiffened. "Dang it. I can smell the noodles. Hang on." She handed Layla to Mason and rushed out of the room.

Mason looked at Layla, who stared back, those fingers still in her mouth. "Sorry about the diaper," he said. "But Harper knows better than I do how to fix it." *I can't fix your diaper, our sleep or even my love life. I'm starting to think I'm pretty useless around here.*

Layla wiggled and Mason put her down. She immediately followed the path Harper had taken and Mason kept up.

"Hey, baby," Harper said as they entered the kitchen.

Mason blinked, until he realized she was speaking to Layla. *Idiot*, he told the warmth in his chest, pushing it aside.

Harper was at the sink, draining the meal. "You want to help me mix this up?"

Layla grabbed at Harper's leg and Harper set everything down to grab her.

"Has she always been this quiet?" Harper asked over her shoulder after settling Layla on her hip again.

Mason shrugged. "I don't know. Since getting her home, she either screams, cries or is silent."

"Hmm…" Harper went back to her work. In no time at all she had mixed the macaroni and cheese and was fishing through the bags. "I bought a booster chair. Can you go find it in the car?"

"Booster chair?"

Harper nodded. "Yeah. It's a seat that can be hooked to one of your dining chairs so Layla is tall enough to eat. It's a box. You'll see it easily."

Mason nodded and headed outside once again. How had Harper known everything to buy? He didn't even know the names of the products, let alone that he needed them. After finding what he thought was the right box, he went back inside.

Difficult as this was, Harper was proving to be an absolute angel and it made him wish, once again, that things had worked out differently between them. He couldn't let Layla down, but having Harper in his life would have been such a good thing.

You have her…for just a little bit anyway. Better just enjoy it.

Mason nodded at his own thoughts. Harper said she'd spend the evening with them and help him get settled. That would simply have to be enough. Her friendship was proving invaluable and hopefully could help him get his life back on track. By the time her work was done, he'd be able to let her go and simply be grateful. Yep. Grateful. That was probably all he was feeling towards her anyway. She was saving his bacon. Who wouldn't be a little attached to the person doing the saving? It was a normal response and he was a normal guy. This would all work out…he hoped.

CHAPTER 10

"Okay…" Harper wiped her hands on her pants and turned to look at Mason. Layla was happily sitting at the table smashing macaroni and cheese into her mouth. Half with her hand and half with the plastic fork Harper had given her.

"That's the most I've seen her eat since she arrived," Mason muttered. He scratched his beard.

"What have you been feeding her?" Harper asked.

Mason shrugged. "Whatever I ate."

Harper nodded. "While you won't want to feed her mac and cheese all the time, it's almost always an easy hit."

"Almost?"

Harper grinned. "I had a cousin who hated cheese. This wouldn't have gone over well at her house."

Mason shook his head. "How do you women keep it all straight? I'm so far under water I don't know which way is up."

Harper grabbed Mason's forearm, ignoring how much she enjoyed feeling the muscles there, and guided him to the couch. They could still see Layla, but could also talk without worry about what the child would hear. "Why don't you tell me everything that happened. I think it might help if I know where you're coming from and you have a friend who understands." She paused and tilted her head with a grin. "Of course, I know you and Ethan are buds. Maybe he's a better choice?"

Mason chuckled and settled against the couch cushions. "Somehow I'm guessing Ethan would be as lost as I am."

Harper just waited. She might hate the fact that she was here in a friend capacity, but she loved being able to help. It would have to be enough. She glanced over her shoulder to see Layla throw some pasta on the floor. "You might need a dog," Harper murmured.

Mason sighed. "Somehow I think another responsibility is the last thing I need right now."

Harper shrugged. "Sometimes adding a responsibility lessens the impact of another, so life ultimately becomes easier."

Mason's eyebrows pulled together. "That might be too deep for my tired brain right now."

Harper just smiled. "Just tell me what happened."

And he did. For almost half an hour, Mason talked. It might have been more than Harper had ever heard him speak in one sitting and she knew she could listen to him talk forever. His deep, slightly rumbling voice resonated in her chest and made it ache for what she knew she could never have. That little flicker of hope that had always been sitting in the back of her mind had been extinguished when she'd had to negotiate with her mother just to keep getting a paycheck.

"Wow…" Harper knew her eyes were as wide as dinner plates as he finished his story. "That's…insane."

"Yep."

Harper pinched her lips in thought. "What did your parents have to say about all this?"

"They weren't happy at all," Mason said with a harsh laugh. "They fought with the lawyer for close to an hour after the will was read, demanding Layla be given to them. If my brother Crew hadn't helped run interference, I'm not sure I'd have made it out of the house with her."

"Do you think they'll come here?"

Mason shook his head, his eyes half closed. "I doubt it. Mom hates small towns." He huffed. "I didn't think about it until now, but that might have been what drove me here. Growing up, I didn't have any problems with my mom, but I was naturally the quiet, obedient one. Going back to living with her, even for such a short time, made me realize just how difficult it must have been for Aimee."

Harper's eyes stung with tears for Mason, Aimee and little Layla. This whole situation was a nightmare and a pushy, overly difficult grandmother wasn't going to help matters. It was a good thing Mason's mom lived clear on the other side of the country. "I'm going to get Layla bathed. Why don't you put together the crib I bought?"

Mason jerked upright. "You really think she'll sleep in that?"

Harper nodded. "Yep. I'm sure it's what she had when she was with her mom." She started to walk away, but Mason grabbed her hand. A little jolt of electricity ran straight up her arm and Harper had to work to keep her face calm.

"I know I've said it already, but thank you," Mason said in an almost reverent tone. His golden eyes were soft and framed by those dark lashes that made girls jealous. "I was trying to do this all by myself, but the more you explain, the more I realize that I wouldn't have made it. You're an amazing friend."

Harper's smile was shaky, but she kept it on her face. Who knew how badly one word could hurt. "You're grateful that I'm a pushy know-it-all, who doesn't know when to quit? Awesome. I'll have to tell my mom those particular personality traits actually did come in handy one day."

Her deflection worked perfectly as Mason chuckled, standing to his feet. "I'm assuming I'll need tools?"

She nodded. "Yep. I have some in the car, but I'm sure you already have everything you need."

"On it." Mason glanced at Layla, turned to Harper and shuddered. "Is she going to get messy like that every night?"

"Maybe," Harper admitted, laughing. "She's just at an age where she's learning to feed herself. Though sometimes she might let you take care of it, odds are she'll want to be involved. Half the food will go in, half will be washed off in the bath."

Mason rubbed his forehead. "I might need a hazmat suit."

Harper's smile continued as she walked over to the little girl. She studied Layla, who watched back with large, brown eyes. She really was a beauty. Brunette hair that would probably only continue to darken as she got older. The coloring definitely ran in the family, since it was similar to Mason's. Though, Layla's eyes were darker than Mason's. It made Harper wonder exactly what Aimee looked like, or maybe Layla's dad.

Harper shook her head. "It doesn't matter, does it, sweetie?" Harper cooed. Her smile faltered when Layla continued to stare. It worried Harper that Layla spoke so little. Harper picked up the bowl. "Cheese? You like macaroni and cheese?"

Layla smiled a toothy grin.

Harper sighed but smiled back. For now, she would set the speaking on the back burner. When she was ready to, Layla would more than likely talk. But her world had just been turned completely upside down. It made sense she might be a little quiet for a while. The words would come back in time…hopefully.

* * *

Mason grabbed his toolbox and headed to the extra bedroom. He glanced at the picture. Looked simple enough. He should have this together in no time. "Hey, Harper?"

"Yeah?" she hollered back.

"Be sure and give me the receipt for this stuff, okay?" Mason was more than a little uncomfortable with the idea of her paying for everything.

"Okay."

He blew out a breath, grateful she hadn't fought him on it. Layla was his responsibility and he had enough resources to take care of her just fine. He just hadn't known what he needed in order to do that.

As he took the pieces and tools out of the box, he noted that for the first time in several days, he felt better. Lighter. More hopeful. How he had ever thought he could do this alone, he didn't understand. He must have been too drunk on grief to truly understand what it was going to be like to take care of a young child.

Even feeding Layla had been a challenge and yet Harper had stepped right in, knowing exactly what to do. Someone needed to create babysitting classes for boys, because this was ridiculous. He knew there were single fathers in the world. How did they learn it all?

From the women they had children with, Mason thought wryly. He didn't have that resource, but he had Harper. She was never going to understand how glad he was that she had burst her way in, wielding her knowledge with the same expertise she wielded a paint brush.

She'll also never understand how hard it is for you to keep referring to her as a friend.

Mason had been determined when he brought Layla home to not be distracted by anything else. Layla deserved all his attention, at least until she was a little older and Mason could breathe again. But even in the short time Harper had been there today, he'd realized just how hard it was having her around.

Every time she touched him, his heart jolted, like he'd been shocked by an electric current. And when he'd grabbed her hand to say thank you, he almost pulled back when an extremely pleasant warmth had begun to climb his arm.

He shook his head and opened the instruction booklet for the crib. As sweet as she was, Mason couldn't do it. It simply wouldn't be fair to ask Harper to wait. She was a beautiful, wonderful woman and deserved more than what he was capable of offering at the moment.

"How are we doing in here?" Harper stood in the doorway with a freshly washed Layla on her hip.

Mason blinked at the image. Harper looked so natural with the little girl, like a mother with her daughter, though they were a picture of contrasts. Layla's wet hair was darker than normal, but combed nicely with the ends curling into small ringlets, while Harper's straight blond hair was scraped over one shoulder, looking brighter than ever against the dark little girl.

That warm feeling was back and Mason almost couldn't bring himself to push it away. It was a welcome feeling after so much grief and loss. He cleared his throat and looked down at his project. "A little slower than expected." He picked up the instructions. "I don't think the person who wrote these spoke English."

Harper laughed. "Probably true. But I think you'll figure it out." She started to walk away, but Mason wasn't ready for her to go.

"Hey!"

Harper turned back, her eyebrows raised.

Idiot, he scolded himself. *Now what?* "Uh…what's the thing Layla has?" The little girl was holding onto a handle that seemed attached to a cup and was holding it up, a small lip in her mouth.

Harper frowned. "A sippy cup."

"A sippy…what?"

Harper's frown turned into an amused smile. "You really haven't been around children, have you?"

Mason scratched his chin. "Uh…no. I'm the oldest, but not old enough to remember my siblings as babies. And I don't have any nieces or nephews, and my cousins are all back East." He shrugged, once again feeling completely inept.

Harper waved him off. "Sorry. I'll remember we're starting from ground zero, I just forgot." She jutted her chin to the cup. "It's a cup that has a special lid so the child can drink without making a mess. It's kind of a learning step between a bottle and a regular cup."

Mason didn't want to tell her about his attempt at helping Layla drink earlier today. He'd put his ignorance on display enough today. "Well, give me a half hour or so and I'll have this together."

Harper laughed softly. "Okay." She walked away and Mason scowled, wondering why she had a skeptical tone.

He looked at all the pieces once again, but shrugged. He built giant totem poles out of wood. How hard could a crib be?

An hour and a half later, he shuffled into the sitting room, finding Harper reading a woodworking magazine to Layla. He made a note to get his niece a few books when he could manage to get to town. "It's done," he grumbled, dumping himself on the couch next to her.

"Oh good," Harper said. "Because the little lady is definitely ready for bed."

"She won't sleep," Mason said, opening one eye. "She hasn't since she got here."

"That's because she could get out," Harper said. "Come help and I'll show you what to do."

Mason sighed, but pulled his aching body back up and walked down the hall. Getting Layla to sleep would take a miracle and a small petty part of him wanted to see Harper actually run into a problem she couldn't fix.

Mentally smacking himself, he amended his jealousy and joined her in the tiny room.

"Oh shoot." Harper spun and handed Layla to Mason. "Hold her a moment. I forgot the blankets." She disappeared down the hall before Mason could stop her.

His eyes automatically went back to Layla, who was watching him with those serious eyes. They blinked slowly, and he realized Harper was right. She was ready for bed.

"Okay, here we go." Harper pulled the tag off a small pink sheet and followed it with a soft blanket. She handed the blanket to Mason. "Let her touch and cuddle with it for a moment."

Mason offered Layla the blanket, but she just stared.

"Throw it over your shoulder and gently tip her head down," Harper suggested.

Not knowing how that would help, Mason did as instructed. Layla resisted only for a moment before relaxing against the soft fabric. He could practically feel her body melt into his chest and a small protective fire lit inside of him. This was all so new, but Mason couldn't deny that having Layla around was already changing him.

"Great," Harper whispered, having fixed the sheet over the mattress. She patted the side of the crib. "Now let her down with the blanket."

"That's it?"

Harper nodded. "Yep. She's so tired she'll probably sleep a good long while."

Mason walked over and gently eased Layla up and over the side, placing her on her back, the blanket tucked into her shoulder and side of her face.

"Come on." Harper walked to the door and waited.

Mason looked at Harper, then back down at Layla. He was suddenly afraid of leaving her. Would she be alright? Would she start to cry as soon as he left? He watched those eyes blink slowly again, but just couldn't seem to walk away. A small, soft hand on his pulled his attention away.

"She's going to be fine," Harper insisted quietly, though she was smiling at him. "Come on and let her sleep." When he still didn't move, she grasped his hand and tugged, pulling him into the hallway.

Harper closed the door and there wasn't a peep from the other side. She pushed her hair away from her face. "Okay. I think maybe you should go to bed as well and in the morning I'll come help show you how to create a schedule that you can both work with."

Mason looked at the door. "You're sure she's fine?"

"Absolutely." Harper's response was so matter of fact that Mason felt he had no choice but to believe her.

He nodded, forcing himself to take a couple of steps away from the door and Harper's alluring presence. "Thank you…again. I don't know what I'd have done without your help."

"Been too sleep deprived to function," Harper teased. She nodded toward the front of the house. "I'll let myself out. See you later."

Mason watched her go, wanting to say so much and yet not knowing how. She marched into his home like a whirlwind and yet somehow, had set everything to rights. The only thing that would be better was if Harper could become just as permanent a part of the household as Layla now was.

The sound of a soft sigh behind him, however, reminded Mason why that wasn't possible. At least not right now. Maybe, hopefully… after all was said and done, lightning would strike twice and he'd find someone just as wonderful as Harper to help give Layla a feminine influence in her life. If only he could be so lucky.

CHAPTER 11

Harper pulled her hair up into a bun before swiping on a bit of lip gloss. She pursed her lips and spread the raspberry creme gloss on. She loved how it made her lips pop. "Not that he'll notice," she muttered as she put her make up away. Mason had said the word "friends" so many times yesterday that Harper had wanted to shout that she got it.

"Geez, sensitive much?" she scolded herself in the mirror. She wasn't even supposed to be going over to his house today. But after putting Layla to bed, it had been clear that Mason was exhausted and would need to wait to go through creating any kind of schedule. "I can spare a few hours this morning," she muttered, grabbing her oversized purse and stuffing it with snacks from her cupboard that would be a good fit for Layla. Mason would need to go grocery shopping and learn how to get food that Layla could and would eat.

She paused, realizing just how deeply Layla's arrival was going to affect Mason. Every aspect of his life had changed in a split second. He'd need a sitter to go anywhere by himself again, and the odds of it being a last minute thing were basically gone. Travel, work, food, sleep…there really wasn't any part of his life that wouldn't change. A dull ache built in her chest and Harper rubbed her sternum. Sympathy and a longing to help ease his burden nearly overwhelmed her and she had to grip the counter until her knees quit shaking.

"And to go through all this while mourning his sister's death?" She blew out a breath. What kind of superhero was he? He might have been a mess when she arrived, but it was only because he was trying. He hadn't complained, he hadn't wanted Harper to just do it all. He could have simply given Layla to his parents and washed his hands of the matter, but instead Mason had decided to honor his sister's wishes and raise her daughter. A daughter no one even knew existed.

Harper closed her eyes and manually brought air in and out of her lungs. She had always been one to sympathize, but this...this was different. Harper didn't just feel bad for Mason. She *hurt* for him and yet admired him at the same time. If she could choose the perfect man, one who was masculine yet gentle, intelligent yet humble, and knew how to work, Mason Turley wouldn't just be at the top of the list...he'd be the whole list.

She shook her head and gathered her keys. She couldn't do this. Couldn't continue to torture herself with fantastical wishes that would never come true. Her feelings for Mason were so much more than she thought. This feeling didn't come from a simple crush, she'd had those before.

No...this pain and admiration were the result of something deeper, something she didn't want to name, because naming it made it real and no matter how much she yearned after the lumberjack, he still couldn't be hers.

It only took a few minutes to arrive at his house. Harper's heart began to pound in her chest as she walked up to the door. Unlike yesterday, there was no screaming and wailing coming from inside and she hoped that was a good sign.

She knocked, but no one came to the door. Her rapid pulse began to speed for a different reason. Had something happened? She knocked a little harder, the sound slightly frantic. After what seemed like forever, the door creaked open. "Mason?"

He scrubbed a hand down his face. "Yeah. Come on in." He backed up, showing off his pajama pants and tight T-shirt.

Just friends...just friends... Harper had to chant the reminder. Mason was all too delectable first thing in the morning, especially after her realizations this morning.

"Sorry." He covered a yawn. "I wasn't expecting you quite so early."

Harper laughed softly. "It's nine o'clock. I was expecting Layla to be up and demanding breakfast."

Mason stilled. "It's nine?"

She nodded.

"Huh." His hand went through his unruly hair. "I can't remember the last time I slept this late."

She patted his chest as she walked by him. *Oh, man...that was unnecessary torture.* Harper tried not to appear as if she was yanking her hand back, but if she didn't get herself under control, she wasn't going to make it through breakfast let alone anything else she was supposed to help with. "Let me go check on Layla and I'll meet you in the kitchen. We can go through some things while she sleeps."

Mason nodded and shuffled away, another yawn breaking loose.

Harper laughed under her breath, turning away so she didn't run into a wall from watching him walk away. It would be all too easy to just stand there all day and enjoy his boyish behavior. Why was it so attractive to see big men act adorably little?

The world may never know.

Harper grasped the doorknob to Layla's room and carefully eased it open. Layla was standing in the crib, watching her. Her eyes were bright and refreshed, a far cry from yesterday's red rimmed look. "Hey, sweetie," Harper said with a smile. Once again, she had a moment of worry that the child wasn't responding. *Time. Just give her time.*

Layla smiled and waited for Harper to approach before raising her arms.

"Such a good girl," Harper said, pulling the cutie close. She kissed the warm forehead, brushing the curls back from Layla's. "Let's give your uncle another lesson in diaper changing, huh?"

Layla bounced against Harper's hip, so Layla set her down and took the girl's hand. "Let's go." Harper guided her down the hallway, but Layla wasn't going to be held back, eventually ripping her hand away from Harper's grip and racing into the front room. "Careful!" Harper called, lengthening her steps to keep up.

In a flurry of curls, Layla ran to the couch and crawled up, settling herself proudly on top.

Mason came from the kitchen. "What's going on?"

Harper waved a hand toward the couch. "You might have a climber on your hands."

He frowned. "Is that good?"

Harper shook her head. "Uh, not usually."

Mason's shoulders slumped. "Just give it to me straight."

Harper tried to hold back her laughter, but there was nothing for it. She walked over and grabbed Layla off the couch, still giggling under her breath. "Sorry. You just look so…resigned. Like you're prepping for someone to punch you in the face."

Mason joined her with a chuckle. "It kind of feels like that. Every time I turn around, something new is throwing me off my game." He sighed. "So, does being a climber mean exactly what it sounds like?"

Harper nodded. "Yep. There are some children who like climbing things and that can be anything from the couch to the fridge."

"That can't be true," Mason argued.

Harper raised her eyebrows. "It is."

"Why do I get the feeling you were a climber?"

Harper smiled. "I didn't manage the fridge, but I did have a tendency to climb the bookcases. Mom says I almost sent her to an early grave."

Mason turned and walked back to the kitchen. "I don't even want to hear it."

"You'll be fine," Harper assured him, following his path. "I lived to adulthood, didn't I?"

"Yeah, but I'll bet your mother knew more about children than I do." He began grabbing food out of the fridge. It looked like it was an omelet morning.

"You'll learn," Harper pressed. "I promise not to back off until you're comfortable with it all."

"Might as well move in then," he said with his head still inside the fridge. "Because I don't know that I'll ever get there."

Harper swallowed the emotions that followed his joke. He obviously had no idea how those words would affect her. "Before you start breakfast, you need to change Layla." There. Dirty diapers were a perfect way to move her mind away from living with a handsome lumberjack into focusing on reality.

Mason jerked upright. "Right." He cleared his throat, his cheeks slightly pink. "I should have thought of that." He walked over. "Come on, Tiny. Let's see if Harper's lesson yesterday stuck."

Harper watched from the entrance to the kitchen, that same unnamed feeling swirling through her belly as he talked and teased the little girl, all while changing her diaper perfectly.

You're only going to end up more broken hearted if you don't stop it, she scolded herself.

The thought was sobering. She really needed to keep her hormones under control. She was only here for the morning. If she didn't get a good handle on that painting today, she'd be scrambling to get it ready at all. She'd keep that as her plan. Help Mason, go home and paint and *stop* noticing every sweet thing that Mason did with little Layla.

* * *

Mason brought Layla to her feet. "All set," he said with a grin.

Layla lunged forward and threw her arms around his neck, starling Mason. He rubbed her skinny back, feeling like a bull in a china shop. She was so small, so breakable, but dang it if her little hug didn't fill him with a little bit of parental pride.

"Ready for some breakfast, Tiny?" he whispered.

Layla stepped back and stuck two fingers in her mouth.

"I'll take that as a yes." He stood and offered his hand, which she obediently took. Why couldn't things have been this easy when she first got here? Instead, it had been nothing but complete chaos. It was amazing what a little direction could do.

Speaking of...

Mason looked up to see Harper watching them.

"You're a natural," she said, though her smile looked a little sad.

Mason shrugged. "Or you're just a really good teacher."

She shook her head. "That's not it, but thanks for the boost." Turning, Harper led them back to the kitchen. "I'll scramble some eggs for Layla. Were you wanting an omelet for yourself?"

"That was the plan," Mason said. He sat Layla at her seat. Her curls were kind of a wild mess. Much different than the combed ones Harper had given her last night. He grinned. It was kind of cute.

Layla slapped her hands on the tabletop.

Harper laughed from the stove. "Are you ready for your eggs?"

Layla frowned and Mason's eyes widened. He'd seen this look before. Layla slapped the table again.

"Uh..." Mason turned to Harper.

Harper faced them fully this time and looked at Layla firmly. "Eggs. Do you like eggs? Should we have eggs?"

Layla let out a grunt and shook her head.

Harper turned back to the stove.

"What do we do?" Mason whispered.

She glanced over her shoulder. "Nothing. She's eating eggs. We'll work through it."

"What if she starts to scream?"

Harper smiled and pulled the pan from the stove. "She's two, Mason. There's going to be lots of screaming and lots of tantrums. It's not called the terrible twos for nothing."

Mason pushed a hand through his hair. His was probably just as wild as Layla's and he knew he should be completely embarrassed that Harper was seeing him in his pajamas, but even with a long night's sleep, he was still too tired to care. "There's no way to stop it?"

"Oh, you can give her everything she asks for," Harper said easily. "It'll stop it for the moment, but then you'll have one spoiled kid on your hands and you'll pay for it later."

He slumped into a chair.

Layla shouted and began to buck in her seat.

"Why did Aimee do this to me?" he grumbled. Layla was a sweet little thing...when she'd slept and when Harper was reading her a story. But dang it! He didn't know a thing about raising a child. He didn't know about sippy cups, or the fact that she still needed a crib. He didn't know what to do when she screamed, cried and demanded things. What about when she started talking back? How was he going to handle that? Harper seemed to think Layla should already be talking, yet all he'd heard were cries and shouts, no actual words. Was she traumatized from her mother's death? Was there something wrong mentally? How in the world did a parent know how to keep track of it all?

He groaned and let his forehead hit the table. *This is impossible.*

"Hang in there, Daddy," Harper said, patting his shoulder. "You'll get the hang of it. You're already a master diaper changer. After a bit, this'll all be old hat."

He straightened. "My life has always been quiet and orderly. This is the exact opposite." He looked at Layla, who was still slapping the table. "I just don't see how this is going to work." He shook his head. "But it's also not like I can send her back."

Harper stood watching, as if processing everything he was saying. "Do you want to let your parents take her?"

He jerked back. "I..." He paused. "I don't know." The words tasted bitter and made his stomach slightly nauseous. He didn't want to go against his sister's wishes, but surely his mother, an experienced parent, would do a better job than Mason could.

Harper held up a finger, then went back to the kitchen. She scooped the eggs onto a plastic plate, bringing it and a child's fork to Layla.

Layla wrinkled her nose at the offering.

Harper smiled wide. "Mm, mm! Eggs!"

The toddler wasn't convinced.

Harper shrugged and took the plate and fork, bringing a bite to her lips. She closed her eyes. "Mm, mm. Eggs!"

Layla narrowed her eyes, but she didn't respond.

Harper took another small bite. "*My* eggs," Harper said. "Mm. *My* eggs."

Layla shook her head. She held out her hands, grabbing for the plate.

Harper stopped, another bite almost to her mouth. "Oh. You want some?"

Layla made grabby hands again.

"Eggs?" Harper prompted.

Layla's lips turned down and she strained for the plate.

"Good enough," Harper murmured, putting the plate in front of Layla. She leaned in with an open mouth, but Layla wasn't about to share. The little girl stuffed a handful in her own mouth, then grinned triumphantly.

Harper pulled back, chuckling softly. She held up her hands. "Layla's eggs."

Layla continued eating, ignoring Harper.

With the baby busy, Harper turned back to Mason. "Is it okay if I offer my opinion?" she asked softly. "I don't want to overstep my bounds as your friend." She gave a self deprecating grin. "Even though I already did when I burst in here with diapers and a crib."

Mason folded his arms over his chest. "Go ahead. I value what you have to say." And he did. Harper had a good head on her shoulders and Mason was already relying on her knowledge with Layla. Why not hear what she had to say in this case?

Harper glanced to make sure Layla was still occupied, then looked at him with a stoic face. "I think more than anything, right now you're overwhelmed, under rested and still grieving." She shifted. "You've barely had time to process the fact that your long lost sister is gone, let alone that she had a child. You're sleep deprived not only from the trip but from dealing with Layla. And yes…your life has been turned upside down with her becoming yours, but when Aimee said you were the best choice, I believe her." Harper leaned forward. "As a *friend*, I think you're amazing. You're kind. You're a hard worker. You look before you leap and while Aimee might have lived a little different than that, she recognized that a steady foundation was something that would be good for her daughter."

Harper reached across the table, her hand resting on Mason's forearm. "You're good for Layla," Harper insisted. "Things are tough right now, but I have every faith that they'll get better. You two will get to know each other and settle into a routine. Every parent everywhere has managed it and I don't think you're some kind of exception. You're just as capable as everyone else and it bothers me that you don't feel the same."

Mason said in stunned silence. Why couldn't he have this woman in his life? There was a literal ache in his chest with the desire to kiss her. But Layla was there, smashing eggs into her hair and Harper had just made it very clear that her words were from a friend. He couldn't cross that line. If he thought his life was chaotic now, trying to nurture a relationship during this transition would be a nightmare. Still…he couldn't help but wish.

"Thank you," he said hoarsely. "I needed that."

Harper nodded and removed her hand…much to his disappointment. "Good. Just take it one day at a time. It'll all turn out just fine."

Eggs hit the side of his face, seeming to punctuate Harper's words. "Right," he drawled sarcastically. "It'll all be fine."

CHAPTER 12

Harper stepped back to examine her display. The sun was shining and spring was definitely in the air, yet Harper couldn't seem to enjoy it. She was restless, jumpy, and truthfully, she wanted to walk out of the market and head straight back to Mason's house.

She missed Mason…and Layla… Somehow the little tot had wormed her way into Harper's heart all too quickly. Those large eyes and silky curls were a constant in the back of Harper's mind.

"It's only been two days," she reminded herself. "Give it time." That had been her mantra for the last forty eight hours. *Give it time.* She'd done a good deed in helping Mason, and now she needed to put her focus back where it belonged.

The fact that he hadn't called or texted for help since she left only attested to his ability to grow and adapt, but would Harper be okay? With the way her heart was hurting, she wasn't so sure.

Once she had taught him a few basics, Harper had forced herself to go home and focus on her career. But her heart wasn't in it. The painting for the competition wasn't going well, and for the first time that she could ever remember, Harper didn't want to be a vendor, selling paintings and interacting with customers. She had always loved this aspect of her job, but not today.

Unfortunately, her heart was two hours south, locked up in a cabin with a man and a baby, and neither of them had any clue.

"It looks great."

Harper gasped and spun. "Oh my gosh, Mason. What are you doing here?" Harper had been positive Mason wouldn't attend any more live exhibitions that summer, which was part of why she'd been brave enough to come. It was taking all her willpower to stay away from him and she knew that seeing him in person would ruin her.

He adjusted Layla, who was grinning wildly, and looked around. "I, uh, I'm carving today."

Harper frowned. "With Layla?" She reached out and took the girl without thinking. Those little arms were reaching for her and Harper was far from immune to the cuteness. "You're going to try and work while watching her?" Harper snorted. Mason still had a lot to learn, apparently.

"Yeah, well...I figure it'll all work out." Mason squished his lips to the side where they nearly disappeared into his beard. "I know I don't really have any right to ask, but we were wondering if you would help us."

Harper automatically swayed Layla on her hip. "Oh?" She couldn't explain how her heart skipped a beat and her ears perked up. Okay... that was a lie. Harper knew exactly why her body was responding that way, but she was trying not to think about it. Wanting things to be different just made it harder.

He reached out and caressed Layla's cheek.

A corresponding sensation ran down Harper's face and she held back a shiver.

"Both Layla and I have missed you," he said softly.

"Has there been trouble with your schedule?" *Please say no, please say no.* Once again, Harper's heart was yo-yo-ing. She felt as if she had no control of the organ. Mason had been a point of joy and pain and yet this tiny bit of hope had it speeding up like a runaway freight train with only one destination in mind, and her career completely forgotten in the rearview mirror.

His head shake was slower this time and he took another half step closer. "It's not the schedule."

Harper waited, that freight train nearly bursting through her chest.

"Layla keeps looking for you and wandering the house like she's lost," he explained. "And we've had a couple of close run-ins when I had no idea what she wanted." He huffed. "She's still not speaking and I don't read minds very well."

Harper blinked and stopped bouncing Layla. That runaway train had come to a screeching halt. "What?" she whispered hoarsely. This was not where her hormones had thought this conversation was going. Her cheeks were flushed and Harper felt too warm. She hoped Mason would attribute it to the glorious sunshine, because she certainly wasn't going to explain her overactive imagination.

"I guess I just wanted to ask, if you're not too busy, if you wouldn't mind stopping by once in a while." He rubbed the back of his neck. "You know, show me what I'm doing wrong and help me make sure I'm giving her everything she needs." He raised his eyebrows, those golden eyes pleading. "What do you think?"

Harper had no words. Her mind went through every reason why she should turn him down. She was on a deadline. She needed to spend more time trying to advertise her business. Her social media accounts were lagging. She had a competition to enter. Her mother was threatening to take away her income. She was sending out paintings to new art houses, hoping to be included in their exhibits.

"Sure."

Wait, what? That was *not* what she had planned to have come out of her mouth.

Layla began tugging on a piece of Harper's hair and Harper leaned her head down, resting it on the child's silky crown. She wanted to sigh in contentment. She had missed this. Something about having a tiny person rely on her made Harper feel…needed…and wanted. Two things that always seemed to be missing from her life. Her mother only wanted her to change careers. Her customers wanted the paintings. Even Mason only wanted her help. But Layla? Layla seemed to simply enjoy Harper. It was a heady sensation.

"Great!" Mason said with a wide smile. "Uh, I mean...great." He nodded, looking slightly embarrassed. They stood staring at each other for the next few seconds.

Layla was still pulling on Harper's hair, but Harper barely noticed. She was caught in a golden gaze that was drawing her in like a bee to honey. The air began to grow thick and heavy, like maple syrup, and Harper found her body leaning forward ever so slightly.

Mason blinked. "Yeah. Let me grab her from you." He reached out and took Layla, lifting her off Harper's hip.

"Oh, yeah...thanks." Harper cleared her throat. *Oh my gosh, can I get any more pathetic?* She mentally face-palmed herself. If she got out of this conversation with any pride still intact, it would be an absolute miracle.

"I gotta run do my stuff, but...see you around?" Mason asked, looking slightly worried, like she had changed her mind in the last two minutes.

Harper nodded. "Yep. I'll be around."

"Great." That heart-stoppingly wide smile was back. Really, if she was going to be stupid enough to spend time around him, the least Mason could do was have a crooked tooth or something. *Anything* that would take away from his attractiveness.

Harper gave a little wave as Mason walked away, Layla hanging on around his neck. Her heart lurched and Harper admitted, once again to herself, that her heart was no longer hers. She had thought it was back at Mason's log cabin, but now she knew better. It was here at the festival, but it was walking around, handsome and cute as sin, doing whatever it pleased.

"Excuse me, miss," a voice called.

Harper spun, grateful for the interruption. "Good morning! How can I help you today?"

"I was curious about that painting in the back," the woman said, pointing with a gnarled finger. "The one with the pine trees?"

Harper smiled, but there was a distinct lack of joy behind the effort. This was her life. Pleasing patrons and talking about painting....all by herself. Somehow, the realization hurt more than it usually did. Her bright, career driven future had suddenly turned very dreary and lonely.

* * *

MASON WALKED AWAY from Harper feeling excited, but also idiotic. He'd been honest when he said he wanted her to visit, but his reasons had nothing to do with more help. Not that he considered himself an expert on parenting now, but using the schedule and tips that Harper had given him a few days ago, he and Layla were doing alright.

But Harper was missing. She had only been around a few days, but with her gone, the house seemed quieter, if that was possible, and Mason was struggling to control his desire to have her close. The idea of being something more than friends just wasn't going away any time soon, even though logically he knew it was a bad idea. He really should be using this time to continue getting to know Layla and becoming more comfortable with his new role as surrogate dad.

Just this morning, he'd realized how much he was going to have to adjust his time in the mornings when leaving the house. It had taken three times longer than usual to pack up Layla and her gear just to get to the car, instead of just being able to grab his coat and go. And then, as he began to buckle her up, she'd filled her diaper and he'd had to go back inside and start all over.

Now he was going to have to start planning in advance just for him to be able to work. He'd probably need a babysitter or nanny eventually, but Mason wasn't even sure where to start with something like that. He worked from home most of the time. Could he simply watch Layla on his own? Or was he going to have to adjust to having a stranger plus the baby running around?

Mason felt himself pale and he swallowed hard before looking at his niece. Her wide eyes, so reminiscent of his sister, looked straight back. Without conscious thought, Mason reached up and tucked a piece of her thin hair behind her ear. He'd tried combing it this morning, but…

"We can do this. Right, Tiny?" he whispered.

Layla stuck two fingers in her mouth and looked around at all the hustling happening at the event.

Mason chuckled softly. "Yeah. We can do this." He strode back to his vendor area and spent the next hour trying to keep Layla from touching sharp objects and talking to potential customers as they walked by. It should have been a disaster. He was constantly darting around, scooping her up before she killed herself or broke something and Mason soon realized exactly why Harper had been so amused that he thought Layla could entertain herself while he worked.

Luckily, most of the customers were understanding and even talked and laughed with Layla. She never spoke, but she smiled and giggled, charming everyone who said hello. When it was time for him to start up the chainsaw, however, Mason was definitely ready for a break. This parenting gig was no joke.

"Hey, sweetie," Harper cooed, walking up like the angel she was and holding out her arms. "Let Daddy work his big chainsaw and you come help me, okay?"

Layla didn't complain a bit at Harper's invitation.

"Uh…" Mason felt his cheeks grow hot. "Don't you have a booth to run?"

Harper nodded. "Yeah, but unless you're asking for a trip to the ER, there's no way you can run that saw and let her be loose."

He frowned even while knowing Harper was right. His pride, however, demanded that he argue. "I brought stuff for her to play with."

Harper grinned. "Do you really think she'll stay in one spot? Has she done that at all this morning?"

He sighed, his shoulders lagging. "Are you sure this is going to be okay?" Mason asked under his breath. "She's cute, but can be a terror for something so small."

Harper smiled. "I'll be fine. Just go and do what you need to do."

Before he could talk himself out of it, Mason leaned down and kissed Harper's head. "Thank you." Spinning on his heel before he did something stupid like try to give her a real kiss, Mason marched to his work site. He needed to do something manly. Something that involved a lot of testosterone, like handling killer wood-carving machines. His life was being run by two females who had no idea just how wrapped around their little fingers he was. One of them couldn't even speak yet, but she still demanded all his time and attention and Mason gave it all too willingly.

Jerking on the cord to start his chainsaw, he felt a thrum of satisfaction. His niece might be worming her way into his heart and Harper wasn't too far behind, but geez…there was something so satisfactory about feeling the hum of that engine in his hands. Time to do some carving.

By the time he'd finished his demonstration, Mason was feeling much better. His burdens felt smaller and his energy greater. He was ready to grab lunch and take on being a dad again for the afternoon. He'd always heard men complain about their wives wanting "me time," but after this…Mason got it. He'd only had Layla a little under two weeks and this hour for himself had done wonders.

Maybe hiring a nanny won't be such a bad thing, he thought as he headed to the food area. He wanted to be the main adult in Layla's life, but he still needed to put a roof over their head and food on the table. In time, hopefully he could figure out how to do both. Layla wasn't going to end up like her mother, at least not if Mason could help it.

Deciding the least he could do was bring Harper lunch, he carried a couple of plates of food back to Harper's booth and walked around back since she was with a customer. After setting everything down, he grabbed Layla so Harper could better concentrate and plopped her on his lap, handing her a french fry to gnaw on while he waited for Harper.

"Oh, my goodness." Harper sighed as she came around back. "I'm starved." She sat down and tucked her hair back. "Today has been crazy busy."

"Is it too much with Layla? Do you need me to keep her?"

"Do you have another demonstration this afternoon?" Harper asked.

He nodded.

"I'll be fine for that time, but we might want to consider bringing a sitter next time. She was darling and drew in customers, but it's hard to answer questions when I'm trying to keep her from knocking everything over."

Mason chuckled. "I had the same thought. It hadn't even occurred to me to pass her off to someone else, but now I'm starting to understand."

"That's alright," Harper assured him. "We'll figure it out. Is this for me?" Harper pointed to the extra plate.

Mason nodded. "It's my way of saying thanks."

"Well, thank *you*," she said with a grin, pulling the plate into her lap. "I'll take free food anytime."

Mason watched Harper from his peripheral vision, keeping most of his attention on the child in his lap. He had no idea if she realized how she had lumped them together as a team when it came to Layla. The words had flowed so easily that Mason was positive they were completely sincere, but also completely innocent.

He couldn't deny how much he enjoyed them either. But how was he supposed to win Harper's heart if he didn't have enough time to date her? No. He shook his head. He couldn't think like that. He couldn't let himself hope…could he? Was there really a way to make this work? For him to have it all?

He was still debating with himself, but when Harper pulled Layla into her own lap and began to bounce the little girl until she laughed, Mason knew he would regret not giving it a try.

CHAPTER 13

"Am I going to have to clean up like this after every meal?" Mason grumbled, sweeping under the table.

Harper held back a laugh, though she couldn't seem to stop a grin. "Probably. Children, especially little ones, are definitely not easy on the cleaning bill." She'd kept her word and stopped by two days after the festival on the pretense of helping him clean the house and work through any other issues he was having. As far as excuses went, it was pathetically flimsy, but even Harper's career-determined side hadn't cared. She just wanted to spend more time with the duo who held her heart, even if the feeling wasn't returned quite the same way.

Mason snorted and bent over to sweep the excess of eggs and other crumbs into the dust pan. "Now I get why you said I need a dog."

"They do help," Harper offered. "I had a dog all my growing up years."

"Why don't you have one now?" Mason asked, though his attention was still on his work.

Harper tucked a piece of hair behind her ear, wondering how vulnerable to get. They were friends, but not necessarily confidantes.

Though, he did share everything with you. This isn't that big of a deal by comparison.

"I always figured I'd wait until I wasn't single to get a dog," Harper said. She shrugged and grinned. "Don't want the pooch to get tired of seeing my face."

Mason paused, his eyes growing intense for just a split second, before he nodded. "Yeah. I'll bet pets are easier when there are more people involved."

"You didn't ever have a pet?" Harper asked, grateful he hadn't pressed her single issue, or acted weird that she brought it up. Sometimes guys seemed to have funny ideas about that kind of thing.

Mason shook his head and set the broom and dustpan back in the closet. "No. Mom didn't want the mess." He paused. "Huh. I guess Aimee was right." He snorted. "I was kind of offended when she said I was the most like Mom, but now I'm starting to see it." He pushed a hand through his hair.

"From what you've said, I don't think you're like her at all," Harper argued. "She sounds a little…difficult." Harper shrugged. "You're pretty easy to get along with."

Mason gave her a half grin. "Thanks for that." He looked around. "Now what?"

"Layla isn't dressed yet."

Mason grimaced. "We've sort of worked that one out, but it's ridiculous how long it takes."

Harper laughed and walked toward the sitting room where Layla was playing with several Tupperware containers. They were the only "toys" that Mason had. "Let's get this party started." She took Layla by the hand. "Let's get dressed. Okay?'

Layla happily tripped along beside Harper toward her bedroom.

"So…" Harper paused. "Her clothes?"

Mason's cheeks turned red and he pointed to a suitcase.

Nodding, and choosing not to point out the fact that he needed to get her a dresser, Harper rifled through the pile. "Looks like today is laundry day."

"At the rate she gets dirty, every day might be laundry day," Mason muttered.

Harper just smiled. He was just as cute when cranky as he was when being sweet, though she'd take that thought to her grave. She pulled out a couple of pants and shirts. This was probably a good time to try and get Layla to speak. Turning, Harper held up two shirts. "Do you want to wear the pink shirt? Or the purple one?"

Layla pushed her hair out of her face and pointed to the pink.

"A pink girl, huh?" Harper helped unzip the pajamas and Layla sat down, kicking her legs. "Whoa, there." Harper wrestled with the child a little until she was undressed. "Arms up!" Making silly faces, Harper wrangled the shirt onto the small body, snapping the buttons under her diaper. "Now. Pants." Harper grabbed two pairs. "Do you want the pink ones? Or the yellow ones?" To her surprise, Layla picked the yellow. This was going to be an eyesore. "Awesome. Pink and yellow."

She turned Layla around, setting the girl on her lap, and Harper helped get the small legs into the openings. "Stand up!" With a final pull, Harped pulled the pants over the diaper. She bit back a smile at the thought of Mason handling potty training sometime during the next year. *That's going to be fun.*

"All done!" Harper threw up her hands and clapped.

Layla also clapped, but still didn't speak.

"How much should a two year old talk?" Mason asked. "And is it just the guy in me, or does her outfit look hideous?"

Harper stood and laughed. "It's pretty sad. But does it really matter? She picked it out, and wanted to wear it, and who's she going to see anyway?"

Mason shrugged and stuffed his hands in his pockets. "No one, I guess, except me and you."

"And I think we can handle it," Harper assured him. "Letting her feel like she's in control will help her cooperate."

"So no more tantrums?"

"Oh, there'll be tantrums. But this at least can lessen some of them."

"And the talking?" He bent down to pick up Layla, who was holding out her arms to him.

Harper pursed her lips. "I'm not sure. My gut instinct is to give it time. She's had just as much upheaval as you but isn't as mature. I'm hoping she shut down because she just lost her mother. But only time will tell."

Mason went pale. "And if it doesn't change?"

Harper shrugged. "You need to get her in with a pediatrician anyway. The doctor should have better suggestions."

Mason nodded. "Thanks. I don't know what I would've done if you hadn't come to help."

Harper patted his shoulder as she left the room. "What are friends for?" She was starting to hate that word. Sweet Layla was tugging at Harper's heartstrings and every time Mason learned how to do something new, it made Harper fall just a little bit more for him. She had only spent a few days with this makeshift family, but Harper already knew that if given the chance, she could love this whole household without even trying.

She rubbed her forehead. It was going to take a miracle for her to walk out of this situation with her heart still intact.

"Bring Layla out here and we'll see if she'll play with something," Harper called. "Then we can talk about the rest of the equipment you're still missing."

Heavy footsteps behind her told Harper that Mason was following her directions. Poor guy. He was trying so hard. Why his sister thought she could simply dump a child in his lap and all would go smoothly was something Harper couldn't comprehend.

No one plans to dump a child, her inner voice scolded. *There's no way Aimee ever thought this kind of thing would happen. Layla's just lucky her mother thought to have a will at all. Otherwise, prickly Granny would be turning the little girl into a perfect little princess and there'd be no pink and yellow outfits at all.*

Harper had to give it to the voice in the back of her brain. Sometimes it impressed even her.

"Where can I find a sheet of paper?" Harper asked.

"My desk is in the third bedroom," Mason offered.

Leaving him with the baby, Harper walked down the hall to retrieve the supplies she needed. Mason would enjoy this part. Lists and structure were right up his alley and Harper knew having something to refer to would help get him back on his feet…without her…and once she got some distance, the pain in her chest would subside…eventually.

* * *

Mason looked down at the list he'd been working with Harper on. It was such a relief to have everything mapped out for him. He was usually comfortable being in charge, but this time, he was so far out of his element that he hadn't even known where the starting line was. Dresser, books, booster seat…the list was clear and concise and Harper had even helped him know why the equipment was necessary. *Geez, kids are expensive.* It was a good thing he didn't live a lavish lifestyle or this would have put him into debt.

He glanced at Harper, who was playing with Layla. She had slid from the couch to the floor and together the females were building with wooden blocks that Harper had brought over. Layla was enjoying pushing them over, giggling at the destruction.

One side of Mason's mouth pulled up into a grin. His niece was more enjoyable than he thought she would be. Her eyes lit up when she smiled and sometimes, when he wasn't paying attention, Mason could see stark reminders of Aimee in the child's behavior. Harper's idea to give Layla a choice in getting dressed had been brilliant.

Just like his younger sister, Layla didn't like being told what to do. Having options helped make her much more cooperative. *And will hopefully waylay any tantrums,* Mason prayed. Harper had assured him they would still happen, but Mason decided he'd keep hoping for a miracle.

"Are we keeping you from your work?" Mason asked, the thought bringing with it a slew of worry. "It just occurred to me that while you're here, you're not painting."

Harper shrugged, looking slightly uncomfortable. "I do have a project I'm working on...but I've kind of been stumped with it anyway. Helping a friend has been a nice break."

Friend. More and more, that was starting to become a curse word in Mason's vocabulary. He didn't want Harper to just be his friend. Even during the last few days, his attraction to her had shifted from *she's really nice and pretty and would make a great girlfriend* to *I'm not sure what I'm going to do when she's not in my life anymore.*

You're still adjusting, he reminded himself, using Harper's words. *Once you get settled into a good routine with Layla, life will be easier, and then it won't matter that Harper's not here.*

The words made his stomach churn. Mason wasn't fooling himself at all. He didn't want to do this alone, but he couldn't imagine trying to navigate a new relationship with two girls at once. No woman should have to play second fiddle and that's exactly what Harper would be. Their time together would revolve around a child and Mason's attention would be split and their alone time almost nonexistent. He was still trying to get to know Layla, let alone how to handle being a father.

And maybe that was part of the problem. Mason hadn't known that Layla existed. He didn't see her as a newborn. He didn't hold her and hear from Aimee about her likes and dislikes. He was starting completely from ground zero...on everything.

And Harper deserves to be treated like the only woman in the room. Not the one I turn to when I have a couple of minutes during naptime.

Mason sighed and slumped a little deeper into his seat. His life was such a mess.

"I think maybe it's time for lunch and a nap," Harper announced, climbing to her feet.

Mason blinked and looked at his phone. He'd obviously been lost in his thoughts for a while. "Wow. Time flies."

Harper smirked. "Especially when you're napping." She picked up Layla.

"I wasn't sleeping."

She chuckled. "You were snoring, Mason."

He rubbed his forehead. "Really? I thought I was just lost in thought."

Harper shook her head. "Nope. But that's alright. It gave Layla and me a chance to get to know each other a bit." She looked down at the little girl on her hip. "Who wants peanut butter and jelly?"

Layla scrunched her nose.

"She obviously understands us," Mason said.

Harper looked thoughtful. "She does, but I haven't figured out yet why she's not repeating everything she hears." Harper turned to Layla and rubbed noses with her. "Can you say lunch?"

Layla laughed and the sound did odd things to Mason's stomach. Slowly, but surely, he was positive the little stinker was worming her way into his heart. Mason had taken her on out of a sense of duty and to fulfill his sister's dying wish, but somehow, the organ in the middle of his chest was starting to get involved.

He had to be getting soft because he felt as if it were the same struggles he was having with Harper. His heart wanted her, but his brain said to handle things more rationally. Layla needed Mason to be a protector and guardian, not a softie who let his overactive feelings run the show.

Logic had gotten him far in life and Mason knew he couldn't abandon it if he wanted to be able to handle the many years of parenthood ahead of him.

An hour later, they were cleaning up peanut butter sandwiches, which Harper had somehow convinced Layla to eat, and suddenly it was nap time.

"So…I just put her down?" Mason whispered, Layla tucked tightly into his chest. "I've been trying, but she cries and doesn't sleep well."

"You don't have to whisper," Harper said, but nodded. "Yeah. Just like the other night. Let her know it's naptime, put her down, tuck her in. You can sing her a little song, or read a book, you know…create a pattern."

Mason felt the blood drain from his head. "I have to sing to her?" he asked hoarsely. He hadn't considered that. He'd been doing his best to follow the schedule she had given him, but naptime was still a fight. Harper showing up to help today was an answer to prayer.

Harper's twitching lips told him just how much she was enjoying his discomfort. "You don't *have* to sing. But kids enjoy it." She leaned in. "And Layla won't care what your voice is like or how off key you are. They just like music."

Mason swallowed hard and nodded. He was a grown man. He could handle this. He marched down the hallway, knowing he probably looked like he was going to the guillotine, but unable to help it. "Okay, Layla. It's naptime." He stopped at the edge of the crib when she started to squirm. "Naptime? You ready for naptime?"

Layla shook her head and Mason looked for Harper.

"Give her her blanket," she said softly. "Like you did before."

Mason grabbed the soft piece of fabric and tucked it over Layla's shoulder, then laid her down. Layla immediately jumped to her feet and held up her arms, starting to cry.

The tears bit at Mason's resolve. He hated it when she cried. She was so tiny. They had to be doing it wrong. He started to reach for her, but Harper hissed at him and Mason pulled his arms back, feeling like a little boy caught at the cookie jar. "She's crying," he said, as if it wasn't obvious.

"She's going to cry," Harper explained. "You just need to stay in charge. If you give in every time she cries, you'll be back to chaos in no time." Harper raised an eyebrow. "A two year old isn't a good boss."

Mason scrubbed his face, trying to ignore the sounds coming from the little girl. "Then what do I do?"

"Read or sing," Harper pressed. "Give her clear boundaries. Then tuck her in and leave."

Mason groaned. He didn't have any books yet. He'd have to sing instead. *Crap.* Closing his eyes, he tried to remember one of the little ditties most kids knew from their childhood, but he wasn't feeling very confident "The Itsy Bitsy Spider" was going to help him out. Singing it twice, he put Layla down again and tucked in her blanket, then walked toward the door.

He closed his eyes once in the hall, hearing her sniffle and whine.

He hated it. How did parents do it? How could he handle this day in and day out? Warm fingers touched his cheek, and Mason's eyes snapped open.

Harper was there, looking at him with sympathy. "That was great. Give her a few minutes and she'll quiet down. The first few times will be rough, but sticking to your guns will give you both some sanity."

Mason nodded, and his eyes dropped to her lips. She was so close. So...close... He could smell the fruity scent of her shampoo and the warmth of her body was starting to permeate his shirt.

As if realizing she was in his bubble, Harper pulled back, ducking her head and putting space between them.

Mason wasn't sure what came over him, but he couldn't let her create that space. Reaching out, his hands grabbed her hips, stopping her. Harper's beautiful eyes widened and she looked up at him...questioning...begging...

Mason was positive he hadn't made the conscious choice to kiss her until after his lips brushed hers. But the jolt of the touch brought every nerve ending to full alert, causing him not to care how it began. All he knew was he wanted more. One little peck wasn't enough. Harper's breathing was shallow and erratic, but she didn't pull away and Mason decided that was as good as any "yes". He slowly lowered his head, bringing their mouths together for longer.

Heaven help me...

Harper was an angel. She fit perfectly into his arms and their mouths fit perfectly together. Why, oh why did life have to be so cruel as to not only take Mason's sister, but to take away his chances for having this woman in his life?

He should have let her go. Should have stepped back instead of continuing something that couldn't last, but instead he found himself tightening his hold. If he couldn't have her for a lifetime, at least he could have her for a moment. And despite how much it would hurt later, it would have to be enough.

CHAPTER 14

*H*arper's hands tightened on Mason's shirt as she raised herself on tiptoe to get closer. What in the world was happening? She hadn't meant to get quite so close to him when he came out of the bedroom, but he'd looked so defeated. All she'd wanted to do was offer a little comfort, but somehow she must have pushed a little too far and the tension between the two of them finally snapped. Only instead of shoving them apart, it pulled them together.

By the lips.

Harper wasn't even close to being sorry about it. Excitement and pleasure rushed through her veins as Mason's arms held her close. She felt cherished…adored…beautiful…everything those romance novels she read said she would feel. No other man had ever managed to reach quite so deep before and she and Mason weren't even dating!

We aren't dating!

The words ricocheted through Harper's mind until she finally pulled back with a gasp. They weren't dating. She was supposed to be pursuing her career. She'd been helping him with Layla. Harper's knees were shaking as she stepped back, trying to breathe some sense into her brain, but it kept screaming for her to go back, to kiss him again.

If she'd harbored any hopes of leaving this mess with her heart somewhat intact, they'd just been shattered in a matter of moments.

"I'm sorry," Mason said gruffly. He pushed his hands through his hair. "It's just…" He waved toward her, but didn't speak. "I…" Groaning, he closed his eyes and shook his head. "I'm sorry. I've been wanting to do that for so long…"

Harper held up her hand to stop his ramblings, her brain latching onto his words. *He wanted to do…* She didn't bother asking him to clarify. Stepping forward, she grabbed the front of his flannel shirt and jerked, bringing his mouth back to hers.

Mason groaned and his arms banded around her, picking right up where they'd left off, as if that moment of panic had never happened.

Harper had no idea how long they stood in the hallway, so tightly wrapped in each other's arms that she was positive someone watching wouldn't be able to tell one person from another, but when they finally came up for air…it still wasn't enough.

Mason brought his forehead to hers, closing his eyes and breathing heavily. "I don't know why you did that, but a mere thanks definitely isn't enough."

Harper laughed, shaking her head and breaking their touch. "I can't say I've ever been thanked for kissing someone before."

Mason's arms wrapped around her waist again. "Just because every other guy you've dated has been an idiot, doesn't mean I'll follow in their footsteps." He lowered his head and left yet another lingering kiss.

Harper practically whimpered when he pulled away. All the heartache, all the self control, all the longing from afar for a life she could never have…none of it prepared her for what she was really missing. How had she ever thought she could continue to resist him?

Yes, she still needed to finish that painting, but she could do it. Even if it meant losing hours of sleep, this moment right here would make it all worth it. She'd never felt so alive. As if she could simply float away from happiness. This was a feeling worth fighting for.

"I should probably let you get home," Mason whispered as he

nuzzled her neck. "But now that I know what it's like to hold you, I'm not sure how to let go."

"Oh my gosh," Harper breathed. "If you keep talking like that, I won't be able to leave."

"Then don't."

The words hung in the air between them. Could she? She had come this morning planning to assuage her crush by spending a few hours with them on the pretense of helping. But she had planned to do work this afternoon. Her painting was waiting and she had a couple of emails she wanted to send. Could she throw away yet another afternoon just to have more time in his company?

There's only so much naptime.

Once again, the rational part of her brain came to the rescue. "Okay."

Mason's smile was enough to make every worry pop like a fragile bubble. The woman that followed him to the family room, snuggled into his side and sighed in contentment was not the same woman who had bargained with her mother for more time, for a chance to win a competition in California.

Mason's arm lay around her shoulders, holding her close, and when he turned on the television, Harper didn't even care what they were watching. She just wanted to be close to him. Wanted to enjoy the woodsy smell in her nose and the strength of his chest against her cheek. Her fingers drew patterns on his shirt as her mind reveled in the all the new sensations swirling throughout her body.

"Mason?"

"Hm?" By the lazy sound of his answer, he was just as content as she was.

"What did you mean when you said you'd wanted to do that for a long time?"

Mason stilled, then shifted a little. He chuckled and Harper raised herself up so she could see him. Mason gave her a sheepish grin. "I, uh...might have had a crush on you for a while now."

Harper's jaw dropped. "Are you kidding? I thought it was all in my head!"

Mason tickled his fingers along her cheekbone. "Nope. That pull between us...it was as real as the baby sleeping in the other room."

Harper pushed a little more until she sat completely upright. "Then why didn't you say anything? I mean, there were a couple of times I thought...maybe...but then you'd throw out the 'friend' word and I'd smack myself for being too eager."

Mason let his head fall back, groaning. "I haven't been in a good place." He came back down, his golden eyes begging her to understand. "Long before I became interested in you, I told myself I wouldn't get involved with anyone until I had found my sister. I've been looking for three years. My money, my extra time and all my energy have all been spent on her behalf." He took one of her hands, threading their fingers.

Harper couldn't deny the way his touch made her feel. Her heart sped up and she felt a surge of sympathy for what he must have been going through. It made her own life decisions look so selfish.

"I didn't want to date someone and have her play second place to Aimee." Mason jerked his chin toward the bedroom. "And when I came home from her funeral, I had the same excuse, but a different reason."

"And now?"

He gave her a soft smile. "And now I'm seeing that I was an idiot." He leaned forward, stealing another kiss that Harper was too happy to give. "I can't promise you date nights or long texting threads into the night," he whispered against her mouth. "In fact, my time is probably even more taken than it was when I was searching for my sister." He kissed her again. "But I can promise that what time I do have...is yours...if you want it."

Harper wrapped her arms around his neck, letting him pull her forward until she was half laying on his chest. "I want it," she said, letting her fingers play with his hair. "I've wanted it for so long."

"Then take it, baby," he said with a grin, coming closer until their lips were all but touching. "It's yours."

* * *

MASON WAS positive he would never come up for air. He could drown in all things Harper and die a happy man. But eventually, his lungs won out and he pulled back so they could both catch their breath.

Harper curled up like a kitty cat into his side, her legs tucked under and her head resting on his sternum with one arm slung around his chest. He held onto her back, keeping her secure and enjoying every point of contact. How had he held back from this for so long? People made this type of situation work all the time. As long as Harper knew what she was getting into, there was no reason why they couldn't be together. Layla made things complicated but not impossible...right?

Their little slice of heaven seemed far too short when Layla eventually woke up. They'd had a couple of hours on the couch, but as he walked down the hall, Mason knew it wouldn't be enough. That thought was why he knew this was going to be a problem. His time with Harper would never feel like enough. She'd been here all day and he still wanted more.

Just take what you can get, he told himself. *It'll all work out. I'll make sure of it.*

"Hey, Tiny," Mason said as he walked into Layla's room.

Her face was bright red and her hair matted to her cheeks, but when she held up her arms, she might as well have reached into his chest and squeezed her heart. *Stick a fork in me, I'm done.* There was nothing for it. Layla had turned him into a lap dog and Harper was right behind.

He carried Layla out, her fingers in her mouth until she spotted Harper. Wiggling against him, Mason put her on the ground and the little girl ran over, flopping her head into Harper's lap.

"Hey, pretty girl," Harper said with a laugh. She pulled Layla onto her lap, nuzzling her neck and getting laughter in return. "Want to go for a walk?" Harper asked, glancing between Layla and him. "The sun's shining. We should take advantage of it."

Mason nodded. "That's a good idea."

"Great. You change her and I'll pack some snacks."

Mason gave her a wry look. "I know that trick."

Harper laughed and stood, bringing Layla to him. "Tough luck, handsome. I only said I'd help with the schedule."

Mason took Layla, but also grabbed a kiss when he leaned close. "To motivate me," he said with a smirk and pump of his eyebrows.

Harper walked away, glancing over her shoulder with a flirty smile. "I'm happy to keep you motivated all the time."

Mason whistled low enough Harper wouldn't hear it and shook his head. He turned when Layla squirmed. "You women are going to be the death of me," he told her. "I think I should be more upset about that." With a shrug, he went to the corner where he had diapers and other baby stuff, getting Layla changed and ready for an outing.

Once again, it took far longer than it should have, but eventually they were walking along the boardwalk, Layla swinging her legs out in front of her stroller. This was the first time Mason had really gone out with Layla, other than the market the other day, but that hadn't been in his hometown. A light breeze played across their skin, which felt good to Mason, but Harper was having a hard time with her hair.

"I should have pulled it into a ponytail," she muttered, rolling her hand around it.

Mason let go of the stroller with one hand and tugged on her beautiful blonde locks. "I like it down." He stared at the pink color that crept across her cheeks. The fact that she blushed was oddly attractive. It brought her skin alive and he wanted to touch it to feel the heat. He knew from experience only a couple hours ago that her skin was like silk, and he wanted to touch it again.

They were quiet after his admission, but it wasn't uncomfortable. He wished he could take her hand, but the stroller kept him from it. Just another reminder that having a child was going to interfere with his love life.

Can we really do this? he wondered. After knowing what it was like to kiss her, he wasn't sure if he could stop, but he also wasn't sure how this would look going forward. He wanted to see Harper every day, but between their work and Layla's schedule, what if he only saw her once a week? Would that be enough to build a relationship on? What if Harper couldn't handle it? What if she needed more than he could give her?

"You're thinking awfully hard over there," Harper said with a grin. She tried once again to tuck her hair behind her ears, but it only lasted a few seconds.

He smiled back. "Just thinking about how tame this situation makes me look." He waved his hand toward the stroller. He couldn't tell her about what was really going on in his brain. It would only make him look like he was unsure of his feelings, which wasn't the case at all. He was halfway in love with Harper. He just wasn't sure if their lives would allow it to actually progress.

Harper's laugh was heavenly, which fit perfectly with his comparing her to an angel so often. "The great lumberjack has been domesticated. Whatever shall he do?"

"I feel like I need to carry one of my chainsaws around with me," he continued. "Just to prove that I'm not a sissy."

Harper whacked his arm. "You're giant. No one thinks you're a sissy."

"I don't know..." he murmured. "I know what I've thought when I've seen guys like this."

"And what was that?"

Mason widened his eyes and leaned over a little. "That they were whipped."

Harper rolled her eyes. "You men. So dramatic."

He gave an extra big shiver. "No man wants to be held back."

Harper sobered and her eyes dropped to Layla. "And are you being held back?"

Mason regretted his words. He'd been trying to tease, but apparently it had been the wrong topic. One of these days he'd remember that his situation was unique. But it *was* a good question and he wanted to give her an honest answer. "I think it would be easy to think I am," Mason said. He paused, yanking the stroller out of a rut. "But it wouldn't be entirely truthful."

Harper glanced his way, obviously waiting for an explanation.

Mason squinted into the sun, trying to come up with the right words to express his thoughts. "I think it's all about a person's attitude, though." He swallowed hard. "My life has taken a complete one-eighty," he explained. "But it doesn't have to be bad."

Layla squealed and bounced in her seat.

They stopped and Mason watched the bird that had caught her attention. "My time isn't my own anymore. It's full of diapers and naptimes, tears and tantrums." He huffed a laugh. "But it's also full of taking time to stop and watch a seagull. Reading books in funny voices, cuddling and laughing much more than I ever have before." He turned, making sure Harper could see the sincerity on his face. "It might not have been what I expected my life to be like at this point, but it isn't holding me back. It's opening a whole new world."

Harper's eyes were misty and she laughed when she sniffed. "Sorry." She wiped at her face. "I don't know why, but that might have been the sweetest thing I've ever heard."

Mason smirked, his chest puffing out a little. "I never turn down brownie points."

Harper's laugh grew and she stepped up, rising on tiptoe to give him a soft kiss. "Mason Turley, you're an amazing man."

Yeah...there's no way we're not giving this a shot. He began to push the stroller again. "Just trying to keep up, Angel. Just trying to keep up."

CHAPTER 15

Harper raced around her small home trying to make sure there was nothing on the floor that Layla might try to grab, break or simply put into her mouth. The child still seemed to be at the age where she tasted everything. *Everything!*

Today was Sunday and Harper was glad for the day off. After working another exhibition yesterday, she was eager for a chance to relax. *And keep ignoring my nonexistent painting.*

"Poor Mason has it rougher," she reminded herself. He dealt with the toddler after work, while Harper got a break. It was easy to see why single parenting was so difficult now that she was watching Mason go through it.

The doorbell rang and Harper's heart skipped a beat. She took a moment to collect herself. This was the first time they would be together…together. Yes, Layla would be there, but after that kiss a couple of days ago, their relationship had completely shifted and Harper found she had never been happier. Even with the deadline looming, her days were simply…better. Even with dirty diapers, sticky fingers and almost no alone time, she felt more fulfilled than the day she sold her first painting and realized she was now considered professional.

Harper adored little Layla and her feelings for Mason were stronger than ever. Their dating story might be full of interruptions and difficulties, but she was just grateful they were going to have a story at all.

Harper pulled open the front door. "Hey." *Talk about the lamest greeting in the history of greetings.* Harper wanted to palm her forehead. What was she? Some sixteen year old kid?

Mason grinned, Layla laying against his shoulder. "Hey."

Why did it sound so much better when he said it? Mason sounded sexy, Harper sounded like an idiot. "Come on in." She pulled the door open farther and closed it behind them. "Wow." Harper smiled. "You look like a full fledged dad."

Mason was sporting a diaper bag, which was so full of stuff he couldn't zip it, plus another bag that contained more supplies and, of course, a baby in his arms.

Mason's cheekbones turned pink. "I'm learning."

She leaned in slightly. "I think you're succeeding."

Mason bent down and left a quick kiss on her forehead. "Thanks. I couldn't have done it without you." He straightened with a frown. "I feel like I'm always saying thank you to you."

Harper laughed softly and took Layla, who was about to fall out of Mason's arms in her attempt to get to Harper. "I'm just grateful you didn't kick me out when I came bursting in with unwanted help."

"I didn't realize I needed it," Mason admitted, unloading his gear like a pack mule. "Now I know better."

Pleasure swirled through Harper's chest. She'd been so consumed in helping that she hadn't realized how bold she'd been during the beginning few days of their dealing with the baby. "Have you two eaten breakfast yet?"

Layla bounced and kicked.

Mason scratched his beard, smiling sadly while he shook his head. "I'm starting to think I should make that doctor's appointment."

Harper nodded. "Yeah...if she doesn't start saying things soon, I think that's a good idea." She shrugged. "I mean, you'll need a pediatrician anyway, but I keep hoping she'll adjust and start speaking."

The mood had gone from amused to somber and Harper once again felt dumb. What else could she mess up?

"Breakfast," Harper said decidedly. Walking forward, she led the way to the kitchen. Pancake batter sat next to a griddle, all ready to go.

"I don't think I'm the only one who plans things well in advance," Mason teased.

Harper smiled sheepishly. "Guilty."

He walked to the griddle. "Want me to take care of this since you're holding Layla?"

"You make pancakes?"

Mason winked at her. "I used to be able to flip them in a pan when I was younger." His face fell a little. "Aimee loved it."

"Let me grab a pan," Harper hurried to say. "I'll bet Layla will follow right along in her mother's footsteps." She found what she wanted and held it out to him, but instead of just taking the dish, he held onto her hand.

"Thanks," he said softly. "But I haven't done it in ages. What if I make a mess?"

Harper shrugged. "We'll clean it up."

He looked around, his smile relaxing as he stepped away from the sadness of his sister. "I don't see a dog."

Harper laughed and set down Layla, who was squirming. "Not yet. Maybe someday."

Mason's eyes were smoldering as he replied, "Right. Maybe someday."

Harper had to turn away. The words felt like a promise and she liked it a little too much. "Layla!" The little girl was in the process of climbing onto the table, having already conquered the chair. "Good grief," Harper said, grabbing the toddler.

"You haven't been over in a couple of days," Mason said as he began heating up the pan. "I've had to kid-proof the entire house." He paused long enough to give her a significant look. "And that includes making it climbing proof."

Harper's smile widened. "What did you do?"

"For one thing, the chairs are all up on the table."

A bark of laughter broke free and Harper shook her head. "That's original."

"Actually, that's YouTube," Mason said with a snort. "I found a video about it." He shrugged. "Who knew? Parenting according to social media."

"Oh, I'll bet you could find all sorts of things about parenting on social media," Harper retorted. "And very little of it will be useful."

"Are you trying to make sure you keep your job?"

Harper loved this back and forth. The teasing, the light heartedness. It was exactly what she had always imagined when she fell for a guy. "Maybe. After all, who would I be if I wasn't the baby saver?"

"Oh, I don't know…" Mason tilted his head as if truly having to concentrate. "A beautiful artist?"

Heat began to climb Harper's neck.

"A pretty neighbor?"

She shook her head at him.

"Or what about just a stunning woman?"

Mason had turned around now and was facing Harper with that intent look in his eye again. Oh, how she wanted to kiss him. She had every confidence it would actually be even better than their first. But with Layla bouncing on her lap, Harper finally understood his initial hesitations. A baby made a huge difference in how a relationship progressed.

But Harper wanted this. She wanted *them*. And she wasn't willing to give up quite so easily despite the struggles in her career. Naptime would come soon enough.

* * *

MASON HAD BROUGHT his computer with him in order to get through a few emails while Layla took a nap this afternoon, but right now he couldn't even begin to think about work. The welcoming look in Harper's eyes said she absolutely understood what he wanted and felt the same way.

His hands twitched, aching to hold her and kiss her and cherish her all the ways he wanted to. How he had ever thought he would be able to stay away was a mystery. At every turn, Harper was there. Building him up, helping him through things, and proving she was the perfect person to have in his life no matter how crazy it was.

"Your pan is starting to smoke," Harper said softly, her lips twitching.

Mason spun, and sure enough, it was getting too hot. "Hang on." He took it to the sink and winced at the sizzle and steam when he stuck the pan under the cool water. Carefully, he patted it dry and put it back on the stove. "Okay." He held a hand over it. "Should be ready in just a minute." He forced himself to hold still when Harper came up on his left, Layla on her hip.

"I have to say, I never would have expected you to be such a pancake expert."

He smirked. "I was kind of a big kid…"

"Let me guess. You were hungry all the time and those sugary carbs were the best way to satiate you."

He tilted his head from side to side. "I can't say I ever thought of it that way, but yeah." He pulled his shoulders up. "I just like pancakes."

"Not waffles?"

"I eat waffles."

Harper laughed. "Is there anything you don't eat?"

Mason poured some batter into the pan while he considered the question. "Um…I don't like oysters. Tried one on the half shell when I first moved here and decided then and there it was never happening again."

Harper pinched her lips between her teeth, but her smile still broke through. "My mom used to call those expensive snot balls."

Mason chuckled. "It's a good word for them."

She pointed to the pan. "Is it ready?"

Mason took in the amount of bubbles and the edges of the pancake. "Okay. Yep. Back up."

Harper followed his directions. "Watch, Layla. Uncle Mason is gonna show you a trick."

Even in his periphery, Mason could see what a beautiful picture the two of them made. One dark, one light. Their faces cuddled close together. It was a good thing his life was never going to be the same, because *he* was never going to be the same.

His brother had once described Mason as an ultra big teddy bear, and now Mason understood what he meant. He was a big guy, but he had led an orderly, exacting life. Even in his search for Aimee, it had all been organized carefully. Now, however, other than the schedule Harper helped him with, Mason's days were all over the place. He'd been completely honest on their walk the other day when he'd told Harper his life had taken a one-eighty. But he wasn't exactly regretting the view.

He gripped the handle of the pan, sending a prayer heavenward that he wouldn't stick the pancake to the ceiling or something. "Here goes." Pulling on rote memory, he clenched his jaw and gave the pan an upward jerk.

"Oh my gosh!" Harper said with a laugh. "You did it!" She turned to Layla, clapping her hands. "Yay! Yay for Uncle Mason!"

Layla grinned, still sucking on those two favorite fingers of hers.

Mason made a face and rubbed his heated neck. "I sort of made it." The pancake was half in and half out of the pan. He quickly grabbed the spatula and did his best to fix it, but the poor thing was permanently scarred. *It'll still taste the same.*

"It was great," Harper reassured him. "I'd have missed the plan completely. Plus, the pancake won't taste any different, so we're all good."

Having his own thoughts parroted back at him had Mason once again wanting to kiss the daylights out of his pretty artist. Naptime couldn't come fast enough.

They shared a smile-filled breakfast and then worked together to get things cleaned up.

"Syrup and toddlers," Harper moaned. "Who knew?"

"I'm surprised you didn't," Mason quipped. "You seem to know everything."

"I didn't deal with breakfast when I was babysitting. It was usually dinner, but I still should have known better."

He nodded. "That makes sense." He straightened from wiping down the sticky table. "You must have babysat a lot."

Harper nodded. "I had an afternoon nannying job during the summer. It got me out of the house and usually left me with a lot of time for daydreaming." She smiled, but made a face. "I wouldn't have been a good employee at a place where I had to be ultra focused all the time. But when I took the kids to the park, or they were napping or playing games…it allowed my mind to wander."

"And what did it wander to?" Mason was fascinated. Despite her talk about daydreams and lack of focus, Harper was a hardworking, well-educated woman. He was struggling to see her as the artistic dreamer she liked to portray.

"Painting," Harper replied automatically. "Brushes and color and anything else that caught my fancy."

"When did you first know that painting was going to be your career?"

Harper frowned. "Um…I don't really know. It just was always there." She laughed and set Layla down on the floor, drying her hands with the towel. "I have pictures of me painting as a tiny little girl. Layla's age."

"So your mom was into painting?"

Harper shook her head. "No. But she indulged me when I was little. As I got older, I had to fight for what I wanted."

Mason huffed. "Interesting."

Harper shrugged it off. "My mom is a nice woman, but she has expectations that I don't necessarily follow."

Mason nodded. "I hear that. I think this thing with Layla is definitely going to put a wedge in my relationship with my parents."

"Speaking of…" Harper put her hand on her hip. "Have you heard from them since getting home? You said your mom was talking about fighting the will."

Mason grumbled. "She's still talking about it, but I guess my dad is trying to convince her to leave it alone." He shook his head. "I'm not sure why she cares." He pushed a hand through his hair and watched Layla walk around, examining the kitchen.

"Her estranged daughter had a daughter," Harper said. "I can see how that would be painful. And then...after finding out Layla existed, your mom wasn't chosen as guardian?" Harper whistled low. "Any woman who enjoys control would be livid. Li-vid."

Mason couldn't help but chuckle a little. "Livid, huh?"

Harper made a face and nodded. "My mom enjoys control as well, though from your stories your mom might be a bit...more heavy handed."

"I'm seeing it more and more," Mason muttered. He didn't want to keep talking about this. He was at Harper's house on a beautiful Sunday in order to spend some quality time together. His mother was *not* the kind of conversation he was interested in. "Want to go for a walk?" he asked, craning his neck to look out the window. "It's sunny again and I don't think the wind is too bad either."

Harper followed his gaze. "Another walk sounds great. Did you bring the stroller?"

Mason gave her a triumphant look. "What kind of uncle would I be if I didn't have a stroller sitting in my car at all times?"

"Not an experienced one, for sure," Harper teased back. She began walking toward the hallway. "Let's get Layla's diaper changed and then we can head out."

"Why do I get the feeling that by *we*, you really meant me?" Mason hollered after her.

"She's your niece!" Harper responded.

Mason was beginning to think that his smile was becoming a permanent part of his face. Even when he realized Layla's diaper wasn't going to be a quick change, he couldn't stop the light, bright feeling that was floating through his chest. He liked it...a lot.

CHAPTER 16

The morning seemed to fly by, most of it with their walk, though Harper wasn't complaining. The sun was out and the day was beautiful, just perfect for strolling down the boardwalk and listening to the ocean. In fact, it had been a little too perfect.

Layla had discovered a grand love of the water and sand...especially the sand.

"Upsy-daisy," Harper said as she helped Layla stand in the bath. Holding on firmly, Harper poured bucket of water after bucket of water, trying to get the little girl's skin clean from every tiny grain. It made Harper feel bad for those mothers who had two, three or more children who tracked sand in every day. Living on the beach was beautiful...but messy.

"Out we go." She lifted Layla out and wrapped her in a fluffy towel, making faces to encourage the toddler to laugh. Once the sound began to emerge, it only encouraged Harper to get even more silly. Was there anything better than a baby's laugh?

A deep chuckle came from the doorway.

Okay...there might be something better.

Embarrassed, but knowing she wouldn't change her behavior even with an audience, she sheepishly grinned up at him.

"I had no idea you were such a comedian," he teased.

Harper rolled her eyes and rubbed her nose against Layla's again. "Only to two year olds." She grinned back up at Mason. "Adults don't find my sense of humor quite so appealing."

"I do."

Those two simple words sent such a rush of pleasure through Harper that she almost jumped to her feet to kiss him then and there. Only Layla's yank on her hair was able to pull Harper's attention away from the intensity of Mason's eyes. "Ouch! No, no, Layla. Owie."

Layla frowned and tried to reach for Harper's hair again, but Harper pulled back.

"Nope. Not happening." She turned the child around and scooped her up. "Time to get dressed."

"What can I do?" Mason asked.

Harper plopped Layla into his arms. "Get her dressed and I'll get her a sandwich. I think she's starting to get hangry."

Mason gave her a half grin. "Yes, ma'am." He turned and walked back to the sitting room where his bags were, chatting with the little girl the whole way.

Harper almost hit a wall as she followed, her eyes unable to leave the scene. Mason might still be learning, but he was definitely going to be a wonderful father to Layla. And the thought of that warmed Harper's heart in a way that she couldn't quite express. This wasn't something she would be able to transfer onto canvas, or write about in her poetry notebook. This was...she rubbed her sternum.

It was pleasant, and anxious and good and eager...it was so many things at once that Harper didn't even know how to name them. One thing she did recognize though, was that her heart felt so full, she was positive it would burst as she watched Mason and Layla.

I don't know if there's any other way to describe it...I'm falling in love. Harper knew she should be shocked. She should be angry. She should turn the other way and run for the hills, but she couldn't. Her heart had been attached for a while now and putting the feeling into words was just her finally being honest with herself.

It wasn't just his looks, or his size, or the careful and methodical way he went about life. Harper was starting to see him on a deeper level and everything pulled her in. She didn't just enjoy looking at him, she wanted his touch. She didn't just enjoy chatting, she wanted his opinion, wanted to share the hidden parts of herself and know the hidden parts of him. She found joy in watching him work with Layla, in his learning and growing and willingness to adapt. Each and every thing he did called to her and Harper realized she was starting to think on a much more permanent level than she had before.

There's no other word for it, she told herself. *It's love. And it goes for Mason AND the cute little tot.*

Holding back a sigh of pleasure, Harper went to the kitchen to grab that sandwich. A hungry baby wasn't going to care that she'd just had an emotional revelation. Layla would want to eat and eat now.

"Here she is," Mason said, holding his niece in the kitchen entryway.

Harper smiled. "Great. Put her in her chair. I've got a sandwich and some strawberries for her."

After Layla was settled, Harper turned back to the fridge. "I'm assuming you're hungry as well?"

Mason scratched his beard. "Maybe."

Laughing softly, she opened the fridge. "I'm just going to assume from now on that the answer is always yes."

"I hate to say it, but that will always be a safe assumption."

Harper began grabbing sandwich fixing out of the drawers. "Turkey or ham?" She turned when he didn't respond. "Let me guess. Both?"

Mason shrugged. "Sorry. Should I offer to help pay for groceries?"

Harper shook her head, a too-wide smile still on her face. "Nope. I invited you two over. This is my day." She set the containers on the counter. "Besides, you've paid for my lunch several times now."

She set up an assembly line on the counter and began putting mayonnaise on bread. "Come on over," she said. "Help me know what you want."

A broad arm rested against her shoulder. "I had no idea that building a sandwich could be so intriguing."

Harper glanced up from under her eyelashes. "Intriguing?"

Mason raised a playful eyebrow. "Usually I'm focused on the food. But this time, there's something even better pulling my attention."

Harper dropped his gaze and bumped her hip against his leg, since she was too short to bump his hip. "Stop flirting and get lunch."

"I can't help it," Mason said, reaching around her to grab the lettuce. "You bring out an appetite that I didn't know existed."

Harper's hand hit the counter and she dropped her head back. "Oh my gosh, stop!" she cried while he chuckled in that low tone she adored. "I think you're going to have the dad jokes thing down pat by the time Layla can understand them."

"That's a low blow," Mason said, feigning being offended. "I'm not making up puns."

"No. Just cheesy flirtatious remarks."

His beard twitched. "Sorry. I can't seem to help myself."

"Where's the famous self control of yours when we need it?" Harper grumbled, making Mason laugh again.

"Fine, fine," he said, then bent down, his mouth to her ear. "But I'll only behave until naptime. Once Layla is sleeping, all bets are off."

A shiver ran down Harper's spine. She gave him her best coy look. "I think I'm alright with that." The silence between them grew heavy and thick and oh, so delicious. Harper's pulse was already beating hard in anticipation. She wanted another kiss from Mason and she wanted it now. Perhaps she needed to borrow a little of Mason's self control just to get her through the next hour.

Layla slapped her hand down on her sandwich, causing a loud *smack*.

Or not... Layla was proudly smearing peanut butter and jelly in her freshly washed hair and Harper realized the time would pass, and would probably pass both quickly and slowly at the same time.

Still...she and Mason hadn't had a moment together in several days and no matter what, Harper was determined to make the most of the few moments they would get.

* * *

MASON KNEW he should probably be embarrassed that he was in the hallway bouncing on his toes like a young school boy, but he couldn't help it. He was restless with the desire to have some time with Harper.

Harper came out of her spare bedroom, softly closing the door, then looking up at him with a wide smile. "She was pretty tuckered out."

"So she's asleep?"

Harper shrugged. "Close to it. She didn't give me any trouble about laying down even though she isn't used to the playpen."

"Thank heavens." Mason didn't even bother to take Harper to the couch or somewhere more comfortable, he simply grabbed her and pulled her in, covering her mouth with his.

Apparently, she didn't mind his lack of finesse, since her arms were around his neck immediately and she rose up on tiptoe in her eagerness.

"This is so much harder than I thought it would be," he murmured against her skin, his lips moving across her face, kissing her cheeks, her cheekbones, her eyelids, her forehead…anything and everything. He wanted to feel her soft skin and he wanted to make it his.

His time with Harper felt so limited and yet, each and every moment had him falling deeper and deeper. Watching her bathe Layla had nearly brought him to his knees. The two year old was Mason's top priority, and seeing Harper fit so well into that part of his life was like putting honey in front of a hungry bear.

"Then I guess we better make the most of what time we have," Harper replied breathlessly.

Mason brought his mouth back to hers, then shifted his body so he could scoop her up, cradling her against his chest while he walked them to the sitting room and away from Layla's door. He grinned at her squeak of surprise, but didn't miss the opportunity to deepen the kiss.

Carefully, he sat down, keeping Harper in his lap. His hands came up to cup her face and rubbed his thumbs against her cheekbones. "So…soft," he murmured, tilting his head for a better angle.

He nearly groaned when Harper's hands found his hair. She ran her fingers through it and the sensations were overpowering.

"Do that again," he whispered.

Harper laughed softly and followed his orders. "You like that?"

"Mmm…" Mason rested his forehead against hers, his eyes closed in contentment while she continued to play with the locks. "Harper, I—"

A knock on the door had them both jumping to their feet. Harper pushed her hair out of her face. "Geez, that nearly sent my heart through the roof."

Mason cleared his throat and tried to get himself back under control. "I, uh, guess you better answer it." He couldn't quite bring himself to be grateful for the interruption, since he'd been looking forward to this time with Harper, but he'd been about to confess his feelings for her and now that the moment had passed, he found himself a little reluctant to take that leap forward.

To declare his love would be moving *much* faster than he was ready for, especially when he wasn't even sure how deep Harper's feelings went yet.

"It's probably just a package, or something," Harper assured him before heading to go find out.

Mason waited next to the couch, fully planning to resume their interlude when she returned, until he heard, "Aspen! Maeve! Hi!"

Letting his chin hit his chest, Mason gave up. If the sisters had come for a chat, he knew there would be no more kissing or holding until somehow they managed another break. A heaviness settled within him. His fears were coming true. How was he supposed to win Harper's heart if he couldn't ever spend time with her?

"Mason!"

Mason jerked upright. "Oh, hey, Aspen. Hi, Maeve." He swallowed hard, trying to bring moisture back to his dry mouth. His embarrassment at being caught on Harper's couch brought heat up his neck, but Mason knew his beard would cover it. He stood, feeling incredibly awkward among so many women.

But Layla's asleep. I can't just leave.

He bit back a curse. He was stuck. With three women who probably wanted to gossip, and two of them didn't even know he'd become a guardian in the last two weeks.

"What brings you here?" he asked, trying to break the silence. Aspen, for her part, didn't look particularly surprised to find him there, but Maeve was grinning like a madman.

Aspen put her hands on her hips and tilted her head. "We came to visit. How about you?" She jerked when Harper whacked her arm. "Sorry," Aspen said through her laughter. "We didn't know you were entertaining."

Harper rolled her eyes and walked over to Mason. She took his hand and rested her head against his arm. "Come on in, ladies. Grab a seat."

Aspen held up the box in her hands. "Does it help that I brought treats?"

Harper smirked at Mason. "Considering he's always hungry, I think you're probably forgiven."

Harper brought the box to Mason. "It's strawberry lemon. See if you like it."

"I'll grab forks!" Maeve announced, walking toward the kitchen. It was evident the sisters had been there before. She came back and handed forks to Mason and Harper. "Dig in."

Mason looked wide eyed at Harper. "Uh…" It felt weird to eat in front of the ladies, while they didn't have anything.

Harper shook her head. "This is how it goes with Aspen. She brings food, but never eats it herself." Harper shrugged. "Might as well get used to it."

Aspen crossed her ankle over her knee. "I eat all day long at the shop. It's someone else's turn."

Mason opened the box and took a large bit of the cake. As usual, it melted on his tongue and he groaned. "So good."

All of the women laughed.

A thud brought the noise to a halt.

Every head jerked toward the hallway, where Layla slowly shuffled out of her room, her blanket clutched in her hands and her eyes half closed. She rubbed them with her free fist and yawned.

"What in the world are you doing up?" Harper scolded. She set her fork on the coffee table and went over to scoop the little girl up. When she came back to the couch, Layla began to crawl into Mason's lap and he hurriedly set the cake aside.

Once the tiny head was resting against his chest, Layla's fingers in her mouth, Mason turned to address the two wide eyed women on his right. "Aspen, Maeve. I'd like you to meet Layla. My…sort of daughter."

CHAPTER 17

*A*spen's body language said she was as curious as she was confused. "What do you mean, your daughter?" Her dark eyes darted between Harper and Mason. "Were you married before?"

Harper pinched her lips between her teeth. She didn't want to overstep her bounds by answering–after all, it was Mason's story–but Aspen was Harper's best friend. She looked at Mason, who gave her a half grin.

"Layla is actually my niece," he said, turning back to the visitors.

Maeve fell backward, her tense posture relaxing. "Oh no."

Mason nodded. "My sister was killed in an accident a few weeks ago." He paused and took a deep breath, the words obviously still causing him pain.

Harper rubbed his shoulder. She knew it would take a long time for him to get through this grief. The biggest problem was, he hadn't been able to grieve, he'd been too busy adapting to becoming a single father.

"In her will, she asked that I take Layla." He rubbed the child's back, who had promptly gone to sleep on his chest.

Harper bit back her jealousy. She knew exactly how good that chest felt and it was supposed to be her time right now. *It's life,* she reminded herself. *If I'm going to be with Mason, I'll have to get used to it.*

"Fact is, I, uh, didn't even know Layla existed." He scowled. "My sister had a falling out with my mother and ran off as soon as she graduated. Her passing was the first any of us have ever heard from her."

"Oh my goodness." Aspen's hand came up to cover her mouth. "How sad. And now you're her guardian."

Harper and Mason nodded.

Aspen rubbed her forehead. "I feel like I just fell into a telenovela."

Mason chuckled. "It sounds like it, doesn't it?"

"But he's doing great," Harper inserted. "He's a wonderful father, or uncle, or whatever you want to call him."

Mason gave her an appreciative smile.

"Why haven't you told anyone?" Aspen pressed. "We're all your friends. We would've helped."

Mason sighed. "I wasn't really trying to keep anything a secret. I was just…" He looked around as if searching for the right words.

"Too busy trying to survive," Harper offered.

"Exactly."

"I can't even imagine." Aspen leaned in. "But you're set up now? You have all the equipment you need? Your house has been child proofed?"

His big shoulders shrugged. "As much as it can be, I suppose." He looked at Harper. "Harper helped…a lot."

Heat crept up her neck and cheeks as she tried to shrug off his compliment. "Basically, I shoved my way inside until he realized how much help he needed."

Aspen slapped the arms of the chair. "Good." She turned to Mason. "Come over for dinner tonight. At the family house." She grinned. "Mine and Austin's apartment is too small, but we'll feed everyone and they can meet Layla." Aspen tilted her head to the side. "It'll be short notice, but I'll bet most everyone can come."

Harper felt the sting of tears in the back of her eyes and she blinked rapidly. She had never doubted that Aspen and the others would help out, but she'd been so busy helping settle Mason, and then her own work with the art competition, and then trying to figure out how to date while still taking care of Layla...they just hadn't gotten around to announcing her existence to everyone else.

Mason cleared his throat. "Are you sure?" he asked. "No one expects you all to take on any of this responsibility."

Aspen stood, Maeve right behind her. "Did you or did you not step in to help when I was having love life troubles with Austin?"

Mason made a face. "Uh...I guess we did."

"Right. And why did you do that?"

Mason relaxed and Harper smiled. "Because friends help each other."

"And so does family." Aspen walked over and lightly brushed her fingers over Layla's hair. "This little beauty is about to learn that she has a dozen aunts and uncles that will spoil her rotten given half a chance."

Maeve leaned around her sister. "I get to hold her first!" she squealed quietly, so as not to wake the child.

"Yeah, well I get to feed her cake," Aspen argued.

Maeve scowled. "Says who?"

"Says the aunt who actually bakes," Aspen shot back.

Mason held up a hand, laughing softly in that wonderfully deep tone of his. "I get it, I get it," he said, stopping the fight before it got too crazy. "Lesson learned. We'll be there."

"What can I bring?" Harper asked, trying to make herself useful.

Aspen looked to Maeve, raising her eyebrows.

"A salad, maybe?" Maeve offered. She shrugged. "I have no idea what Estelle will want to cook."

"Fair enough." Harper stood and hugged her friends. "You two are the best."

"I know," Aspen said with a laugh.

Maeve smacked her sister's arm. "So conceited."

"Confident," Aspen threw back.

Maeve rolled her eyes. "I don't know how Austin handles you."

Aspen made a face. "If I had a marriage where my husband had to *handle* me, the marriage would never have happened."

Maeve muttered under her breath. "There's a reason the Lord put you as the middle child."

Harper snorted, then made an innocent face when Aspen glared. "So…green salad or fruit?"

Aspen shook her head. "Just because glasses here," she jabbed her thumb over her shoulder, "is afraid to speak up, doesn't mean the rest of us have to be."

Maeve tugged on her sister's arm, all while pushing up her fake glasses. "Come on before you wake the baby with your arguing. It would serve you right if she's totally cranky when you have her tonight."

Aspen followed, grinning. "Yeah, but then I'll feed her cake and I'll be the favorite."

"Until she's bouncing off the walls," Maeve argued.

Aspen held the door open for her sister. "Easy." She winked at Harper. "That's when you give her back."

"Oh my gosh," Maeve moaned. "How in the world are we related?"

Aspen gave her sister a playful shove. "You know you love me. Don't try to pretend otherwise."

"Only because life would be boring without your antics."

"Perfect. You get a front row seat without any of the repercussions." Aspen waved and started to close the door behind them, but not in time to keep Harper and Mason from hearing Maeve's screech of outrage and adamant denial.

Mason turned to Harper as soon as they were gone, his eyes wide. "What just happened?"

Harper laughed quietly. "They're quite the pair, aren't they?"

* * *

Mason rubbed the back of his neck. It was getting stiff from slouching on the couch with Layla. "They're something, that's for sure."

Harper stood and walked toward the kitchen. "Just wait until you see them in action with Estelle. She actually tries to keep them in line." Harper smirked. "It's a losing battle, every time."

Mason shook his head, his brain still swirling. "I can't decide if I've been helped or pranked."

"Helped." Harper disappeared. "Definitely." Her voice carried from the kitchen. "Do you want a drink?"

Mason looked down at the sleeping child. He wasn't going anywhere for a while. "Sure," he said, careful not to shout. Layla was out, but he was positive his voice could snap her out of it if he wasn't careful.

Harper came back with a cold bottle and loosened the lid before handing it to him. She again sat beside him. "So…" She gave him a small smile. "Maybe I'll grab my paint supplies and try to get some work done?"

Mason nodded after taking a drink. "It looks like I'm stuck." He gave her a wry look. "And it looks like the playpen isn't going to work."

"Apparently, our climber isn't held back by mere walls." Harper stood. "I'll bring my stuff in here. We can talk while I paint." She paused at the hall entrance. "Or do you want to sleep? I'll bet you could scooch down and close your eyes. I'll just work in the other room for a while."

Mason debated his choices. The friendly interruption and then Layla's appearance had ruined any chance they had of spending time alone. That little voice in the back of his head that argued this was why he'd avoided a relationship to begin with tried to come out of its corner, but Mason shoved it back. They could make this work. He didn't want to do it alone and Harper hadn't complained once. She understood his position…for now. "Come talk to me," he said with a smile. "I'd like to watch you work."

The blush on her cheeks let him know it was the right choice. Without a word, the beautiful artist nodded and walked down the hall. Mason waited eagerly for her return, wanting to do all he could to show how much he appreciated her. It wasn't much, but he was doing his best, and hopefully it would be enough.

It has to be.

The afternoon flew and soon they were loading Layla in the car to head to the Harrison home. The driveway was filled with vehicles, letting Mason know that Aspen's prediction had been correct.

As he unloaded his charge, he had a moment of hesitation. "Do you think it's okay to introduce her to so many people at once?" he asked Harper.

She gave him one of her gentle smiles. "She'll let us know if it's not. But Aspen was right. They'll all love her, and you and her both are going to need that."

Mason nodded, staring at the house. "I know, but...I just want to do the right thing."

"You are." She tugged on his free arm. "Come on."

"Hang on." Pulling on her hand, Mason brought Harper back and gave her a short, but fierce kiss. "Thank you," he whispered when her eyes fluttered back open.

"For what?" Her blue eyes searched his.

"For being so positive all the time," he whispered. "And for helping me figure all this out."

Harper laughed a little self consciously and tucked her hair behind her ear. "It's far from figured out, but I'm glad I could help even a little bit." Together they walked up the front porch.

Without knocking, she opened the door and the noise of chatty adults came to a screeching halt. "Hey," Harper said, waving and drawing attention away from him and Layla.

Mason was grateful she was taking the lead. These were his friends, but his life had changed so drastically in the last couple weeks that he was feeling a bit awkward and anxious. How would everyone react to Layla? Would they understand what he was going through? Now that he was a parent, was he too different to get along with them anymore? Would Layla like his friends? Would he have to find new ones?

"Yay!" Aspen said, walking through the crowd. "Me first!" She held her hands out with an inviting smile. "Hey, sweet girl," she cooed. "Want to come see Auntie Aspen?"

Layla increased her grip on Mason's neck and his worry shot up a notch.

"Let her breathe," Estelle said, stepping up next to her sister. She smiled kindly at Mason and her gaze softened even more when it turned to Layla. "She's beautiful," Estelle said softly.

"Thanks," Mason muttered. He looked around. Everyone seemed frozen, like they weren't sure how to handle having a child here. His concerns were right. This wasn't going to work. Not that any of his friends were bad, just that he wasn't really a part of them anymore. He took a step back, ready to say he was going home.

Before he could move, another person slipped through. "Hey, Mase." Ethan's grin was easy going and wide as usual.

Mason breathed a little easier. He and Ethan had been good friends for a long time.

"Mind if I try?" Ethan raised his eyebrows and nodded toward Layla.

Mason hesitated, but Harper was nodding at him encouragingly. "Sure."

Ethan turned that wide smile to Layla. "Hey, beautiful." He bent over. "I'm your Uncle Ethan." He winked. "Your *favorite* uncle."

A groan came from the crowd even as most everyone chuckled.

"Are you hungry? Want to grab a snack?"

"She likes cheesy things," Harper whispered.

Ethan acknowledged the help. "Want to get some cheese?"

Layla perked her head up.

Ethan held out his hands. "Come with me and I'll get you all the cheese you can eat."

Layla stuck her middle fingers in her mouth and considered him. The whole room seemed to hold their breaths as they waited for her response.

Her mind apparently made up, Layla fairly leaped across the space into Ethan's arms.

"Whoa." Mason had to shift his hold to keep her from hitting the ground.

"Got her," Ethan said, tucking the little girl onto his arm, supported by his chest. "Alright, pretty lady. I promised you cheese. Let's get to it."

Mason watched, his heart pinching slightly as Ethan walked away with Layla. She was staring at the surfer with an adoring look on her face and it took Mason off guard. A heavy slap to his back brought him quickly out of his thoughts.

"It's the smile," Jayden said with a laugh. "The women can't seem to resist it."

Mason's smile felt tight, but he appreciated the attitude. "How are ya, Jay?" he asked.

Jayden squeezed Mason's shoulder. "Doing better than you, I think." His smile faltered. "I'm sorry about your sister." His eyes drifted to Ethan and Layla. "A part of me wants to say congrats on becoming a father, but…" He shrugged.

Mason nodded. "Yeah…I get it."

"If it helps, I think you'll be great at this." Jayden grinned again and walked away, heading to the kitchen area.

The next half hour was filled with food, laughter and a releasing of Mason's tension. The longer he was there, the more he realized how much he needed this. How much he needed *them*. First, it had been Harper, but even that wasn't going to be enough. Apparently, when they said it took a village, they were talking about a group just like this.

Layla was smiling and laughing and being passed from person to person as each adult took the time to get to know her. It didn't matter that she was a baby. It didn't matter that Mason's life had been turned upside down. They accepted him just as he was and were all willing to help.

His own family might have fallen apart, but Mason was quickly realizing it didn't matter. He and Layla had everything they needed right here.

His phone buzzed in his pocket and he pulled it out. "Excuse me," he said to Gavin, a friend he'd been chatting with. "It's my brother."

Gavin nodded and stepped aside.

Mason rushed outside, the only quiet place he could think of. "Crew?"

"Mason!" Crew shouted. "Where the heck are you?"

"I'm at a friend's house," Mason explained, frowning at the frantic tone in his brother's voice. "Why?"

"Man, you need to get home. I'm in your driveway."

"Crew," Mason said firmly. "What's going on?" Why would Crew have shown up without any warning? Something wasn't right.

"Mom got herself a new lawyer…and she's coming after Layla."

CHAPTER 18

"Three returns!" Harper screeched at her computer screen. She pushed her hands through her hair, tugging at the roots. "That can't be right!" Frantically, she searched for the receipts to the paintings the invoice referred to. While every artist got the occasional return, three at once was unheard of.

Harper's stomach was churning as she looked into the original purchases. Sure enough, she found they had all been bought by the same customer. Harper remembered the woman. She had looked a little fancy in her heels and jewelry as she walked around the outdoor market, but who cared when she bought three of Harper's largest canvases, claiming they would be perfect for her office.

"It sounds like perfect was a bit of a stretch," Harper murmured. She bit her lip, which was beginning to tremble. This was going to put a big dent in her bank account, which was already dangerously low as it was.

Try as she might, Harper hadn't had any luck trying to build her business by using online advertising. Instead, she'd been spending money she didn't have and with her mother's ultimatum hanging over her head, it was money that wouldn't be replaced.

So her bills had been higher, her income the same and now she had to refund three large pictures. It wasn't fair.

She closed her eyes and hung her head. This was why she was supposed to be focusing on her career. She had been so...distracted lately. Her painting was due soon for the competition and wasn't even close to being done, her mother had been calling every single day, nagging about giving up and changing careers, and between her newest discovery and Mason leaving the party last night because he got a call from his brother...Harper felt as if her world was starting to get claustrophobic.

But your time with Mason and Layla has been the happiest time of your life.

Happy. It was such a dangerous word. Logically, Harper knew her happiness didn't rely on anyone but herself, but it was so hard to remember that when Mason came into the room. Her smiles stretched automatically across her face and when Layla hugged her neck, Harper felt herself melt into an ooey puddle of emotions.

No...Mason and Layla might not be responsible for Harper's happiness, but they sure added to it. And that was why it was so hard to stay away.

Today, however, Harper had put her foot down, which had turned out perfectly since Mason said he needed time with his brother anyway. She had all day to paint, to catch up on inventory and make sure her invoices were all sent. She could rework her ads and look into other ways of expanding. Perhaps there was even another art exhibit or two she could send her portfolio to.

Instead...she was sitting at her computer, crying at a stupid email.

She didn't want to work. Painting had lost its luster and Harper wasn't sure how to get it back. She squeezed her eyes shut, forcing the tears to shut down. There had to be something she could do. She had never been confrontational, but she also wasn't one to give up without a fight.

She wanted this. She had *always* wanted this. She hadn't spent her entire life going against her mother's edicts just to lose now. Right?

She had a full twenty-four hours to herself. Her distractions were otherwise occupied.

Harper sucked in a tremulous breath and stood, locking her shaking knees. It was time to paint. It was time to take back what was hers. Women had families and careers all the time and even though all her evidence pointed otherwise, Harper just wasn't quite ready to give up Mason and Layla yet. She could find a way. She had to.

An hour later, her brush lay dormant next to the piles of paint. Harper sat back in her chair, feeling like a failure. When her doorbell rang, her heart jumped, thinking it might be Mason, and Harper forced herself to sit back down.

It doesn't matter if it's Mason, she scolded herself. *You're working today. You can see him tomorrow.*

Her hands twitched and her heart sped up. She wanted…she wanted… She jumped to her feet and raced for the door. She didn't know what she wanted, but Harper knew for sure what she didn't want.

Jerking open the door, she rushed onto the deck.

"Oh! You *are* home!"

Harper's shoulders deflated. "Oh, hey Maeve."

"Hey." Maeve's smile turned concerned when she grew closer. "Are you okay? Did I wake you from a nap?"

Harper shook her head. "Nope. Uh…come on in." Harper tried to straighten her back and pretend she hadn't been looking for Mason, but it was more difficult than she wanted to admit. How ridiculous was she? She was everything her mother taught her not to be. Relying on a man was breaking her!

The front door closed. "Okay, I came over to demand answers about you and Mason, but something else is going on," Maeve said. She folded her arms over her chest. "Why don't you have a seat and we'll talk about it."

Harper sighed and flopped onto the couch. She loved Maeve, she really did. But Harper wasn't sure she wanted to spill everything.

"Harp," Maeve said softly. "I know I'm not Aspen, but while she's at work, I'm here and I'm ready to listen."

Harper cracked an eye open. "It's not that," she said, her voice breaking. "I just... I don't know." Harper sat up. "I'm just such a mess right now. I'm torn between two directions and I don't know which one is better."

"I'm guessing this really does have to do with Mason," Maeve said thoughtfully. She pushed her fake glasses up onto her head. "Is it Layla? Are you afraid if you and Mason get serious, you aren't ready to be a mother?"

"Oh, heavens, no!" Harper immediately cried out. She snapped her mouth shut when she realized how loud she was. "I mean...I hadn't planned on taking on someone else's child, but Layla isn't a problem."

"Then what is it?" Maeve tilted her head. Her brown eyes were deeply curious. "You and Mason seemed so content the other night. You looked so happy."

"We are...were...oh, I don't know." Harper shook her head, tears threatening once more. "How does Aspen do it all?" she finally asked.

"Uh..."

"I mean...how does she manage to keep her career going and still have time for Austin?" Harper leaned forward. Already she was feeling slightly better even though their conversation had just started. "I've wanted to be an artist my whole life," she explained. "And my mom was always against it." Harper paused. "No. That's not right. Mom thought it was great that I painted, but she doesn't think it's a real job. She wants me to have something secure and safe. Something I can support myself with if I ever found myself alone."

Maeve huffed a laugh. "Uh, Harper, you *are* alone."

"Exactly!" Harper cried. "I decided I couldn't do it the same way my mother did. I needed my art. So my solution was to build my career *before* I got involved."

Maeve's eyes widened in understanding. "Oh..."

Harper nodded. "But now..." She sniffed. "Now all I want to do is be around Mason and Layla, and my art is suffering, and I had someone return three paintings today, and my mom is holding my trust fund hostage, and if I can't win this competition down in California, then she's going to take it away completely, and I can't even find the time to paint, let alone the inspiration because all I want to do is kiss a handsome lumberjack and play peek a boo with a little girl because her laugh warms me in ways I didn't even know existed and I can't imagine my days without it!"

Maeve never moved. Her eyes were about to bug out of her head and she was obviously shocked at Harper's confession.

Harper, on the other hand, felt better for having gotten it all out. *Now I just need some kind of solution.* "So I'll ask again," Harper said, bringing her voice down and sitting a little straighter. "How does Aspen do it all?"

Maeve slowly shook her head. "Oh, Harp. I can't...I'm so sorry..." Maeve fell backward. "This isn't going to be what you want to hear, but...she doesn't. Something always has to give. Sometimes it's time with Austin and sometimes it's the business, but no one person can have it all, all the time."

Maeve was right. That wasn't what Harper wanted to hear. And unfortunately, it fed the doubts already building in the back of her mind. If she didn't get this business going first...Harper was positive she never would.

* * *

MASON BROUGHT the ax over his head with a heavy yet satisfying *thud*. The log in front of him split, sending a small spark of splinters into the air just as Layla's laughter rang through the trees.

He paused before picking up the next piece and looked over in time to see Crew pretending to nibble on Layla's stomach, which was the cause of her merriment. The laughter brought a smile to his lips, but the weight on his shoulders never shifted. What was he going to do? Crew was positive that Mom's new lawyer was a shark and would do anything to make a buck.

How in the world was someone like him going to prove to a judge that life with a single lumberjack was better for Layla than the larger, more experienced home of his mother?

You might not always be single...

An ache began deep in Mason's chest. Harper was working today. Mason was supposed to meet with a lawyer in a bit and she needed time to work on a painting for some kind of competition she was entering, and so they'd agreed not to see each other today. It was amazing how such a short amount of time could be so painful. He wanted her here. He wanted to talk about a plan for Layla. He wanted Harper's optimistic attitude. He wanted to hold her and feel like it would all be okay.

Instead he was chopping wood to work off his nervous energy and Uncle Crew was getting to know his niece. Both things were fine, but they weren't what Mason wanted deep down.

"She doesn't talk much, does she?" Crew asked, studying the little girl.

Mason shook his head. "Not yet. Harper said I should think about taking her in to a doctor soon. She thinks Layla might have some trauma issues that are keeping her from speaking."

Crew nodded thoughtfully. "You like this Harper a lot, don't you?"

Mason shrugged, though he knew it had to be written all over his face.

"Mase, you idiot," Crew teased. "You've mentioned her like fifty times since I got here last night. What's going on?"

Mason took in a deep breath and pushed a hand through his hair. "I think I'm falling for her."

"But..."

Mason raised an eyebrow. "Why do you think there's a but?"

"Because you don't sound excited to have finally found a woman who doesn't run from your giant size."

If Layla hadn't been in Crew's lap, Mason probably would have chucked a piece of wood at his brother's head, but he held back. "But I'm worried she doesn't feel the same."

"Why wouldn't she?"

Mason rolled his eyes. "Is this really what we're going to talk about? I thought we needed to discuss Layla and Mom?"

Crew put Layla on the ground and she began to run around, checking out all the dandelions growing in Mason's yard. "We'll get to that when the lawyer arrives. Why don't you think Harper feels the same?"

When Layla came his way, Mason set the ax down and picked the little one up. "Hey, Tiny."

"Quit avoiding the question, Mase," Crew shouted.

"Because I can't give her enough of my time," Mason shouted back.

Crew's eyebrows shot up. "What do you mean?"

"I mean...that Layla will always come first," Mason said, his voice back to normal. "Harper deserves to be wined and dined like a princess and all I've got are sippy cups and cracker crumbs. She deserves one on one attention and I can only offer a few minutes while Layla's napping." He shook his head. "It just isn't fair to her."

Crew snorted. "Don't you think that's for her to decide?"

Before Mason could respond to his brother's ludicrous question, Mr. Thomas came marching around the corner.

"Mason!" the older man shouted, holding up a hand. "Good to see you." He walked up with his hand outstretched.

"Hey, Mr. Thomas," Mason said. "Thanks so much for coming. I know working with family law isn't your specialty, but…"

Mr. Thomas waved him off. "I actually studied it before I went into corporations, so it's fine. Makes me brush up on other aspects of the law." He smiled and tickled Layla's side. "This must be the little lady."

Mason nodded. "Layla, this is Mr. Thomas. He's going to be helping us in court."

Mr. Thomas turned. "And you must be Crew."

Crew stood and shook the man's hand. "That's right. I'm Mason's younger brother."

Mr. Thomas nodded. "It's good you're here. Having family support is always positive in the courtroom." He took a deep breath. "Let's get this nightmare started, huh?"

Mason made a face. "I hate that that's an accurate term."

"Me too," Mr. Thomas agreed. He moved to the wooden picnic table and set down his briefcase, pulling out a large folder. "I've gotten the papers from your mother's lawyer, Mr. Thornbull." Mr. Thomas tilted his chin down and gave Mason a look. "It appears he's pushing for the fact that you're single and inexperienced. He'll be trying to convince the judge you're incompetent and incapable of taking care of Layla." One eyebrow shot up. "Don't give him any reasons to be right, okay?"

"Is that your way of saying stay out of trouble?" Mason asked with a chuckle.

"More or less."

"Don't worry. I never go looking for trouble."

"That's what we lawyers like to hear. Now..." He flipped through his papers. "I read your sister's will and I can't find any loopholes, so Mr. Thornbull is going to have his work cut out for him. You have a good record of employment, your boss had only good things to say, you own a home and have the means to take care of the child." He paused. "The biggest cons are that you're not married and that your mother has more money than sense at her disposal."

Crew snorted a laugh, then tried to cover it. "Sorry." He shrugged at Mason. "But he nailed it."

"There isn't anything you can do about the single issue?" Mr. Thomas pressed.

Mason hesitated but shook his head. "I'm...dating a woman, but it's brand new. We're not even close to getting married."

"Would she testify on your behalf in the courtroom? You know, talk about what a great guy you are?" Mr. Thomas asked, grabbing for a pen.

"Maybe," Mason said. "As long as she has the time, I don't see why not." He offered Harper's name and number. "I'll ask her, so she's not caught off guard with everything."

"Wonderful." Mr. Thomas finished making a few notes. "Let's go over their case and then we can build our defense, alright?"

Mason glanced at Crew. Crew was just as serious as Mason was, but he slapped Mason's shoulder. "We can do this," he said. "Mom has no right to take Layla from you. Every single one of us knows why Aimee left Layla to you over Mom. This is for her."

Mason nodded curtly. "For Aimee *and* Layla." *And myself. I'm far from a perfect father, but I love the squirt and am not ready to give her up.*

CHAPTER 19

Harper's phone buzzed again and she pinched her lips together. Mason had texted three times this morning and she had been studiously ignoring him. But it seemed the more she ignored him, the more determined he became and the less focused she managed to be.

They had spent all day apart yesterday and Harper had struggled all day long. Her brain had been at her canvas, but her heart had been elsewhere, and it had shown in everything she'd done.

She was ready to throw her canvas away and start over, but with the deadline looming, she couldn't do it. There was absolutely not enough time to come up with something new.

Her phone finally stopped making noise and Harper let out a breath of relief. Maybe now he would leave her alone. She wasn't trying to stay away from him forever, just…until she got herself figured out. Talking to Mason, having him touch her or even hearing Layla's laugh, wouldn't allow Harper to make a good decision. She'd be swayed by how much she enjoyed all those things, and then her heart would lead her head and she'd once again find her business crumbling at her feet.

No. This needed to be done in a much more strategic manner and that meant providing her own company for a little bit longer.

Harper studied her canvas. She had ditched the Impressionist idea. Yes…the winner of this particular competition usually had an Impressionistic vibe, but Harper just couldn't wrap her head around it.

Nature was her specialty and that was going to be her best bet. She decided a few more trees on the mountain would be a good idea and began squirting green paint onto her work table. She wanted it a little lighter and added just a touch of white so there would be a greater contrast.

Just as she was lifting her hand to paint, there was a knock on the door and Harper sighed. She probably needed to ignore it, like she had her phone, but…

The knock sounded again.

Closing her eyes, Harper shook her head. "Coming!" she called. Setting down the brush, she wiped her hands on her smock and rushed to the door. "Oh! Hey, Mason." Her heart lurched in her chest at the sight on her front porch.

Mason looked good enough to eat in his tight T-shirt and freshly combed hair. His beard was neatly trimmed and showed off his amazing jawline. He might be a big guy, but Harper knew she would enjoy staying inside his protective arms forever, if given half a chance.

"Harper!" Mason grinned and bounced Layla, who was reaching for Harper.

Harper stepped up and took the little girl. "Hey, sweetie. Come on in, guys." She stepped back. "This is an unexpected visit."

Mason rubbed the back of his neck. "Yeah. I know, sorry. I tried calling, but…" He waved at her apron. "You've obviously been working, I'm sorry to interrupt it."

Harper shook her head. "It's fine. I needed a break anyway." The words weren't a lie, but Harper felt torn anyway. This was exactly what she had been afraid of. Now all she wanted to do was play with Layla and spend time with Mason. But what about her painting?

"I promise not to take your whole afternoon," he said. "But I needed to talk to you about something."

"Okay." Harper tilted her head and swayed back and forth, glancing at Layla with a smile when the little girl began playing with her ponytail. She seemed to have a thing for Harper's hair and it was fun as long as Layla didn't pull too hard.

"I'm not quite sure how to say this, but..." Mason blew out a breath. "Mom got a new lawyer and she's coming after Layla."

Harper's jaw dropped and she stopped moving. "Say what?"

He nodded. "Yeah. You know how Crew showed up at my house the other night, when I left the party? He called when I wasn't home and told me about it. That's why I ran out so quickly."

"Mason," Harper breathed. Shock couldn't begin to describe the numbness that was taking over her system. She couldn't believe what she was hearing. Mason had mentioned before his mother had threatened to come after Layla, but Harper hadn't believed it would truly come to that. Now here it was...staring her in the face and she could barely wrap her brain around it. "What are you going to do?"

Mason swallowed. "I've got a lawyer friend helping me out. He's actually the lumbermill's lawyer, but he studied family law early in his career, so he was willing to take on the case." Mason shrugged. "I'm going to fight. What else can I do?"

Harper nodded. "That's the only thing you can do." She looked at Layla, who was watching them with her two favorite fingers in her mouth. "You can't let her go, Mason," Harper whispered. "You just can't."

"I know," Mason choked out. He scrubbed his hands down his face. "It's just...hard to feel like I have a chance of winning. My mom has money, experience and stability on her side. I'm just...me."

Harper set Layla down and walked over, resting her hands against Mason's chest. "Mason, no one is more qualified to take care of that little girl."

He snorted. "Harper, you had to come over for days to show me how to take care of her. I'm not sure the word 'qualified' should be used in conjunction with me at all."

Harper playfully slapped his chest. "None of that." She pointed to Layla. "No one loves that little girl like you." Harper shook her head hard. "Your mother might have more money, but she doesn't have Layla's best interest at heart, not even close. Don't you dare give up before you've even fought. Layla needs you."

Mason's eyes grew intense in a way that put butterflies in Harper's stomach. His hands landed on her hips and he flexed them several times. Why, oh why couldn't it be naptime?

"Thank you," he said in a low tone. "I needed to hear you say that."

Harper gave him a small smile. The air was still too heavy for levity, but if she didn't say something, she would rise up on her tiptoes and kiss him whether or not Layla was around. "I know."

Mason barked a laugh and let go of her. "I never quite know what I'm going to get with you," he said between laughs.

Harper's smile was more relaxed now. She could think better now that he wasn't touching her. "Come on. I'll feed you two lunch. My stomach's been growling for hours."

Mason picked up Layla and pried the magazine she was shredding out of her hands. "Sorry."

Harper waved him off. "No worries. It's an old one anyway." She took it from him and tossed it in the garbage. "Quesadillas okay?"

"Works for me," he said as he followed her into the kitchen. "How's the painting coming?"

The question was completely innocent, but made her pause. This was one of the times that Maeve had been talking about. Only one thing could be important. Either Harper could usher them out of the house so she could paint, or she could set aside the painting and enjoy their time. With Layla's nap hitting soon, Harper knew Mason would have a few ideas of how to pass the time, and the thought sent a thrill up her spine. She wanted it too. She wanted the kiss she had been denied just a few minutes ago. She wanted him to hold her and tell her it would all be okay, the same way she had done for him. She wanted…

"It's fine," Harper said, turning toward the fridge so he couldn't see how strained her smile was. "It's coming along just fine."

* * *

MASON SET Layla at the table. Harper sounded slightly off, but he couldn't quite figure out why. His mind was so caught up in their little missed moment that he was struggling to think of anything else. He didn't want to give up Layla, but man…he wanted to kiss Harper.

This was exactly the conundrum he'd been trying to tell Crew about when they'd been talking yesterday. Crew seemed to think Harper should simply be given a choice, but Mason was torn. Yes, he was falling for Harper, and despite the fact that they were dating, he really didn't feel like it had been fair of him to ask her in the first place.

All he could do was hope Harper knew what she was getting into. She had been such an angel with Layla, he had to believe that she understood why he waited instead of simply kissing her whenever he wanted to.

"What can I help with?" Mason asked, straightening and stretching his back.

"Do you want to grab some salsa and sour cream out of the fridge?" Harper called over her shoulder. "Or do you have some other topping in mind?"

"Those work for me." He dug through the shelves until he found what he wanted and glanced back to see Layla playing with the napkin holder. "Crud." Napkins were flying everywhere and he ran over to stop her.

Harper laughed. "Let her go. They're just paper and she's happy."

Mason scratched his beard. "You sure? It's gonna be a mess."

"I'm sure." Harper was still laughing under her breath, so Mason decided to follow her advice.

"You're awfully chill about messes and stuff," he said, coming back into the kitchen.

Harper smiled. "Art is messy," she said. "It's a part of life."

Mason shrugged. "I suppose so."

"You're a neatnik, aren't you?"

He scrunched up one side of his face. "Maybe." He held up a finger. "Or maybe *was* is the better term. But being neat while I was a single guy living alone was easy. Now it doesn't matter how much I clean, Layla can mess it up within seconds."

Harper nodded. "Imagine when you're married and have multiple kids. Those poor stay at home moms."

"Or dads," Mason muttered. He couldn't seem to stop his brain from taking her sentence a little further. As in…imagine if he and Harper got married and had more children…

His neck heated and he cleared his throat. That future didn't sound too bad…but he and Harper weren't even close to that deep of a relationship yet. He'd barely managed to spend more than an hour with her at any given point in time.

He looked over to see Layla still happy as a clam with her shredded napkins, and then scooted next to Harper. "Need any help?" he whispered. He could smell her shampoo and almost bent down for a deeper sniff.

Yeah…that's not creepy at all.

Harper sent him a flirty smile. "Are you saying I don't know how to make quesadillas?"

Mason opened his eyes wide and shook his head. "Nope. I'd never say such a thing."

Harper laughed just like he hoped. "Alright, hot shot. If you can do better, be my guest." Harper stepped back, handing him the spatula. "Don't tell me you can flip them like you do a pancake."

Mason shook his head. "Not a chance. I'd probably throw hot cheese everywhere."

Harper wiped her forehead dramatically. "Thank goodness. I've been shown up in the kitchen enough for one lifetime."

Mason chuckled and turned the tortillas. "Tell me something I don't know about you."

Harper pursed her lips. "Hm…something you don't know…" She tilted her head. "I hate the color black."

Mason paused. "Really? Don't you use it in your paintings?"

Harper nodded. "Of course. But it's my least favorite color."

"Why's that?"

"Because it's the absence of every other color," Harper explained. "I don't like how too much black makes things feel heavy or takes away from the bright happiness of something like, say, yellow. A little black can help the yellow pop, but too much causes the yellow to look sickly and the entire painting suddenly drags."

Mason moved the quesadilla to a plate. "Wow...I didn't realize painting was so philosophical. There are probably some metaphors for life in what you just said."

Harper grinned. "Even a blind squirrel gets an acorn now and again."

Mason shook his head with a smile and the next few minutes were quiet while they finished cooking and setting up lunch.

Harper cut the first, and now cooled, quesadilla into small pieces and took the plate to Layla before coming back. "Looks like that's about it," she said. "We should be covered."

Mason slipped the last one out of the hot pan, set it aside and turned off the stove. "Great. I'm starving."

Harper punched his arm. "You're always starving."

No man was strong enough to let that line go. He shifted and caged her in against the counter with his arms on either side. "Maybe my appetite is for more than just cheese and tortillas."

Her blue eyes sparkled with joy and it only urged him on. "Oh?" Harper asked innocently. "What else could you possibly be hungry for?"

Mason leaned down until he was hovering just above her mouth. "You," he said before giving her a quick peck. That was all it took. That one small second was enough to remind Mason of exactly what he'd been missing the past couple of days.

Harper must have felt similarly because they'd barely pulled apart before both of them reached for each other.

Mason couldn't get his arms tight enough around her. He had one hand in her air and one wrapped around her back and still couldn't get her close enough. When her hands went to his own hair, his knees shook and he worried he would take them both to the floor.

All his worries and concerns fled. He had Harper in his arms. His angel was right where she belonged and that meant the world was right again. The anxiety he'd been trying to drive out by chopping wood fled and he knew that no matter what life threw at him, he could handle it as long as Harper was by his side.

A scream tore through the air, followed by a thud, then silence, and Mason jumped away from Harper so fast that she almost fell over.

"Layla," he breathed. Turning, he sprinted around the countertop to find Layla on the floor with a pool of blood around her head.

The little girl's face was red and her mouth open, but sound didn't emerge for three eternally long seconds. When her cry finally rent the air, it was as if the world came back into focus. Horrible, bloody, traumatic focus.

Mason grabbed his niece and cradled her in his arms. "Call nine-one-one," he said hoarsely, not bothering to look up. "Call nine-one-one."

CHAPTER 20

It took less than five minutes for the ambulance to arrive, but it might as well have been an hour. Harper was trying to stay calm, but it was more difficult than she would have imagined. Children got hurt all the time…but this wasn't just any child. It was Layla.

Mason had refused to let go of her, so Harper had been pressing a cloth to the cut on the toddler's forehead and fighting the instinct to hold her the same way Mason was. *But she's not yours.*

The little voice in the back of her head was the only reason Harper was staying sane. She felt responsible for what had happened. After all, Mason had been kissing *her* when Layla had gotten hurt. They'd tried so hard to be good while she was awake, but the pull between them had been so strong…

Harper bit the inside of her cheek to keep the tears at bay, but now she had tears and a shredded cheek. "She's gonna be fine," Harper tried to reassure Mason, though the words fell flat. They felt like a lie, though Harper knew they weren't. Layla's life wasn't on the line, the little girl would probably be running around within the hour, but somehow those words of reassurance weren't enough.

Layla whimpered and Mason looked as if the sound gave him

physical pain. "I've got you," he whispered. "Daddy's got you. It's gonna be okay."

Harper's tears picked up again. Her heart was breaking as Mason hurt for his little girl. It was amazing to see how deep their connection was in such a short amount of time.

The door opened and Harper jumped to her feet. "In here!" she called. "We're in the kitchen." She rushed to the entrance and a couple of first responders walked inside. "She fell from the chair and cut her forehead," Harper explained, though it was unnecessary.

Staying back to give everyone room, Harper wrung her hands until her knuckles ached. She didn't have the right to be closer, but all she wanted was to be in the inner circle.

"Hey, sweetheart," the EMT said to Layla with a smile. She nodded at Mason before reaching out for Layla's forehead. "I'm just gonna take a look at this, okay?" A tension-filled moment passed before the woman smiled again. "Yep. Looks like we're gonna need stitches!" The EMT rocked back on her heels. "Why don't you bring your daughter into the ambulance. We'll get her to the hospital faster and she'll be taken care of in no time. We can actually do stitches, but they'll have better equipment to deal with a child. Plus, since it's on her temple, they might want to watch her for a while."

"You think she's hurt more than with just the cut!" Mason shouted.

Harper started forward to reassure him, but stopped, forcing herself back. Right now she would only be in the way. Best to let the professionals handle this.

The EMT took out a flashlight and shone it into Layla's eyes, humming. "Yeah…she might have a slight concussion. They'll be able to study her a little further." The EMT shook her head. "It's gonna be fine. This happens to kids all the time."

Layla shifted and let out another wail, stopping Mason from responding. "Fine," he said tightly. "Let's go."

He stood and began to walk after the EMT's. Harper rushed to his side. "Can I come?" she asked him softly. "I want to…" How did she tell him it was all her fault? She shouldn't have kissed him. Shouldn't have encouraged him! In fact, she should have just ignored his knocking in the first place! If she'd been focusing on her career, this would never have happened.

Mason made a pained face. "I...just...whatever. Just meet us there, I guess."

Pain hit Harper's chest. That wasn't exactly the glowing endorsement she was looking for, but it was enough. She needed to see this through. Layla held too much of Harper's heart for her to not make sure the little girl was okay. "I'll be right behind you," Harper said softly, though she was sure that Mason didn't hear her. He was too busy climbing into the back of the ambulance.

Harper locked up behind them and grabbed her keys, rushing to the garage. The least she could do was be there to help. After that... well...Harper wasn't sure what would be after that. How could she make this up to Mason and Layla? Mason would need some guidance, he'd never dealt with this before. Layla would need a mother's touch.

Harper wasn't her mother and Mason wasn't her husband, but Harper could still help. She had helped before and she would do so now.

Just as she was getting in the car, her phone buzzed with an email. She started to ignore it when Harper realized it was from an art house she had sent her portfolio to. Taking the few seconds necessary, Harper clicked on it and her heart sank even further than it already was.

She'd been rejected. Again.

Her work wasn't the style they were looking for. Typical. It was an automatic response and Harper knew it was simply a polite way of saying she wasn't good enough.

She shook her head and tossed her phone into the passenger seat. This had to be the worst day in the history of worst days. They say the night is darkest before the dawn, but Harper was starting to wonder if there was a dawn.

Her eyes blurred as she drove and Harper wiped the tears with the back of her hand, not caring in the least about her makeup. Was there anything in her life worth salvaging anymore?

Was her mother right? Did Harper need to simply give up and move on?

An image of Mason's look right before he kissed her came to mind. Despite the torrent of despair in her chest, a slight warmth built as she recalled the intensity in his eyes. How his look made her feel like the only woman in the room. How she felt precious and adored, and how even the thought of Mason or Layla brought a smile to her face.

That's worth salvaging.

A broken sob ripped itself from Harper as she realized she wasn't just falling for Mason. She had already fallen. She loved him with every piece of her being and Layla was right behind him. Her art, which had taken such priority for so long, wasn't enough. It didn't even come close to helping her feel so fulfilled and satisfied as a lumberjack and a two year old did.

Harper knew she would always paint–it was part of who she was–but it could no longer be the most important thing. She had stayed back when the EMT's were at the house because she didn't have the right to be in the middle, but right here and right now Harper knew that she'd give up anything, even her career and art, to be granted that right.

She pressed down a little harder on the gas pedal, praying no police were close by. Mason was going to need her and Harper was going to be there. From now on, she would always be there. She didn't even have to think about it anymore. She'd find another way to appease her mother or pay the bills, whatever life came down to.

But right now, Harper had a family to get to. One that she hoped would be hers permanently.

* * *

MASON FELT like an elephant had taken up residence on his chest. He could barely pull in enough air not to keel over and suffocate. How could he let this happen? How could he have let himself be so distracted with something as stupid as a kiss?

A kiss.

He was so disgusted by his lack of control that for a brief moment in time, he'd thought of calling up Mr. Thomas and simply handing Layla over. How could he claim to be a fit parent if he couldn't keep his hormones in check?

Harper hadn't meant to distract him. She'd only been making them lunch and he had to go and turn it into something more. Where was Crew with a good punch to the face when Mason desperately needed one? Isn't that what brothers were for?

The ambulance lurched to a stop and the EMT in the back pushed open the doors and climbed down. "Step down and we'll bring the little one."

Mason shook his head. He couldn't stand the thought of letting Layla go. She was holding his hand and Mason didn't want to scare her by letting go. She needed him right now and he'd already failed her once. He wasn't going to do it again.

The woman looked at him sympathetically. "It's going to be okay," she assured him.

The words brought Harper back to mind. She'd said the same thing. Even when Layla had been screaming and Mason could barely speak from staring at the cut and all the blood, Harper had been cool and collected. She'd called emergency services, wiped Layla's face and then pressed a clean cloth to the wound until the paramedics had arrived.

His angel was more than he could ever deserve.

"Sir," the woman said again. "She's going to be fine. Step down and we'll bring her inside."

Mason's mouth felt full of sawdust. He couldn't seem to swallow properly. He looked at Layla, whose dark eyes were droopy, but steady. "I'm just going to wait for you right there, okay?" he asked hoarsely.

Layla slowly blinked, but the paleness of her skin scared Mason and he scrambled down, desperate to get her inside and under a doctor's care. "Careful," he blurted out as the workers lifted Layla down.

"We've got her, sir," the woman said patiently. "She's gonna be fine."

Mason nodded and took Layla in his arms when all was said and done.

"Right in here, sir." The EMT waved him inside and they headed toward the check-in desk.

It didn't take long before they were in a room with a nurse bustling about setting everything up. Mason tried to be patient during the process, but he felt as if his world was shattering. The fears and doubts that he'd pushed away when Harper had landed in his arms were growing stronger and right now he didn't have the energy to fight them.

If only...if only...

The words were a harsh refrain. If only Aimee hadn't died. If only his mother wasn't so set on taking Layla. If only Mason had more self control. If only Harper wasn't such an angel. If only…

"Sir?"

Mason snapped out of his internal scoldings. "Yes?"

"The doctor will be in soon." The older woman smiled. "Can I get you anything while you wait?"

Mason shook his head. He looked down at Layla, who was still awake, though barely, and tucked into his side. "We're fine."

The woman patted his shoulder as she left. "These things happen," she assured him. "Your daughter will probably end up with a few stitches, but will be fine."

Mason nodded, but the words stung. Why wasn't anyone more upset about the fact that there was blood dripping down Layla's face? Was he the only one who wanted her well and safe? No wonder parents got all up in arms about the healthcare system! None of them cared! Layla could be bleeding out and the doctor was probably taking a break somewhere.

He grit his teeth and forced his runaway thoughts to slow down. Layla was okay. She was hurt but okay. Surely if it was dire, the nurse would have done more than tell them to wait.

"Mason?"

Mason's head jerked around so quickly, something pinched in his neck. "Harper," he said flatly. *If only I wasn't in love with Harper, this would never have happened.*

Harper gave him a timid smile. "I'm so sorry it took so long, but I had trouble getting through the front desk." She rolled her eyes. "I'm not technically family, so they didn't want to let me back."

When her hand landed on his shoulder, Mason had to fight to keep from pulling away. If this experience taught him anything, besides the fact that Layla had to be watched at all times, it was that his initial worries had been correct.

He couldn't have it all. He couldn't have Layla and Harper. Not only was it not fair to Harper, it wasn't fair to Layla. She was the one who had ended up hurt because of Mason's inability to stay focused. No child should suffer like this. Mason's love life would just have to be one of the things he would give up in order to make sure that Layla's childhood was better than her mother's.

"I'm assuming the doctor hasn't been in yet?" she asked.

Mason shook his head. How was he going to tell her it was over? The hospital didn't seem like a good place for it, but he really didn't want to pretend things were okay when they weren't either.

Harper scooted a chair closer and leaned into him, caressing Layla's cheek. Layla whimpered and tried to sit up, then reached for Harper.

"No, Tiny," Mason whispered. "I got you."

"I don't mind," Harper said, moving to take Layla.

"I don't want you to get blood all over your clothes," Mason said, trying to come up with an excuse that wouldn't hurt her feelings.

"Mason," Harper said again. "It's alright. I don't mind. They're just clothes."

"It's not alright," he said fiercely. "She's not yours to hold," he blurted out before he could think better of it.

Harper jerked back. "What?"

The timing of the doctor's arrival was a blessing or a curse depending on one's perspective, but Mason decided it was better this way. He didn't actually want to hurt Harper. She'd been nothing but wonderful, but he was going to have to. The only way to take care of Layla was to let go of Harper and either way he looked at it, it was going to hurt. But Harper was an adult. She could survive being hurt much better than Layla would.

"Well, little lady," the doctor said with a smile, scooting forward on a stool. "Let's see what we've got."

Layla leaned back into Mason's chest and he held her close. "Is this going to hurt?" Mason asked.

The doctor smiled kindly, if not with some weariness in his gaze. "I'm sure it will hurt a little, but we'll get her patched up in no time, and then she'll be back to her normal self quickly."

"The EMT seemed to think there might be a slight concussion," Mason added.

The doctor nodded. "We'll check that too." He reached out again. "May I see her for a few minutes?"

It took all of Mason's self control to hand Layla over. Layla was clinging to him and crying and it broke his heart even worse than it already was.

"Don't worry, Daddy," the doctor assured Mason. "You can stand right there and watch. It'll all be fine." The doctor laid Layla down and the nurse began chatting with her, helping calm Layla down so the doctor could inspect the wound. "Yep. A few stitches and she'll be right as rain."

Mason blew out a breath. "Okay. Thanks."

The doctor chuckled. "Don't worry. This happens all the time."

CHAPTER 21

Harper pinched her lips together. She tapped her foot. She folded her arms and chanted calming words in her head, but nothing was helping. Mason's words had *hurt*. Like, really, really hurt. She knew he was upset. She knew he was worried, as many first time parents were. She also knew that this was her fault. *And apparently Mason thinks so too.*

On her way over here, she had been ready to give it all up in order to be with Mason and Layla, but now Harper was having doubts. Mostly because it looked like Mason wasn't ready for her to give up everything to be with them.

"Mason?"

He barely glanced over his shoulder. His stance next to the bed portrayed every bit of his anxiety. His muscles were tight, his fist was at his mouth and he looked like he kept biting it as if to stop from saying something he shouldn't say.

"Can I talk to you for a moment?"

Mason's eyes finally met hers. "Not right now," he said hastily. "I don't want to leave her."

Harper nodded and forced herself to remain in her seat. She could wait it out. The doctor was busy sewing up Layla's forehead. It wouldn't be too much longer. Once Layla was back in his arms, Harper was positive that Mason would be reasonable enough to talk with.

An hour later, Mason was receiving instructions on how to care for the child at home and how to watch for signs of a concussion. The doctor felt that she was fine, but it was best to be safe.

"Thank you," Mason said over and over again. "I'll do that. Yep. Everything. I've got it."

Harper stayed back, not wanting to agitate him, but she was glad to see he was starting to relax now that Layla was done with her visit. It was a nearly forty-five-minute drive back to Seagull Cove. They could talk in the car.

"Are you ready to go home?" Harper asked once they'd reentered the waiting room. She smiled at Layla and pinched the little girl's knee.

Layla grinned, but continued to gnaw on the sucker they had given her as a parting gift.

Mason shifted, pulling Layla out of Harper's reach. "Actually, Crew is on his way. He'll take us home."

Harper stopped moving, stunned by his words. "I…" *So it wasn't something just said in the heat of the moment.* "Mason…I know her accident was my fault, but mishaps with kids happen all the time. Can you really not forgive me for that?"

Mason's face darkened. "None of this was your fault," he said fiercely. Looking around, he moved them to a corner of the waiting room where others wouldn't be able to hear their conversation. "This was all my fault. Plain and simple." Closing his eyes, he dropped his chin to his chest. "If I hadn't let myself get so distracted by you, this wouldn't have happened."

"No…Mason…" Harper reached out to touch his chest, but Mason stepped back again. She let her hand drop. On her way to the hospital, Harper had thought she knew what pain was. Layla being hurt was her fault and no adult who loved a child didn't feel pain when the child did. It was a part of life. When Mason pulled Layla away the first time, it had hurt. When he said Crew was picking them up, it had hurt. All of them combined was starting to steal her breath.

But nothing could have prepared Harper for the direction this conversation was going and what it was doing to her already bruised and confused heart.

"What are you saying?" Harper asked. "Just spell it out."

Mason took several breaths before he finally answered her. "I can't do this, Harper. For years I held back because I was afraid to split my time, but a couple weeks ago I made the biggest mistake of my life by giving into my attraction to you." He shook his head, looking away. "I should never have kissed you. I've always had such good self control, but you were there and helping me and…gah!"

Harper's muscles tensed so hard she was afraid she was going to pull something. Each and every word coming from his mouth was like another stab wound. He wasn't just upset about Layla getting hurt. Mason regretted *everything*. Every moment, every touch, every kiss… all the things that Harper had decided were worth fighting for. They meant nothing to him.

Mason pushed a hand through his hair. "Do you even understand?" he asked. "Layla was given to me. *ME!* I was asked to care for her and I'm facing a battle in court, trying to prove I'm a fit father, and yet what did I do? I turned my back over a stupid kiss."

Harper actually stepped back at the venom in his words. She didn't need to hear anymore. She understood. Straightening her shoulders, determined not to show how much he was breaking her, Harper stuck her chin in the air. "Thank you, Mason," she said, proud that her voice wasn't shaking. "I understand completely. Take care."

Spinning on her heel, she marched out of the emergency room, not bothering to wipe the tears flowing freely down her face. Mason couldn't see them anyway, so what did it matter if she allowed herself to cry?

She got back into her car and found her way back to the main road. The ocean was on her left and the road looming ahead of her.

For once she didn't see the beauty of the sand or the waving grasses. The waves crashing into shore or the families playing in the surf might as well not have been there.

Harper could barely see through her tears to stay on her side of the road. Wiping at her eyes, she took a deep breath. She needed to stay in control enough to drive, but she would also allow herself the tears.

The drive was all she was going to get. Once she got home, Harper would apologize to her mother. She had been right all along. A good, solid career was going to be all that mattered. Steady and dependable. Something that wouldn't turn around and bite the hand that fed it.

She had tried. She'd tried to make a career of her painting and had failed. She'd tried to help Mason and had failed. She'd given Mason and Layla her heart and it had been returned in a bloody pulp.

Everything had failed.

And when everything fails, there's only one thing to do. Harper was going to pick herself up, learn from her mistakes and move forward in a new direction. A *completely* new direction.

And she would never turn back.

* * *

MASON COULDN'T WATCH Harper walk away. It hurt too much to know that it was over. Even the relief over knowing his actions wouldn't lead to another incident like this wasn't enough to overcome how much it had pained him to send Harper home.

She hadn't even argued with him. If Mason had scolded Aimee that way, she'd have ripped him up one side and down the other until he backed off, but not Harper. She'd listened to his ranting with a stoic face, then had wished him well and left.

That almost hurt worse than if she'd cried and fought back.

"Dude." Crew rushed through the doors. "What happened?" He grabbed Layla and held her up, examining the stitches.

"Can we just get in the car?" Mason asked. He needed to get out of here. Away from the smell of antiseptic and the blanket of despair hanging over the entire waiting room. He found himself fitting in a little too well with the emotion and he didn't like it. All the people there were trying to have a physical wound repaired. Layla's cut had been taken care of. It was Mason's wound that still stung and a couple of stitches and a lollipop wasn't going to help.

"Yeah, alright," Crew said. He turned and walked them out to his rental. "Good thing I asked for a car seat when I picked this up," he teased. After strapping Layla in, Crew slid into the driver's seat and started the engine. "You know, I'm surprised Harper didn't come with you. I thought you were at her house."

Mason turned his head to watch out the window. He didn't want to talk about it.

"Mase," Crew said in a low tone. "What did you do?"

Mason scowled and faced his brother. "What do you mean?"

"You turned away and refused to answer," Crew responded, maneuvering the car while he spoke. "What did you do? Why wasn't Harper here?"

"She was."

Crew frowned and glanced sideways. "Where is she now?"

Mason shrugged. "Probably halfway home."

"Why didn't you ride home with her?"

"Look, can we talk about something else?" Mason asked.

"Suuure," Crew said, sarcasm dripping from his tone. "Would it be better to talk about how this isn't going to go over well with Mr. Thomas? How if Mom's lawyer got a hint of what went on today they'll rake you over the coals in court?"

Mason cursed. "No. I don't want to talk about that either."

"There're children in the car," he said with a grin. "Better clean up that potty mouth."

"Crew, if you make another joke, I swear I'll punch something."

"You're paying for the repairs," he said easily, not the least bit concerned about his brother's temper. They drove in silence for a couple of minutes. "What happened?"

Mason sighed and closed his eyes. The window felt cool against his forehead, but it still did nothing to help the empty hole in his chest. "I sent her away."

"Who? Harper?"

"Of course, Harper. Who else would I mean?"

"Mason, you're not making sense. You told me just yesterday that you were falling in love with this woman. You go visit her today, ask her to uphold your case in court and end up in the emergency room. Lover girl, I might add, is nowhere to be found, yet you say she was here and you sent her away." Crew glared at his brother. "Tell me how anything is making sense right now?"

Mason knew from years of experience that if he didn't share it all, Crew would never let up. So the next twenty minutes were spent with him telling the story and twisting until his neck hurt so that he could check on Layla in the back seat.

The fact that she had fallen asleep with the sucker stuck in her hair was a testament to how tired the little tyke was. Mason, however, cringed at the idea of washing the candy out. He wasn't sure how he was going to do that.

Harper would know.

He shook his head, rattling the thought out of his brain.

"Let me get this straight," Crew said. His voice was low and full of steel. "You sent away the woman you love because one distracted kiss led to a child getting stitches? You're a special brand of stupid, aren't you?"

"Watch it," Mason warned.

Crew shook his head. "Mason, little kids get stitches. *All. The. Time.* While the timing isn't ideal because of the court case, it's also something that you'll probably do several more times over the years." He barked out a laugh. "Do you really think that being a single parent means that she'll never get hurt? Do you never plan to go to the bathroom or take a shower? What about fixing dinner? How's that going to work? Or what if Layla stays up when she's supposed to be napping and climbs out of the crib?" Crew gasped dramatically. "Heaven forbid our niece actually explore her room or run around outside."

"You weren't there," Mason growled. "You didn't see all the blood, or the way she couldn't breathe at first because the wind had been knocked out of her. You weren't the one knowing it was all your fault she was hurt because you couldn't control your urges."

Crew held up a hand. "I get it, Sasquatch. And you're right. I wasn't there. But having Harper there didn't make it worse. Two parents are always better than one. *Always.* I could parade a dozen studies in front of you that show that exact thing, but I don't really think this is about keeping Layla safe."

Mason stiffened. "What do you mean?"

Crew breathed in slowly, then released it. "You might be as big as the Jolly Green Giant, but inside you're a scared little boy."

"You think I'm scared of Harper?" Nothing could be further from the truth. Harper was an angel on Earth. There was nothing frightening about her except how easily she pulled his attention away from what was important.

"No. I think you're afraid of losing control."

"I did lose control," Mason practically shouted. "Did you not hear the story? Losing control is exactly what led to our being at the emergency room."

"No. An accident led to you being in the emergency room. Aimee was right when she said you're like Mom. You don't like life to shift or change, but you aren't as rude about it as Mom is."

Mason turned away. He didn't need to hear this. Brother or not, Crew had no idea what he was saying.

"You don't have to believe me," Crew continued. "But if you look back, you know I'm right. You're terrified of losing what little control you have left in your life. Layla forced you to change, in a good way, I might add. I'll bet before she showed up, you had every minute of your day planned down to when you would scroll social media."

Mason huffed. So what if that was right?

"Having a child in your home shook you up a bit, but with Harper's help, you adjusted and got a schedule back to help you keep your sanity." Crew rested his elbow on the window and put his head on his fist while he drove one-handed. "But you can't control Harper. And you can't control Layla. And as time went on, it wasn't the fact that your attention was split, but the fact that the deeper you got, the less you were able to control anything at all."

"I think we need to stop talking about this."

Crew nodded. "Fine. I won't bring it up again, but I just want you to know that I think you're making the worst mistake of your life." He paused. "And I pity you for it."

CHAPTER 22

*P*aint was splashing on the floor and the walls and possibly even the ceiling, but Harper didn't care. This was her studio, she could do what she wanted with it.

"I was willing to give up my business for you." A streak of red went across the canvas. "I sacrificed my time and energy!" A clash of purple mixed into the fray. "Do you have any idea how hard it is to live up to a mother's expectations?" she yelled, dipping her already dirty brush in yellow and smearing the colors across the fabric.

Exhausted, she fell back into her seat, slumping against the hard back. "What's wrong with me?" she whispered into her quiet room. "Why can't I ever be enough?"

Her drive home hadn't been as cathartic as she'd hoped. Instead of feeling ready to push ahead, Harper had dragged herself into the house like a zombie. Her body ached almost as badly as her heart and all she had wanted to do was lie down and sleep.

A couple hours later, her emotions had moved on and now Harper was angry. She couldn't even quite explain the sudden shift, but instead of wanting to cry, she found herself wanting to scream. She was so tired of giving everything and still coming up short. With her mother, with her painting…with Mason.

Her paintbrush fell from her hands. The harsh colors and slashes were nothing like her usual calming work. But it had felt good coming together.

Harper closed her eyes. She could still see Layla reaching for her, stretching...that bloody cut on her forehead and Mason turning to keep them apart. Harper's hand clutched at her chest. How did emotions hurt so much? They weren't a physical thing yet it affected her body as if it were tangible.

She let her head flop to the side and spotted her sketchbook. Her fingers twitched. Groaning, Harper stood and walked over, grabbing a handful of pencils and the tablet. Instead of going back to her work chair, however, she headed to the backyard. It wasn't much, but it was quiet and the setting sun made a beautiful backdrop. Harper, however, wasn't interested in nature at the moment. Instead, her fingers began to move in large strokes across the pristine, white paper.

Over and over she drew, erasing, smudging, shading. Dark black curls emerged in a round, baby face. A pert nose and perfect set of pouty lips. The eyes twinkled with joy despite the lack of color. Anyone could see how happy this child was. How happy Layla had been during their time together.

Another scene emerged and Harper tore the page out, setting it aside. She was surrounded by darkness now, the light only behind her from inside the house. Her skin was covered in goosebumps from the cool evening air, but Harper couldn't stop. These pictures were doing so much more for her state of mind than the angry painting ever could. She had to get them out of her head and into something tangible.

"If I can't paint the bad," she murmured, "I might as well remember the good." She turned her pencil at just the right angle in order to shade the side of Layla's face as it peeked over Mason's shoulder.

His broad back was more than enough to identify who was holding the little girl. Harper smiled softly. Layla really was tiny compared to her uncle, making his nickname a little too on-the-nose.

Harper frowned, her eyebrows pulling together. Was Crew just as big? Harper hadn't met him yet, though Mason said he was in town. *It doesn't matter now anyway,* she scolded herself. *This is all you'll have. Deal with it.*

Harper paused, running a finger down Layla's cheek that would have been soft and plump in real life. Flat, dull paper was nothing like the vibrant toddler Harper had fallen in love with.

The hours flew and eventually Harper grew so cold she had to come back inside, but that didn't stop her from sketching. Picture after picture littered her floor. Layla by herself. Layla knocking down blocks. Mason kissing Layla's head. Mason playing peek-a-boo. Mason eating a stack of pancakes.

Every good memory from their couple of weeks together manifested itself through her paper and through the long night.

By the time Harper had spent all her creative energy, the sun was starting to peek over the horizon. She stood and yawned. Her floor was completely covered with papers, but she didn't have the energy to pick them up.

Finally, Harper knew she'd be able to sleep. She could be honest enough with herself at this point to realize that the next few days would be hard. The first time she ran into Mason in town would be hard. When she saw him at functions with their friends, it would be hard.

"When he dates someone else…it'll be hard." The words caused bile to rise through her throat and Harper swallowed convulsively to push it back down.

But she had survived hard things before. And that was going to be the key. Harper knew she would never quite be the same. Mason and Layla had changed her and taken a piece of her that Harper would never get back. "That's okay," Harper told herself, though the words were like pieces of glass. "They probably need it more than I do."

Padding down the hall, she walked into her room and didn't bother to change, simply fell into bed face first. She eventually managed to crawl up and cover herself with a blanket, but after that, Harper was done.

She breathed slowly, allowing the darkness to claim her. When she eventually felt like rising again, she'd figure out how to pick up the pieces of her life both figuratively and literally, but right now she wanted enough of a break in order to breathe. A dreamless sleep should absolutely do the trick, so despite the nightmare she seemed to be living, Harper sent up a prayer for her rest to be as uninterrupted as possible.

Sleep wouldn't make her whole, but at least it would help her build a little strength and maybe even a bit of courage. Because when Harper faced the world again, it would be a completely different place and she would have to change with it.

***

Mason finished singing his ridiculous lullaby to Layla and tucked her into her bed. She whimpered and his heart lurched, worried that her head was hurting her, but by the time he got to the door, her breathing had already slowed down.

He stepped into the hall and carefully closed the door behind him, but didn't move. Leaning against the wall, Mason slid to the carpet. His body was done. He hung his arms over his knees and let his forehead hit the top. His breathing grew ragged and he felt like someone was squeezing his chest, keeping the air from actually reaching his lungs.

Pots and pans clanged in the kitchen, but Crew's movements weren't enough to pull Mason from his depression. How was he going to do this? Every single thing he'd done since getting home had reminded him of Harper.

When he'd cooked dinner, he'd wanted Harper next to him, teasing at his elbow. When he'd wiped Layla's face, he had imagined Harper watching and laughing. When he'd given Layla a bath, he'd remembered Harper singing and making funny faces. Putting Layla in pajamas had only reminded him of Harper's lessons on getting the zipper up before Layla could climb back out.

He felt torn in two. He needed to take care of Layla, but even more...Mason was beginning to realize he also needed Harper. This wasn't just about his attraction, or how much she had helped him when he'd been underwater with Layla's arrival.

He needed Harper like he needed air. He needed to see her face and hear her laugh and touch her skin. She brought out the best in him and helped a man who was already compared to Sasquatch, feel like he was ten feet tall. Harper made him feel like he could accomplish anything and everything, and with a long, difficult future playing out in front of him...he knew he wouldn't be able to make it without her.

A body slid to the floor beside him. "It's hitting, isn't it?"

Mason nodded.

Crew sighed and a thud told Mason his brother's head hit the wall. "I'm far from an expert on love, but why don't you just go tell her you made a mistake?"

Mason chuckled, dark and empty. "You didn't hear what I said to her." He brought his head up. "There's no way she'll forgive me. And I can't ask her to."

"All men screw up," Crew pointed out.

"Not like this."

Crew rolled his eyes. "How do you know? Do you own the copyright on being an idiot? I'm pretty sure there's enough of that to go around."

Mason shook his head. "It wouldn't be fair to her—"

"Why do you keep saying that?" Crew snapped. "You stayed away from her because it wasn't fair to ask her to share your time looking for your sister. Then it wasn't fair to ask her to share time with your niece. Now it's not fair to ask her to forgive you for being a word Mama would wash my mouth out with soap for."

Mason sighed and scrubbed his face with his hands. "What do you want from me, Crew? I said some horrible things. Really horrible things. Harper is like a living angel and just kept trying to help until I finally shredded every good part of our relationship, making it sound like it meant nothing to me." He shook his head. "What woman would forgive that? What woman *should* forgive that?"

"What woman shouldn't be given the choice?" Crew shot back. "You don't give her enough credit. She's an adult and if she's as wonderful as you say, then she deserves the right to choose." He held up his hand before Mason could argue. "If she turns you down, then fine. She turned you down. But it doesn't really leave you any worse off than you are now." A half smile tugged at his mouth. "But if she's willing to overlook your idiocy…well…isn't that worth the risk?"

Mason let the words ruminate before answering. "She's worth any risk."

"Then go get her."

Mason pulled his phone out of his back pocket. "It's probably too late tonight. She'll be asleep."

"Any woman who likes romance will be fine losing her beauty rest for the right man," Crew drawled.

"For such a non-love expert, you certainly have a lot of opinions," Mason muttered.

"Some of us actually go on dates," Crew replied with a grin.

"And?"

Crew shrugged. "And I have little to show for it, other than experience."

"That doesn't make me want to take your advice."

Crew shoved Mason's phone in his face. "Call her."

Mason scowled and pulled the phone away, giving his brother a look before going back to the device. He took a deep breath. Before he could do anything, however, a call came through.

"Uh-oh," Crew murmured. "That's not good."

Mason nodded and climbed to his feet. Probably best to take this one in his office. He clicked to answer. "Hi, Mr. Thomas."

As much as Mason wanted Crew to be right, it was probably a good thing he hadn't managed to call Harper yet. This phone call was more than likely not going to be good news and it might go better for everyone involved if he took care of the situation with Layla before trying to win Harper back. Honestly, if he lost Layla, Harper might not want to come back.

He had no idea how much of her attention had been for him or for the child, but until he knew where he was going, he wasn't going to drag her into it. Crew wouldn't like it, but Mason's mind was made up. Fight his mother first, then fight for the woman he loved.

CHAPTER 23

*H*arper nearly jumped out of her skin when the front door slammed open.

"Intervention time!"

Harper put her hand over her heart and walked out of her studio. "Aspen Edwards, you nearly gave me a heart attack." Harper stopped and her eyes nearly bugged out of her head. Her hands came up to cover her mouth. "Ohhhhh…"

Aspen smirked and put her hands on her hips. "I knew that would work."

Harper threw a glare at Aspen, then slowly made her way to Riley. "Where did they come from?" Harper cooed at the basket of adorable gray kittens. She reached in and picked one up. The tiny thing meowed angrily, but settled in against Harper's chest as soon as it touched her.

Riley gave Harper a sympathetic look. "They were dumped in a field and we've been feeding them. Two didn't survive, but the rest are doing great now."

Harper frowned. "Who could do that to such sweet little things?" She picked up the kitten she held and put it in front of her face. "You're much too cute to abandon. People are horrible, aren't they?"

"Yeah…" Aspen agreed. "Like men. They're horrible too."

"You're married," Riley reminded Aspen.

"Oh yeah." Aspen nodded. "All but one man is horrible."

"Amen to that," Harper muttered. "Come on in, ladies. Might as well take a break anyway."

"It's a break with kittens, though," Aspen pointed out. "No one can turn that down."

"I'll bet people with allergies can," Riley stated, setting the basket in the middle of the sitting room. She plopped herself on the floor and helped lift each of the five kittens out, allowing them to crawl over her and begin to explore the room.

"If you lost two, this had to be a big batch," Harper said. She rubbed her eyes. They were still tired and gritty despite the fact that Mason had dumped her almost a week ago and she had stopped crying after forty-eight hours. It had taken her longer than expected to purge the emotions from her system, but after that Harper had thrown herself into her artwork…mostly.

"It was," Riley agreed. "But we take them anyway. They'll be ready for families in a couple weeks." Her smile was far from innocent. "You aren't looking for a housemate, are you?"

Harper gave her friend a sad smile. "I always wanted to get a pet when I had a family. I don't think it would be smart to have one when there's no one around to watch it."

"You're home all day," Aspen pointed out. She tilted her head. "Though I suppose paint and cats aren't really good friends."

Harper didn't respond. She sat down and put the kitten in her lap, enjoying the soft fur and the tiny rumble of a purr. Its whole body shook with the effort.

"Harp," Aspen said, her tone much more serious. "What's going on?"

Aspen already knew about the break up. There was no way to hide that from her best friend, but Harper had never shared everything else. "I…might be getting a job."

"What?" Aspen leaned forward from her spot on the couch. "You have a job."

Harper shrugged, still keeping her eyes on the cat. "You know as well as I do that my art doesn't pay all the bills."

"But you have your grandmother's trust."

"Wait, what?" Riley asked. "I feel like I'm behind."

Harper sighed. "My grandmother was an artist, like me. She left me a trust when she died so I could pursue art school. My mom doesn't think it's a real career."

"Ah…gotcha." Riley nodded. "If it makes you feel better, my mom says I play for a living." She scrunched her nose. "Though she doesn't really give me grief about it."

"Yeah, well…my mom isn't just giving me grief, she's threatening to cut off the money."

Gasps filled the room, startling a couple of the kittens, who mewed their displeasure. Harper pulled the little one back up to her chest. Maybe she would feel better if she just shared it all. So she did. From the very beginning just like she had with Maeve. Everything about her mom, about Mason and even about Layla.

By the time she was done, Harper was exhausted, the kitten was asleep and Riley and Aspen both looked shell shocked.

"How in the world have you kept all this from us?" Aspen asked, her hurt evident in her tone. "What are friends for if not to help?"

"Aspen, you know I love you," Harper said. "But there's nothing you can do about this. My mother is my mother. You have no control over her decisions or my ability to sell my art."

Aspen shook her head. "No, but I could have brought cake therapy. Or kitten therapy."

"Last month it could have been puppy therapy," Riley added. "They were cute too."

Harper sighed. "The point is, there was nothing anyone could do. It wasn't worth dragging you all into my drama."

"Actually, there is something I can do." Aspen put her nose in the air. "You can move into my room at the house."

Harper frowned. "What?"

"Seriously, it'll work," Aspen insisted. "My room is big and completely empty. Why not move in there to save money until your art takes off? If your mom is cutting off the funds, then the best thing you can do is tighten the budget, right? This would make a huge difference."

Harper smiled softly. "Aspen, as sweet as that is, it won't work. I need an art room."

"There's a bonus space above the garage."

"One that I can get messy with paint. Plus, a place to store my canvases." Harper waved a hand around her cabin. "My type of work needs plenty of space, and a single bedroom in an occupied house won't be enough."

Aspen pouted. "I still think it's a good idea."

"I'll keep it in mind, okay? I really appreciate the offer, but it really would be better to keep what I have."

"I know, but the offer stands."

Harper nodded. "Thanks. I appreciate that."

"So what are you going to do?" Riley asked softly.

Harper shrugged. "There's not much I can do. So I'm working on finishing the piece to send to the competition. I won't win, but at least I can say I tried. Meanwhile, I've been researching jobs." She huffed a laugh. "There's actually an opening for an art teacher about an hour south in an elementary school. I'm debating sending in my resume."

"That's a long commute," Aspen said.

Harper nodded. "I know, but hopefully it will only be temporary. I really do want to make a full-time income with my art." She pursed her lips. "Although taking on an outside job will slow it down, but... eventually, right?"

"Right," Aspen said firmly. "It's just around the corner. I can feel it." She paused. "And just for the record...I think Mason's the biggest imbecile ever. Even worse than Austin before we got together."

Harper barked out a laugh that was quickly followed with tears. "Thanks," she said through her hiccups. "This is exactly why we're friends."

Aspen and Riley both came over and wrapped their arms around Harper. "And because I bring kittens and cake," Aspen whispered.

"And that," Harper agreed. No, telling her friends hadn't changed anything, but Harper had to admit that she felt better. Between the kitten and sharing her burden, the world seemed a little lighter, even if the path was the same. Somehow, she would get through this and as she cried in the arms of her besties, she was simply grateful she wouldn't have to do it alone.

* * *

Mason tried to focus on the email he was writing, but Crew's airplane sounds were driving him crazy. Layla's giggles always helped soothe his frustration, but all in all, Mason was just grumpy.

He had been for a week.

Ever since pushing Harper away, yet Mason still hadn't gone after her. Talking to Mr. Thomas that night had made Mason realize he needed to wait a bit, but with each day that went by, he was growing more and more tense.

He knew there would be repercussions from Layla's accident, but the question was…how bad? Their mom's lawyer had sent word that they were working on a court date and Mr. Thomas had advised Mason to sit tight and not make any more stupid mistakes.

"Hey, Sasquatch!" Crew called. "You about done in there? The squirt and I are hankering for an ice cream cone."

Mason sighed and shut down his computer. He walked out. "I don't know if that's a good idea. Maybe we should just stay home until we know what's going on with Mom."

Crew snorted. "We're not under house arrest, Mase. We can go get ice cream." He grinned at Layla and tickled her. "Besides, I'm probably going to have to go home tomorrow and I want to spoil her a bit before I go."

"You're leaving?" Mason asked.

Crew nodded. "I do have a job to get back to, you know."

Mason rubbed his aching forehead. "I know. I just…"

Crew nodded. "I know. I was hoping to be here when it all went down, but…" He shrugged. "Duty calls."

Mason nodded. "I get it. I'm glad you came for a while."

"Me too." Crew continued making faces at Layla. "I'm still not sure why Aimee kept her a secret."

"I'm guessing she was afraid Mom would find out."

"But she was a single mom," Crew said softly, his smile falling. "We could have helped."

Mason walked farther into the room and sat down on the edge of the couch. He leaned his elbows onto his knees. "I'm starting to think Aimee cut ties with all of us in order to cut ties with Mom. I don't think things went well after we left."

Crew nodded. "Yeah...me too. But she was our sister. We would have done anything she needed."

"I know that, you know that, but somehow..." Mason swallowed hard. "Aimee didn't know that."

"I guess we get a second chance, huh?"

Mason nodded, though they both recognized the unspoken words in the room. *As long as Mom doesn't get her.* "You know what? Let's get that ice cream."

Crew's smile was back. "I knew you'd see it my way."

Mason smacked the back of Crew's head as he walked past. "Don't get cocky."

"Did you see that, Squirt? The big, bad Sasquatch hurt me! Don't let him do the same to you."

Mason rolled his eyes. "You're ridiculous."

"And now he's calling me names." Crew stuck out his bottom lip and batted his eyes at Layla, pouting for all he was worth.

Layla squealed and whacked his face, causing Mason to chuckle.

"Even two year olds can see through your act."

Crew pulled back from the swinging arms. "Guess I'll have to work on that."

A knock at the door brought all the laughter to a screeching halt. Mason looked at Crew. "Here we go."

Crew nodded. "Here we go."

Mason went to answer the door and just like they suspected, it was Mr. Thomas.

"Good to see you, Mason," the lawyer said, coming inside.

"You too," Mason replied. "I'm hoping you have good news for us."

"I wish I did," Mr. Thomas said softly. "Where's the best place to talk?"

Mason waved toward the dining room table. "Let's go here." He looked over his shoulder. "Crew!"

"Coming!" Crew came in, carrying Layla. "Mr. Thomas." The men shook hands. Instead of sitting, Crew stood, bouncing Layla.

Mason went ahead and took a chair across from Mr. Thomas. "Just say it," he said. Between the lawyer's greeting and the stoic look on his face, Mason knew he wasn't going to enjoy this meeting.

"News of the hospital was exactly what they were looking for," Mr. Thomas said bluntly. "They've got her records and testimony of the doctors saying it was a completely preventable accident."

Mason bit back a curse word. His fists clenched on the table. "Okay…what can we do?"

Mr. Thomas opened his briefcase. "The character witnesses are even more important now than they were before. I never followed up… Did you talk to your girlfriend? One…" He looked at the papers. "Harper Woodson?"

Mason felt the blood drain from his head. "Um…no. Harper and I are no longer together."

Mr. Thomas stared at him. "You're killing me, Mason."

Mason nodded, still feeling light headed. "I know."

Mr. Thomas shook his head and searched through his papers. "How about Ethan Markle? You mentioned you two were friends."

"Yeah…" Mason cleared his throat. "Ethan would be a great resource."

"Any others?"

Mason nodded. "Jayden Gordon and Gavin Smith. I'm sure both of them would be willing to help out." Jayden was Aspen's cousin and a good friend. He'd been one of the first people to welcome Mason to Seagull Cove. Gavin was a firefighter and had arrived about the same time as Mason. Their similar age, size and quiet ways had drawn them together as friends from the beginning.

Mason's group of friends included several other men, including the town vet and a school teacher, but these were the ones he was closest to, making them the best choice for a character reference.

"But no one closer?" Mr. Thomas pressed. "No one who's been around you and Layla more than once or twice?"

Mason shook his head. The only person who fit that category was Harper and she probably hated his guts right now. He was hoping they could eventually be friends again, but until then? "No. No one else."

Mr. Thomas's sigh was longer and louder than last time. "Alright, well…the will is on our side and you've both added your own testimony about your mother's…controlling attitude, so we'll just have to wait and see."

"Do we have a date yet?" Crew asked, looking far too somber.

Mr. Thomas nodded. "I suppose I should have mentioned that, right?" He turned back to Mason. "This'll all be over next Tuesday."

Mason choked. "That's only a week."

Mr. Thomas nodded. "Evidently your mother's lawyer has some pull because these things often take weeks or even months. But we're on the docket for next week." He shook his head. "Personally, I think they're trying to avoid letting us have much time to build a defense. The longer you spend with Layla, the more examples you have of being a good parent."

Mason pinched his lips. The end was finally close, but just as his mother hoped, he didn't feel prepared. For better or for worse, his future would be decided next week, and Mason was terrified.

CHAPTER 24

All the days were beginning to blend into each other as Harper forced herself to keep moving. Her painting, such as it was, was done and ready to be sent to the competition. She had given herself as much time as possible, trying to overcome her melancholy, but now she was on the very edge of the deadline and had to mail it today or it wouldn't arrive in time to be counted.

She was currently wrapping the piece for transport and would travel to the nearest post office to get it shipped off. It would take her whole afternoon, but it wasn't like it mattered. She had nothing else pulling on her time.

Her resume had gone out to a few jobs within the last week and Harper was waiting to hear back from them. Meanwhile, she moped around the house, pretending to paint, but really doing nothing.

She'd gone to visit Riley and the kittens a couple times and Harper was having a hard time not bringing one home. Sometimes all she wanted in the middle of the night was a tiny, soft kitten to cuddle with, but then the morning would come and sense would return.

She was getting a job. She wouldn't be home. It wouldn't be fair to a pet to be gone all day.

Harper sighed. So for now…she would remain single. Though she would use her friends to help with the loneliness, just like she had always done.

Luckily, Harper had yet to run into Mason, which was a blessing and a curse. She ached to see him but knew it would only prolong the hurt she was still experiencing. "Just like a Band-Aid," she whispered to herself as she wrapped the painting. "Rip it off and get it done."

Her phone rang and Harper ignored it. She'd get back to whoever it was when she was done. Trying to get a painting ready for the mail was no small task.

Her phone went off again and Harper sighed. "Fine," she breathed. Setting down the wooden frame, she grabbed the device and frowned at the screen. Who in the world would be calling her from California? "Hello?"

"Is this Harper?" a deep voice asked.

Harper's frown deepened. Who was this? And why was the tone ever so slightly familiar? "I'm sorry…who's this?"

"This is Crew Turley. I'm Mason's younger brother."

Harper froze.

"Harper? Are you there?"

"Y-yes," she stuttered. "How did you get my number?"

Crew chuckled and the sound was so like Mason's that Harper's knees shook. "I stole it from Mase's phone when he wasn't looking."

"What can I do for you, Mr. Turley?" Harper said coolly. She didn't need this kind of stress right now. If Crew was calling about Mason, then it wasn't anything she needed to hear. Mason had broken up with *her*. Not the other way around. Not to mention, she still needed to get on the road so she could get that painting shipped before it was too late.

"Look," Crew said in a somber tone. "I know Mason probably isn't your favorite guy right now—"

Harper snorted. That was an understatement.

"But he needs your help."

Harper put her hand on her hip. "If he needed my help, why isn't he the one calling?" She wasn't usually so snarky, but Harper's emotions were a little on edge at the moment.

"Because he doesn't think you'll listen."

Harper pursed her lips. "What do you want, Crew?" she asked, her tone softer. "I have several things to do today and some of them are on a tight deadline."

Crew grumbled some things under his breath that she couldn't understand. "Did you know that my mother is trying to take Layla away from Mason?"

Harper's heart skipped a beat. "Yes. He mentioned it once," she whispered.

"Did you know he's at the courthouse right now fighting to keep her?"

Her eyes just about bugged out of her head. "What? Today? How in the world did it move that fast?"

"My mom has connections," Crew said wryly. "But what matters is that he's desperate for a good character witness and doesn't have one. They're using the hospital trip against him and Mason doesn't have a leg to stand on."

Harper's stomach felt nauseous and she put a hand on it. "What do you mean, he doesn't have a character witness? He has friends. Any of them would be willing to speak up for him."

"And they are, but none of them have experience watching him with Layla."

Except you. The words hung in their air between them, breaking down all of Harper's carefully built defenses. "He won't want me there," she said hoarsely. "He practically kicked me out of that hospital."

Crew snorted. "I think you'd be surprised by the reception you'd receive."

Harper shook her head. "Crew...I really don't see how my word means more than anyone else's. I haven't known Mason as long as Ethan or Jayden. Yes, we hang out with the same friend group, but we haven't been close."

"Harper," Crew begged. "You *know* him. You know him better than anyone else. You tell me... How many people in that great big group of yours have seen Mason when he was mopping up spilled orange juice in his pajamas? Or when he was sleep deprived? Or when he was bathing a tiny toddler with jam smeared in her hair?"

Harper couldn't get enough moisture in her mouth to swallow.

"How many have seen him at his worst, but also his best? How many have dealt with his need to be in control and helped him learn to let go?"

"How—?" She didn't even know how to ask the right question. Crew was talking as if he had been there.

"He told me," Crew said softly. "Letting you go was the hardest thing Mason has ever done. The man is a giant on the outside but full of stuffing on the inside. Layla means almost everything to him. He can't lose you both."

Harper bit her tongue. Mason hadn't lost her. He'd pushed her away. But she knew from personal experience that losing Layla would break him. Harper was barely surviving and Layla wasn't even hers. Mason would never recover.

And Layla won't either.

"Where are they?" she asked.

Crew spouted off the directions, obviously having practiced before he got on the phone. "Will you come then? Can I tell our lawyer you'll be here?"

Harper looked at her painting. The courthouse was in the opposite direction. There would be no way to do both. If she went after Mason, she'd lose her ability to enter the competition and any chance she had of talking to her mother about an extension. By not sending in the painting, she wouldn't be fulfilling her end of the bargain and her mother would have the right to cut off funds immediately.

Her stomach churned once more. *He doesn't want you. He has other friends. He regrets kissing you.*

Tears swam in her vision when Layla's dark eyes and addicting laugh broke through the bad memories. She didn't have to do this for Mason, though Harper still loved him…she would do it for Layla. Layla had never let her down and even though Harper wasn't going to be part of the toddler's life, she still wanted Layla to have the best, and it wasn't with her grandmother. "I'll be there."

* * *

DEFEATED. There was no other way to describe how Mason was feeling. A social worker had taken Layla and he was sitting in a courtroom listening to his mother's lawyer talk about every mistake Mason had ever made as a youth, as a teenager and as an adult. His life, which he thought was pretty decent, was being picked apart as if he were a criminal offender.

Pictures of Layla's head wound were up on a screen and had been for the past several minutes. Mr. Thomas had whispered that they were being left up in order to keep the accident in the judge's mind.

Mason's parents were sitting on the other side of the courtroom, his mother pristine and smug.

Mason had never felt such an intense dislike for anyone in his life as he did for his mother right then and there. His mind had slowly been opening the last month to his mother's machinations, but seeing her there, her eyes to the front and her hands folded so primly in her lap while her lawyer argued about her son's incompetence, was almost more than Mason could stand.

Crew's lecture the other day came to mind. Where he said that Mason liked to control things…like their mother. Aimee had said Mason was kinder, and Mason found himself grateful for that, but the longer he sat in the courtroom, the more he was determined to make the differences between his mother and himself even greater.

He wanted to be the complete opposite of the woman in every way, shape and form. He wanted to learn to let go of his control and live life to the fullest. He didn't want to just be kind, he wanted to have full compassion and charity for everyone around him. If he managed to take Layla home, he wouldn't worry about the small messes. He would take pictures when she had food smeared in her hair. He would laugh with her when she knocked over the tower of blocks.

And the next time a woman hands me her heart, I'll treasure it as if my life depends on it.

His own heart sank. He wasn't sure any females would be in his life ever. The case wasn't going well and Harper was gone. Half of Mason's heart was already destroyed and if Layla was taken too, he wasn't sure how he was going to survive. And there'd be no way he could approach Harper after losing his niece.

Even if she could forgive him for being horrible to her, how could she forgive him for losing custody?

"Your Honor," Mr. Thomas said, interrupting another long speech from Mr. Thornbull. "I fail to see how Mr. Mason Turley's seventh grade report card has any bearing on our hearing today."

"It shows a lack of initiative, Your Honor," Mr. Thornbull said quickly. "A history of slothfulness which undermines his ability to take care of a child."

"He was only a child himself," Mr. Thomas argued.

The judge held up his hand. "You'll have a chance to offer your side, Counselor," he said to Mr. Thomas. The judge looked at Mr. Thornbull. "Having said that, I recommend you stick with only those facts which are pertinent, Counselor Thornbull."

Mr. Thornbull nodded, then cast a smug grin at Mason's table. "Thank you, Your Honor." And then he was off again, talking about Mason's delinquent middle school years.

The door to the room opened and Mason glanced back to see Crew slip inside. He walked softly to the front and took a chair next to Mr. Thomas, whispering something to him.

Mr. Thomas nodded and whispered back.

Mason waited until they were done. "What's going on?"

"We might have caught a break," Mr. Thomas said.

"Counselor Thomas?"

The table looked up at the judge. "Yes, Your Honor?"

"Is there something you wish to share?" the older man asked with a raise of his bushy eyebrows.

"Not yet, Your Honor."

The judge nodded. "Then perhaps you could offer Counselor Thornbull enough respect to be quiet during his presentation?"

"Of course, Your Honor."

Mason felt a nerve ticking in his jaw and saw a corresponding one on Mr. Thomas. This judge hadn't been overly friendly since they walked in this morning. It felt as if he was against Mason before they'd even met and it didn't bode well for their keeping the will in tact.

But what did Crew say to Mr. Thomas?

Whatever it was, not knowing was bugging Mason. The whole situation had been falling apart and if they had something good, Mason wanted to know. He looked back to see Ethan, Jayden and Gavin all waiting for their chance to speak on his behalf. They offered him small smiles, which Mason returned. He was grateful they were there, but it was hard to have them listen to every mistake he'd ever made in his life. He'd be lucky if they didn't turn on him by the time they answered questions.

"Thank you, Counselor," the judge said, leaning back lazily in his seat. "Counselor Thomas…here is your opportunity."

Mr. Thornbull sat down and whispered with Mason's parents for a few moments before settling into his seat confidently.

Mason tore his eyes away when his father looked over. There was something decidedly sad in his dad's eyes. Like he was apologizing for their mother, but it was too late for that. They were in court and Timothy Turley had apparently decided not to keep his wife from cutting ties with all their children.

Any respect Mason had had for his dad began to wither. While ultimately, Patricia Turley was her own woman, making her own decisions, sitting by his wife's side meant he supported her, which also meant he didn't support his children.

"Thank you, Your Honor," Mr. Thomas said, standing. "We'd like to present a few character witnesses, if you please." He turned around. "Mr. Ethan Markle, will you please come forward?"

Ethan gave Mason a discreet wink as he walked up and was sworn in.

The questioning began and Mason sighed in relief when Ethan worked hard to make Mason sound as good as possible. Mason owed his friend a steak dinner out. Probably several of them.

Slowly, the minutes continued to tick by as Mr. Thomas worked.

He led Ethan through scenarios and memories they had planned out ahead of time, sharing Mason's strengths and trying to avoid his weaknesses.

The whole process was tedious and slow and from the look on the judge's face, Mason also felt like it wasn't working. The judge looked ready to fall asleep, instead of being interested in anything the defense had to say.

"Does the prosecution have anything to ask?" the judge finally remarked, letting Mason know he was awake.

"Not at this time," Mr. Thornbull said, rising slightly from his chair.

Mason blew out a breath. Good. Maybe the stories from his friends would stick if Mr. Thornbull didn't pick it all apart. Because right now, this was the only thing he had going in his favor.

His hand curled into a fist on his lap. He'd already lost one woman he loved… He prayed that heaven would let him keep the other.

CHAPTER 25

Butterflies were dancing a jig in Harper's stomach as she arrived at the courthouse. Reality was setting in and the fact that she'd just thrown everything away to help a man who didn't want her was giving her cold feet.

What did she hope to gain from this? Mason wouldn't suddenly stop regretting their time together. Layla would still belong to someone else. Her painting would never make it to California. Her mother would still cut off her funds.

Harper laid her forehead against the steering wheel. Maybe if she hurried, she could find another post office? One close enough to this town to allow her to still send the painting. It was sitting in the back of the car, almost ready to be shipped. She could finish it at the post office and mail it off. Was it possible to salvage the situation?

Layla needs you.

A small sob broke through Harper's lips and she clamped her jaw shut to avoid any more. This wasn't about her. She needed to remember that. Mason didn't want her for a girlfriend, but he still probably needed a friend, and right now he *definitely* needed an advocate. Layla deserved a warm and loving home and the only way for that to happen was for Harper to march inside and tell the court everything.

She wasn't naive enough to think she'd get away without sharing parts of her she wanted to keep hidden. The judge would want to know her relationship with Mason, meaning it would certainly come out that she was his ex-girlfriend, and considering she was still in love with him, she was positive there would be no way to hide that either. Somehow...they'd all be able to tell. It was still written all over her face when she looked in the mirror.

Layla needs you.

She sucked in a deep breath through her nose. She could survive this. She might not thrive, but Harper knew she'd survive and for now, that would have to be enough. Layla deserved the chance to be raised with love and that was on Harper's shoulders.

She straightened, forced thoughts of post offices and paintings out of her head and stepped out of her car. She walked inside with her head high, despite not really being dressed for the occasion. *Fake it 'til you make it.* This would have to be her motto today.

Her flip flops slapped against the tile floor and she stopped at the information desk to ask which room she needed to enter. Pausing just outside the courtroom, Harper sent a prayer heavenward and threw back her shoulders. This was it. She would do what she could...for Layla.

She slipped inside quietly, and noticed immediately that Jayden was sitting up front, being questioned.

Harper sat in a seat just in front of the door. An older man, who was speaking to Jayden, glanced her way and gave a subtle nod, which Harper returned. She was going to guess that it was Mr. Thomas, the lawyer Crew had mentioned.

Her eyes traveled over the rest of the room and she saw the back of Mason's head. He was sitting next to a man of similar coloring, but not quite as large. *That must be Crew.* The two heads bent together every once in a while and exchanged whispers, but otherwise the room was quiet and fairly empty.

A well dressed couple sat to the left with a man in an expensive suit. *The Turleys.* Mrs. Turley looked like she'd come straight from a high end fashion show and Harper could only imagine how well a toddler would fit into that world.

"Thank you, Mr. Gordon," Mr. Thomas said.

When the prosecution turned down a chance for questions, Mr. Thomas turned to the judge. "I have one more character witness I'd like to bring up," he explained.

The other lawyer stood. "I don't show any more on the docket."

Mr. Thomas acknowledged the man. "I realize that, but in this case, we had a last minute schedule opening." He waved a hand toward Harper. "Ms. Woodson was previously unavailable, but she managed to work us into her schedule, for which we're grateful."

Harper stood, not missing how Mason's head had jerked around and his jaw dropped. She gave a tiny wave to Jayden, Ethan and Gavin, who were sitting together closer to the front of the room, as she walked forward.

"Your Honor—"

The judge held up a hand. "I'm willing to hear what she has to say," he said. He nodded at Harper. "Take a seat, please, Ms. Woodson."

After all was settled, Harper kept her eyes on Mr. Thomas. She wouldn't be able to keep going if she looked at Mason.

"Ms. Woodson," Mr. Thomas said kindly. "Would you please tell us your relationship with Mr. Turley? Mr. Mason Turley?"

Harper nodded jerkily. This was exactly what she had expected. "I'm…his ex-girlfriend."

"His *ex*-girlfriend?" Mr. Thomas repeated.

Harper nodded.

"Then tell us, Ms. Woodson. Why would you come to a custody battle such as this on behalf of someone you're no longer dating?"

Harper took one last breath, forcing her chest to open and relax. "Because Mason Turley is one of the best men I've ever known and if anyone in this room wants Layla to have even the smallest chance at a wonderful life…they'll leave her right where she is."

The prosecutor stood and started to shout, and it took the judge a few moments to calm him down before he turned to Harper. "I'm guessing you spent a lot of time with Mr. Turley and the girl?" he asked.

"Yes."

"You saw them interact on multiple occasions?"

"Yes," Harper said again.

"And do you find him to be neglectful?" the judge pressed. "The question here is whether she is in danger because Mr. Turley is not yet ready for the responsibility of raising a child."

"He wasn't ready," Harper said softly. "No one is ready to have a two year old thrust on them and go from a completely single life to one where they're responsible for a toddler." She leaned forward, adding emphasis to her words. "But I was with Mason from the beginning and I watched him grow, change and adapt. He not only would put Layla's safety above his own, but his desire to give her a good life, one filled with happiness and love, cannot be matched." She purposefully darted her eyes toward Mr. and Mrs. Turley, then back to the judge. "Not by anyone."

The judge leaned back, studying her. "You and he obviously didn't work out, yet you seem like a very nice young woman, Ms. Woodson. Do you really believe he's capable of loving that little girl?"

Harper knew the answer to this, but it would expose the very inner workings of her heart to say it. *For Layla.* "Your Honor," she said softly. "Anyone, whether adult or child, who manages to have Mason Turley's love, can count themselves the very luckiest of individuals. It's worth fighting for."

* * *

SOMEONE NEEDED to hold Mason back. In a minute, he was going to rush across the room and grab Harper, kissing her until she didn't know up from down, and then he was going to beg her for forgiveness until her muddled brain accepted him into her life once more.

"Easy," Crew muttered out of the corner of his mouth. "There'll be time for that later."

Mason started. "Please tell me I didn't say any of that out loud," he whispered back.

Crew quietly snorted. "No, but the look on your face isn't lost on me."

Mason tried to force his emotions into compliance, but it was a losing battle. Why had Harper come? Why had she been willing to drive all the way up here and spend her day testifying on his behalf when he'd done nothing to earn her loyalty?

Because she's an angel.

It seemed like every time he saw her, the term angel became more and more relevant. He had no idea what was going to happen with Layla and the custody of her, but Mason knew one thing for sure. Layla or no Layla, he couldn't let Harper go. He'd thought he could do it. He'd thought losing Layla would take away his chance for happiness with the beautiful artist, but seeing her again brought all his feelings back to life.

She's worth fighting for.

She sounded so confident, so put together and honest as she spoke of his virtues. By the time Mr. Thomas finished, the very air in the courtroom had changed.

"Mr. Thornbull?" the judge asked.

For the first time since the defense began, the lawyer stood. "Yes, I do have a few questions," he said with a tight smile.

Mr. Thomas walked away and sat down next to Mason. "I don't know why you let her go, but I hope you know that I think you're an idiot."

"I am," Mason admitted. "And I'm hoping she likes idiots."

"She's still in love with you," Crew said from his other side. "Any fool can see that."

Hope surged forward, but Mason held it in check. He wouldn't put the cart before the horse this time. Too often in the past, he'd decided Harper's response before giving her a chance to give her own. He'd controlled his future by simply holding back and he wasn't going to do that anymore. This was exactly what Crew had been talking about.

There was every chance that Harper wouldn't take him back, and in all honesty, he wouldn't blame her.

His words at the hospital had been aimed to hurt. It was the only way he knew to get the always-helping Harper to leave. Small excuses would only have given her more of an opportunity to serve. He'd had to cut the ties completely and his words had been nothing but lies.

How could he ever regret his time with her? His dreams weren't filled with diapers and crashing toddlers... They were full of a stunning artist who was one of the best things to ever happen in his life.

How he had overlooked her for so long while they were merely friends, he couldn't begin to understand, but he was willing to make up for lost time now...as long as Harper was willing to let him.

"Thank you, Ms. Woodson," the judge said. "You may go."

Mason sat up straighter. His wandering mind had missed the whole conversation between her and Mr. Thornbull. Looking over, Mason noticed that the lawyer didn't seem quite as smug as before and he prayed it was because Harper's testimony had gone in Mason's favor.

Mr. Thomas patted his back before standing. "Thank you, Ms. Woodson. We appreciate your time."

Harper nodded, and then she gave a small smile to the judge, Crew and the boys in the back, but not once did her eyes meet his.

Crew chuckled softly. "You've got your work cut out for you."

"That's the understatement of the century," Mason grumbled. He sighed. He deserved that. He actually deserved a lot more than being ignored, but in the least, he deserved her disdain.

"We will take a short recess where I will look over the evidence presented," the judge said. "When I have made my decision, we will come back and settle the matter." The room stood and the judge left in a door through the back.

Mason watched him go, knowing half of his future went with the old man.

"Nothing to do now but wait," Crew muttered.

Their parents walked by and Mason noted that his mother ignored him even more studiously than Harper did. His father, however, paused. "Mason," he began.

Mason raised an eyebrow. "Dad."

Timothy Turley hesitated, then shrugged. "You know how your mother gets."

Mason nodded. "I do. But also know that you don't have to agree with her."

"I don't agree with this," his dad said with a huff. "Having Aimee and your mother fight for eighteen years was bad enough. I'm not ready for another two decades of it."

"Then why didn't you stop her?" Crew asked, stepping up to Mason's shoulder. "Being here means you're supporting her." He shook his head in disgust. "You do realize any relationship you had with us is over, right?"

Their dad's face fell. "I'm not trying to choose sides."

"You already have," Mason said in a low tone. "And in a family matter like this, you can't not choose sides. There are only two choices for Layla. With you or with me. One side or the other."

Their dad sighed and rubbed his forehead, looking older than he had only a few minutes before. "I tried to stop her, but she wouldn't listen." He splayed his hands. "She's my wife."

"Yeah...and Layla's your granddaughter," Mason shot back.

"And Mason's your *son*," Crew added.

Their dad nodded sadly and walked away.

Somehow, it felt more final than it should have. A little voice in the back of his head told Mason that this courtroom would determine whether or not he ever saw his father again, but the notion felt ridiculous.

A low whistle caught his attention and he turned to see his friends waiting. "And I thought Aspen brought drama into the family," Jayden said with a half smile. He reached out and shook Mason's hand. "I'm sorry about all this, man. It stinks."

Mason nodded. "It does, but I'm grateful you're here. Thanks for taking the time to speak on my behalf."

"Not sure why we even came," Gavin said with a grin. Of all their friends, he was the closest in size to Mason, being a firefighter who enjoyed staying in shape between runs on the truck. "Harper put all our testimonies to shame." He leaned in. "Was I hearing things, or did she say she was your *ex*-girlfriend?"

"You heard right," Mason admitted, rubbing the back of his neck.

"When the heck did that happen?" Ethan jumped in. "You were together the night we all met Layla, right?"

Mason nodded. "It's…a long story."

Ethan's right eyebrow rose high. "From your tone, I doubt it's a happy one."

"No…it's a story of how stupid I am."

Jayden chuckled, then shrugged. "Sorry. But I think every guy in existence has a story like that."

"Mason!" Mr. Thomas came rushing back into the room. "He's ready."

"Wait…what? Who? The judge?"

Mr. Thomas nodded and settled himself, standing at the table while Mason's parents and their lawyer came back in as well. "Get ready men, your fate is being decided now."

CHAPTER 26

*H*arper tugged her wagon through the sand. For the umpteenth time, it got stuck and she had to jerk, nearly knocking over her canvas which was balanced precariously on the top. "Stupid sand," she muttered. Her anger was still simmering even though it had been two days since her court appearance.

She didn't know exactly what she had been expecting, but at least a small part of her thought someone would let her know what had happened with Layla. If Mason got her back, wouldn't Crew have called? Or just texted? Texting was fine. Then she wouldn't have to listen to a voice that was a little too similar to Mason's for comfort.

Instead, Harper had been home, trying to spend these last few days of freedom as productively as possible. She had an interview tomorrow with the school for the position of art teacher. She'd also heard back from a fabric store who was looking for someone to manage their yarn department.

Crocheting and knitting weren't high on Harper's artistic talents list, but she felt like it was something she could handle. The income was enough to pay the bills if she lived simply and she'd still have some time to paint and try to turn her hobby into a career.

Her mother hadn't taken the news well. In fact, part of Harper's bad mood came from the phone blow-up she'd experienced just yesterday morning when she'd admitted her lack of painting entry.

While Harper hadn't confessed everything to her mother, she'd told her the pertinent parts. The story of her and Mason, and why she hadn't finished her painting, had *not* been pertinent.

It wasn't like telling her mother about Mason would change the outcome. Mason still wouldn't want her. Harper would still have confessed everything in a courtroom. And she still wouldn't have any idea what had happened to Layla.

With one last jerk, Harper managed to get the wagon through the sand and into the place where she was hoping to paint. She'd have to take advantage of this time before her daylight hours were taken up with other work. If she worked at the school, at least she'd have her weekends free to paint, but if she worked at the store, she couldn't even guarantee that. Customers didn't always wait until Monday.

Harper set up her easel and began putting everything into place. Her small table, her paints, her canvas...lastly she plopped a stool in the sand and sat down, grabbing her sketchbook. She could do a few sketches first, things she'd be able to paint from memory later when she didn't have time to sit by the ocean.

She opened the book and Layla's large eyes greeted her. Harper huffed out a defeated breath. How she missed that girl. Layla would never know what Harper went through to try and help her, but that was okay. Harper didn't need the recognition. All she wanted was closure.

"Soon," she assured herself. Surely she would know something soon.

She traced her finger down Layla's cheek, then couldn't resist doing the same to the broad outline of Mason's shoulder. There was another person who wouldn't understand what Harper had given up. Not that Mason would care, but sometimes it hurt to know he'd never understand. Harper didn't want praise, but at least some mutual understanding would be nice. At least knowing he wasn't disgusted with her, or that he wouldn't turn away if she ever walked into the same room.

She shook her head. "Wishful thinking, Harp. Time to get your head out of the clouds and back on the ground where it belongs." She began flipping pages to get to a blank spot, but the loose picture of Layla caught the breeze and fluttered again. "Crud!" Harper threw the book in the wagon and ran after the loose sheet.

It slapped into a leg and Harper paused. A large hand reached down, picking it up, and Harper followed the hand, gasping when she realized who it was. Her heart slammed against her chest and Harper stumbled back a step or two, as if distance would help her gain control of herself.

"Hello, Angel," Mason said carefully.

Layla squealed and reached for Harper, but she tightened her fists behind her back. "Mason."

Layla bucked and Mason set her down. Her tiny legs struggled in the sand, but eventually she crossed the cavern between the adults and Harper picked her up. A long sigh left her as she cuddled the little one close. "I missed you," Harper breathed, taking in the sweet scent of baby shampoo. She kissed Layla's head and fought back tears. The next couple days were going to be horrific, but oh…the moment was worth it.

As usual, Layla didn't respond verbally, but she bounced, smiled and squeezed Harper around the throat until Harper was sure she'd suffocate.

Mason cleared his throat and Harper forced herself to look up.

"I see you got her back."

Mason smiled and nodded. "Yeah. Thanks to you."

Harper shrugged. "I didn't do so much."

He raised an eyebrow. "No? You didn't give up your chance to enter that competition down in California in order to come to my… our rescue?"

Harper's eyes bugged open. "How did you hear about that?"

Mason took a step forward. "And you didn't lose your chance at regaining your trust money by not entering the competition?"

Harper pinched her lips together. "I see someone's been talking to

Aspen." It had to have been her. Riley, Maeve and Aspen were the only ones who knew the story and Aspen was the biggest talker.

Mason's huge shoulders shrugged. "I thought it good to come prepared." He looked down and Harper realized he was still holding the sketch.

Her pulse skipped. "Um...thanks for catching that. Let me just—" She bit back a curse when he opened the paper and studied it.

"It's beautiful," he said in a low tone. When his eyes came up, they were shining. "She'll adore it."

"Why are you here?" Harper demanded. Her emotions were at a breaking point. She needed him to say his piece and then leave. Layla pulled on her hair and Harper gently broke it free. It seemed some things never changed.

"First of all..." Mason took another step, causing Harper's heart to skip another beat. "I wanted to say thank you." He nodded toward Layla. "Your testimony was a key factor in the judge letting me keep her. I owe it all to you."

"It was nothing," Harper replied. She tried to set Layla down, but the little girl clung like a monkey. Harper sighed. "You'll have to take her. Thanks for searching me out. I'm thrilled that it worked out. She really will be better off with you than your mother."

"I'm not done," Mason said, taking another step. The distance between them had closed to the point where Harper could have touched him with her fingertips if she'd been so inclined.

Her fingers twitched at the thought, but she kept her hands firmly around Layla. "Oh?" How much torture could a person take before they simply broke into too many pieces to fix?

"I also wanted to let you know that the custody came with a condition."

Harper paused.

"I had to have Layla checked out by a doctor within twenty-four hours," he said. "They especially wanted to check on her growth milestones."

Harper swallowed hard. Layla's speech. Something was wrong with it. "And?" she asked shakily.

Mason shook his head. "I don't have answers yet. We went to a pediatrician yesterday, but they're sending us to a specialist in Portland. The appointment is next week." He paused. "But I thought you'd like to know we're working on it."

Harper nodded. "Good. I'm glad she'll be getting the care she needs."

He shuffled forward a little more. "And I also have a proposition for you."

Her heart fluttered. Had he changed his mind? Did he actually have feelings for her? Or was this all about her help in court? How would she know the difference?

"I'd like to hire you."

* * *

OKAY...MAYBE his plan wasn't turning out quite how he had hoped. Instead of looking interested, Harper looked ready to run. He put up his hands. "Hear me out?" he begged. He had a reason for his proposal. He really did. He'd spent all his spare time working this out, but it wouldn't matter if Harper refused to listen.

Harper stepped back, creating more distance where he had closed it. "Fine." She shifted Layla.

Nope. This wouldn't do. He took a big enough step to put them toe to toe. Harper gasped and looked up. "I need a nanny for Layla," he said gruffly. He was fighting the urge to touch her. Being this close was the best kind of torture and he let the anticipation work inside him. Crew, Aspen, even Riley, had assured Mason that Harper still had feelings for him. He was hanging his whole future on the hope that it was true.

"A nanny," Harper said flatly.

Mason nodded. "But there's a problem."

She raised an eyebrow.

"I'm a little picky." He reached out and tucked a piece of hair behind her ear, letting his fingers trail along her jawline. He didn't miss the goosebumps or the tiny shiver she tried to contain. His hopes rose. "I want Layla to spend time with someone who loves her."

"Everyone loves her," Harper said breathlessly.

Mason shook his head. "Not like you do. Only you would be willing to sacrifice your own wants for her own."

Harper blinked rapidly and dropped his gaze.

Mason used his knuckle to pull her chin back up so she was forced to look at his sincerity. "I want someone who understands her. Someone who will play, tickle, laugh and love her the way she deserves to be loved. The way every child deserves to be loved."

"Any nanny would eventually do that," Harper said thickly. "It doesn't have to be me."

"I knew the moment you first stood in my kitchen feeding her mac and cheese that your relationship with her would be wonderful."

Harper sniffled.

"And I knew the moment you insisted on helping me survive becoming an instant father that ours would be special as well."

A flurry of emotions danced through her glassy eyes. "I… What do you mean? You don't want a relationship with me."

How he wished he could take those words back. They hurt as much now as they did then, and Mason was positive they were worse for Harper. "Crew!" he called over his shoulder. It was time to pull out the big guns.

"On it!" His brother emerged from the wild grasses and hurried over with a grin. "Heya, Harper! Nice to finally meet you in person." He snatched Layla, who squealed in delight. "I'll take her." He winked. "Don't do anything I wouldn't do."

Mason rolled his eyes while Harper stood in stunned silence.

"I'm so lost."

He nodded. "I know, and I'm working on that, but first, I needed a set of eyes on Layla besides ours."

"Why?"

Okay…it was make it or break it time. "So I could do this without worrying about her." Mason cupped Harper's face and lowered his mouth to hers before he lost his nerve. Later he would be willing to swear in court that as soon as their lips met, the Earth stood still.

The broken parts of him that he was sure would never heal suddenly came alive and his chest nearly burst with the need for more. More kisses, more touching, more...Harper. His hands trailed down the soft skin of her neck and he flattened one palm against her back, pulling her into his chest. His other hand grasped her hip, anchoring her close.

He pressed forward, trying to be aware of any sign that she didn't want this, but after her initial shock, Harper rose up on tiptoe and grasped his T-shirt in her hands, pulling him down as close as she could get him.

He flexed his fingers, trying not to let his hands wander, but the exposed skin on her arms, her neck and her face was oh, so tempting. Bringing his hands up to frame her face, he pulled his mouth away and began to pepper kisses across her cheeks, her eyes, her jaw...

"I love you," he said hoarsely. "I've loved you since you showed me how to change a diaper."

Harper laughed incredulously, the sound like manna from heaven. Mason hadn't heard it in so long. "You..." She choked on her emotions. "You said you regretted our time together. You regretted *me*."

Mason stopped his ministrations and rested his forehead against hers. "I lied," he said bluntly.

"But why?" Tears began to leak down her cheeks. "I don't know what to think. I don't know—"

Mason cut her off with another kiss. He pulled back just far enough to speak. "I was scared, Harper. I was already fighting my inner voice saying that it wouldn't work between us. That I wouldn't have enough time to build a relationship with you while trying to learn how to be a father." He sighed and straightened. "Then came the pressure of the lawsuit. My mom is a formidable opponent and I was terrified she would succeed in taking Layla away."

Harper leaned forward, her forehead hitting his sternum.

"And then Layla got hurt," he whispered, bending down to kiss the top of her head. "I freaked out. It seemed like everything in my life was screaming that the little voice in the back of my head was right. Layla was hurt because I was distracted by you. I…" He swallowed. "I just wasn't able to have you both."

She lifted her head. "So you gave me up."

Mason nodded. "But I know you. I know how selfless you are and how much you love to help others. I knew that any objection I had would simply be an opportunity for you to help even more than you already had."

She shook her head, dropping her arms and stepping back.

It was like a slap to his face.

"So you hurt me." The words were flat…hard…and filled with pain.

"I did." He clenched his fists to keep from reaching for her. "I wish I could say it was just to protect Layla, but I've learned better." He closed his eyes and dropped his chin to his chest. "It was also a way of protecting me. I was so scared of losing you both that I sacrificed one to save the other."

She didn't respond.

"It was wrong," he continued, desperate for her to understand. "*I* was wrong, and I'll never be able to say sorry enough, but I'm learning." He took a long, slow breath, praying for the right words. "I had several revelations during the trial with Layla and my parents. And I realized I need to change." Her demeanor softened, so he kept going. "I don't want to live in fear. I don't want to control every aspect of my life. I don't want to lose the things most precious to me." He rested his hands gently at her waist to emphasize what he was talking about. "And I absolutely, under no circumstances, want to end up like my mother…or my father."

Her body relaxed even further. "What do you want then?"

"This." He took his time with this kiss. He might be eager to have a future with Harper, but he didn't have to rush in convincing her. She deserved every moment he could give her. Long, drawn out, emotion-heavy moments where he showed her his heart just as much as he spoke it. "And this." He tilted his head and took her mouth again at a different angle.

He loved it when her hands went behind his neck and played with his hair. It tempted him to never cut it again if she would simply keep her fingers moving through it.

They were both gasping for air when he finally pulled back. "It looks like you have those," she said softly.

"Ah, but do I have this?" He tapped at the very top of her sternum. "Because your heart is what I want most of all." He made a face. "Well...that and your forgiveness."

Harper melted into his chest again and they simply held each other for several long moments. "I think we can work something out," she finally whispered.

His heart leapt. "Do you mean it?"

She nodded, not moving from her spot. "I love you too, you know. I have from the moment I saw you playing with Layla even though you had no idea what to do with her."

Gratitude unlike anything he'd ever known worked its way through Mason. He promised himself he wouldn't take this moment for granted, or Harper for granted, ever again. "Then I guess there's one more thing I want," he said.

She looked up. "Oh? It sounds like you're getting a little greedy."

He grinned and let his finger skim along her skin as he memorized the lines of her face. "I really do want to hire you to help with Layla. I can't do it alone, you need a job you can still paint with, and I want you in my life as absolutely much as possible from here on out."

She snorted a laugh, then laughed some more. "I suppose we can talk about that one too, but I seem to remember that dating your boss isn't considered good etiquette."

"In this case, dating your boss is required."

She slapped his chest and he chuckled. "I'll think about it."

He pressed a quick kiss to the tip of her nose. "That's all I ask."

CHAPTER 27

"Do we really have to go?" Mason whined.

Harper pulled on his arm. "Yes! The party is to celebrate you keeping Layla! You can't keep the guest of honor at home!"

Mason jerked her back and Harper squeaked until her mouth was occupied by other endeavors. "Mason," she mumbled against his lips. She laughed when he pressed harder, refusing to give up. Harper shoved against his chest. Geez, the man really was Sasquatch. "Mason," she scolded. "We have to go."

"Layla's in her car seat," he murmured, kissing along her neck. He nuzzled just under her ear. "She can't get hurt or in trouble. I'm not wasting this opportunity."

Harper smiled and tilted her head, allowing him better access. "You're going to hurt Aspen's feelings. She baked all day for us."

"I have no doubt her cakes will get eaten."

"And what about the guys? Ethan and Jay and Gavin will all be wondering where you are."

Mason growled low and pulled her in tight. "Are you kidding? Every guy there is going to know exactly where I am and none of them will blame me for it."

"Mason," Harper tried again, though she was losing her desire to go. Life had been terribly busy the past month as they resettled into a routine. It was why the celebration for the custody battle was just now happening. It was the first weekend they'd had an opening in their schedule where everyone could make it.

Harper watched Layla during the day and worked around the little girl's schedule. It still meant less time for Harper to paint, but it wasn't nearly as bad as it would have been had she been working elsewhere. Plus, despite the hectic schedule, Harper had never been happier. She and Layla were only getting closer and each night, she would drive back to Mason's where they had dinner together and then Harper and Mason got some alone time after Layla went to bed. Harper was becoming more and more sleep deprived as she found herself struggling to go home. The more time she had with Mason, the harder it was to leave.

When Mason had a day with less work, he took Layla early and Harper got more work done. All in all, the shift had been fabulous and had allowed everyone to do what they loved with only a little sacrifice. Layla even had a small canvas set up in the corner of Harper's studio and sometimes they worked together, though Harper didn't usually get much done during that time. She was usually too busy trying to keep Layla from painting everything besides her own canvas.

The memories, however, were priceless to Harper and she wouldn't trade them for anything.

Layla squealed, breaking up the tender moment, and Mason finally pulled back. "Sorry," he said, his voice low and hoarse.

It sent a wonderful shiver down Harper's spine. She smiled at him. "Looks like that plan of yours to live life to the fullest is working."

Mason chuckled and kissed her forehead. "I'm a work in progress, but we'll keep at it." He straightened and when he let go of her, cold settled against Harper's body. "Let's go. I want some of that cake."

Harper rolled her eyes. "Funny how that wasn't much of a temptation only a few minutes ago." She sat down in the passenger seat and pulled down the mirror, trying to fix her hair and lipstick.

"A few minutes ago I had something else to satiate my appetite," Mason said with a smug grin.

Harper gasped. "Oh my goodness." She smacked the side of his arm. "You're naughty."

"And you're an angel," he replied.

Harper never admitted it out loud, but she loved how he called her that.

"Who knew that an angel and a devil could get along so well?" he continued.

Harper laughed and settled back in her seat. How in the world did she ever think that being a famous artist would be better than this? She still wanted to be a full-time painter, but there was no way it could compare to the peace and joy she found with Mason and Layla. They filled her in a way nothing else ever could. Though her work was wonderful, it simply didn't fill her soul.

Maeve had been right. There really wasn't a way to have it all. Sometimes she had to give in the parenting department and sometimes she had to give in the career department. Keeping all the balls in the air all the time was impossible. Learning the balance of priority was becoming one of her biggest goals and Harper was positive that they would get it all figured out. After all, she was certainly hoping to have plenty of time to practice at it.

They arrived at the bakery and climbed out of the car. "Hey, baby girl," Harper cooed as she unbuckled Layla and pulled her out of the car. "You ready to party?"

Layla wiggled to get down and Harper set her down, firmly grasping her hand. Mason took Layla's other hand and together they walked inside.

"Hey!" Aspen shouted. "They're here!"

The bakery was filled with all their friends, which meant it was practically shoulder to shoulder, and Harper couldn't help but feel grateful for all their support. They might not have been able to help much with the custody battle, but each and every person in the room was loyal to a fault and they had welcomed Layla in with open arms, giving Mason, and now Harper, a much needed boost as they took on the responsibility of a young child.

*Well...*Harper reminded herself to be honest. She was dating a man who had that responsibility, but it wasn't officially Harper's...yet. She couldn't deny that she dreamed about it though. Someday, she absolutely hoped to be Layla's mother, but that was a wish for another night.

The important part was that this group was family. Most of them came from different backgrounds, and only a few were actually blood related, but these people supported each other through everything. They'd helped Aspen and Austin when their relationship had blown up social media. And they'd rallied around Mason and Harper in their new roles in life. Something their own families, other than Crew, had failed to do themselves.

Everyone from Gavin, Jayden and Riley, to others that Harper hadn't seen in a while. Eden, who worked at her grandmother's souvenir shop, waved from the corner. Brielle, a dog groomer who was fairly new to town, was smiling widely. Quinn, who had her own antique shop and even Michael, Aspen's cousin who taught at the elementary school, was there. The whole crew, large as they were, had turned out for the occasion and Harper's chest warmed at the support.

Maeve squealed and rushed over, grabbing Harper in a hug. "I'm so happy for you three."

Harper hugged her back. She might be closer to Aspen, but Maeve was like the little sister Harper never had. "Thank you," she whispered. "We couldn't have done all this without everyone's support."

Maeve pulled back. "You two are just the cutest couple." She rolled her eyes. "A little too cute, actually. My mom has been going nuts waiting for you to get here. In fact, she's been lecturing that I'm gonna end up an old maid if I don't get moving."

"Your mom's here?" Aspen asked with a gasp. "They're home?"

Maeve nodded. "In fact..." She turned and pointed to the corner. "They wanted to come say congrats." She dropped her voice. "But Dad won't be able to handle it very long, so they won't stay all evening."

Harper smiled, then rushed over where Mrs. Harrison stood to greet her with a fierce hug. Tears pricked Harper's eyes. This is what a mother was supposed to be like. And if she ever got the chance to be one with Layla, Harper knew exactly what woman she was using for inspiration.

* * *

MASON FOLLOWED Harper's swift run across the room and relaxed when Mrs. Harrison caught her. He hadn't known they were back. He bent and scooped up Layla. "Excuse me a minute," he said to Estelle, Riley and a few others who were gathered around.

Estelle laughed. "You'll lose Layla if you go over there."

Mason shrugged. "There are worse things."

Mr. Harrison saw him coming and stood up, but Mason frowned when he noticed how pale the man was. Mr. Harrison had always been larger than life. A strong, confident man who built chocolate sculptures that made people weep. He looked thin and slightly sickly. When they shook hands, Mr. Harrison's grip was weak and shaky. "Mr. Harrison," Mason said, pushing aside his worries. He'd ask Aspen about it later. "Good to see you."

"You as well, Mason," Mr. Harrison said with a wide smile. His eyes went to Layla. "I can see you've been busy."

Mason chuckled and bounced Layla, who was back to sucking her two fingers. She stared, wide-eyed, at the Italian man in front of her. "You could say that. But I'm happy to say that Layla is here to stay. Everything's official now."

Mr. Harrison nodded and clapped Mason on the shoulder. "Congratulations. I'm sorry about your sister, but what a beautiful way for you to honor her memory."

Mason nodded, though his smile dimmed. He still wished things had been different with Aimee, but Mr. Harrison was right. This was the best thing he could do now.

"Oh my goodness, let me see that baby," Mrs. Harrison cried, stepping past Harper. She put her hands to her cheeks. "Mason...she's a living doll."

Mason leaned his head down. "Layla, this is Mama Harrison. Would you like to go see her?"

Layla looked up at him and Mason tilted his head toward the waiting woman.

"Maybe she'll warm up as the night goes on," Mrs. Harrison said in a disappointed tone. She held out her hands and wiggled her fingers. "Would you come see me, Layla?"

Layla bounced and leaned forward.

"I'll take that as a yes," Mason said and leaned over so Mrs. Harrison could take her.

"Such a sweetheart," Mrs. Harrison cooed. She fingered Layla's curls. "Her hair reminds me of my own girls." She smiled at Harper and Mason. "I think we need dessert. Excuse us!"

She bustled away and Mr. Harrison laughed before sitting back down. He sighed, giving further credence to Mason's thoughts that the man wasn't well. "That child won't sleep tonight," Mr. Harrison teased. "Calling her Mama Harrison gave Emery grandma rights. You've lost Layla for the night."

"She'll need a grandma," Harper said, leaning into Mason's side.

His arm automatically went around her. "She will," he agreed, though the words pained him. His parents had rights to see Layla, but Mason was doing what he could to keep some boundaries in place. For the foreseeable future, they would have to travel to him, and he had no intention of leaving them alone with her. If his mother ever decided to ease up, maybe the rules could change, but until then...

"Emery would never turn down the job," Mr. Harrison said.

"And she'll have a grandpa to boot," Jayden said, coming up on Mason's other side. He grinned. "Howya doin, Uncle Tony?"

Mr. Harrison scowled. "When are you going to settle down, Jayden? Some woman needs to pull that grin off your face." A twitch of his lips let everyone know he was teasing and Jayden laughed.

"Pull it off? I'm pretty sure if it was the right woman, she'd put a smile *on* my face."

Mason chuckled and Harper covered her laugh with her hand. "I can testify to that," he said.

Mr. Harrison smiled. "Glad to see you're doing well, Jay. I haven't been to see your parents yet. Everything okay?"

Jayden nodded. "Yep. The inn just keeps plugging along. You know the drill."

Mr. Harrison nodded. "I do. I've spent quite a bit of time working there myself." He relaxed. "It's nice to have the next generation taking it over, just like the bakery."

"Aspen has done so well with it," Harper assured Mr. Harrison. "You'd be so proud of her."

"I am," Mr. Harrison assured her. He pointed sideways. "Except for that. It's a monstrosity."

Mason laughed. The couch that was dubbed "The A's Place" really was horrible. But it was part of Aspen and Austin's story, so no one complained too much.

Harper smiled. "People come in just to take pictures on that sofa."

Mr. Harrison nodded. "I think I'm too old to understand."

"Are you too old for dessert?" Maeve asked, walking into the group with a plate in her hands.

Mr. Harrison reached for it, but his hands shook slightly. Clenching them into fists, he smiled sadly. "Maybe later, Maeve. Thank you."

She sat down next to him. "Nonsense. Mom's showing off Layla like she's the only baby in the world. Someone might as well take care of you." She began to cut the cake and Mason took that as his cue to move.

"Good to see you, Mr. Harrison."

The middle aged man smiled, though it wasn't as bright as before. "You too, Mason. Come by the house sometime. I have a feeling I haven't heard the whole story about Layla, and I'd be interested."

Mason nodded and took Harper's hand. "We will. Thanks." He guided her away. "Somehow I don't think he'll eat if we're all watching."

"I know," Harper said under her breath. "It's been hard on him."

"Do you know what it is?"

"He has Parkinson's."

Mason stopped. "What?"

Harper nodded. "Yeah. It's why he quit sculpting. His hands shook too much." She glanced around, then leaned in. "That's why they were in Italy. He was seeing family before he reaches the point where he can't travel."

Harper pulled Mason back into motion. His heart ached for the Harrison family. Why did bad things have to happen to good people?

"Come on," Harper encouraged. "It's a party tonight. Leave them be."

Mason nodded. "You're right. Tonight's a celebration." Instead of aching, his heart began to beat a little faster. Tonight was a celebration and he had something he was hoping would be worth celebrating even more than just keeping Layla. Tonight he was hoping to build a complete family, not a partial one.

CHAPTER 28

"She ate the paint!" Riley squealed. "Eww!"

Harper shrugged. "I mean, I got out what I could, but yeah...her teeth were blue for a couple of days."

Gavin laughed. "Kids eat anything."

Jayden was standing behind Harper's chair. "You should have brought her over. I'd have taken pictures for you."

Harper looked over her shoulder. "I'm sure she would have loved that when she's a teenager. Can you imagine Mason bringing them out on her first date?"

Aspen skidded up to the group. "Hey, I forgot to ask you about her appointment last week. What did the doctor say?"

Harper smiled. They had gone to a specialist in Portland a couple of times in the last few weeks and were finally on their way to some answers.

"Ooh, is this about her speech?" Riley asked. She crossed her legs in the chair, curled up like one of her cats. "What did they say?"

"It looks like she has some hearing loss," Harper explained. "We're still running tests, and there'll be more doctors to see, but they think with a set of hearing aids, they'll have her chatting our ears off in no time."

Aspen smiled. "I'm so glad. Not that I want her to have a disability, but still…at least this is one we have medical advances for."

Harper nodded. "I get it and totally agree. She's not completely deaf, but it's enough she has a hard time forming words. She'll more than likely have some speech therapy and the hearing aids, and then hopefully she'll be able to live a perfectly normal life."

"Speaking of…" Mason walked up to Harper's side. Layla was drooping against his chest. "I think someone is wearing out."

Harper stood. "Looks like our evening is about over." She reached out to take Layla, but Mason turned.

"Not quite yet," he said. "Uncle Ethan?"

Ethan came sauntering up. "I love saving a damsel in distress." He held out his hands to Layla. "Come on, Princess. Let the adults talk for a minute."

Harper frowned. "Mason, she'll be cranky all day tomorrow if we don't get her home."

Mason nodded. "It'll be worth it." He scratched at his beard, his hand shaking slightly.

The room had gone quiet and Harper looked around. Her friends were all smiling, but had backed up, leaving her and Mason alone. "What's going on?" Her heart began to pound and when she turned back to Mason, she gasped.

He looked up at her from his place on the ground where he knelt on one knee and gave her a sheepish grin. "So…it wasn't just the schedule that had us pushing back the date for this little party."

"Mason." She put her trembling hands to her mouth. Harper had assumed it would take them a lot longer to get to this point in their relationship. Not that she was complaining. There was nothing Harper wanted in life than to be Mason's wife and Layla's mother. She loved them both with everything in her and making them an official family would only be icing on the cake.

Mason held out his hands, waiting for hers, and Harper obliged. "Harper Grace Woodson." He smiled at her. "I love you. I love you with everything in me." He chuckled. "When we first dated, I thought I would have to split my heart between you and Layla and I struggled to feel like it would be right. Like you deserved better than that. It was part of why I moved so slowly once I realized I had feelings for you."

Her eyes began to mist over.

"But the longer we're together, the more I realize that's not how it works. Somehow, it seems the more I love you and Layla, the more love I have to give."

There was a soft chuckle through the room when one of the women sighed. Harper didn't even bother looking to see who it was. She couldn't look away from Mason's golden eyes.

"I want to continue to give that love to you…to Layla…and to any more people we add to our family over the years." He swallowed hard. "I know you gave up a lot to be with us. You sacrificed your career and your trust fund in order to help me keep Layla and that's only part of why I call you my angel. You were truly heaven-sent." He glanced sideways and Harper followed his gaze.

Jayden walked up with an envelope and handed it to Mason before scurrying back to his spot. The camera around his neck said he was capturing everything.

Mason dropped her hands and pulled out a stack of papers. "I don't have the power to bring back your trust fund. And I'm afraid I wouldn't even know where to begin in trying to further your art career, but I'm hoping this…" He handed her the papers. "Will be a start."

Harper scanned the page, her eyes growing wider and wider as she realized what it was. "A lease?" she asked hoarsely. "You…you bought me a storefront?"

"It has a large room in front for an exhibit and a bathroom plus two rooms in the back," Mason hurried to say. "I figured one could be an office and the other…"

"A nap room?" Harper said thickly. The tears were running freely now. She hadn't gotten into the other exhibits she'd tried for, so Mason had bought her an exhibit of her own. Right off Main Street where she could sell her paintings year-round to any tourists that came through town. She was so overwhelmed that her mind was having a hard time staying in the present moment. "I...don't know what to say."

Reaching into his pocket, Mason pulled out a velvet box and popped it open. A large solitaire winked up at her. "Say you'll marry me," Mason said. He grinned. "And just for the record, the storefront isn't conditional on your answer."

Harper laughed through her tears and a few others in the room did the same. "Mason, I would like nothing more than to be your wife and Layla's mother. I've spent most of my adult life believing that my career was what would bring me happiness and I was determined to see it through before I got involved with anyone, but Layla's arrival helped break me of that notion." She shook her head. "You two are my joy, and my painting simply makes it all a little sweeter." She leaned down, cupping his bearded face, and kissed him. "I would love to marry you." She held up the papers. "And I'd love to open an exhibit."

Mason slipped the ring on her finger and stood up, gathering her into his arms.

The papers were being crushed between their chests, but Harper didn't care. Shouts, cheers and hollers surrounded them as she and Mason continued their own little celebration.

"I think you might be giving Layla more of an education than she needs," Aspen whispered in Harper's ear before clearing her throat.

Harper pulled back from Mason, a smile on her heated face. "Sorry."

He kissed her again. "I'm not. There'll be more of that just as soon as she's in bed."

Harper laid her head against his chest. "I can't wait."

* * *

MASON NODDED and smiled as congratulations flew at him like golf balls on the green, but not once did he let go of Harper. He couldn't. Finally, *finally*, she was his. Not just for the evening, not for a few minutes during naptime...but forever. As soon as they were married, he wouldn't have to say goodnight anymore or swap off babysitting duties. They'd all live together and all their moments would be shared.

He rested his head against the top of hers. "Thank you," he whispered when there was a break in the friend line.

"For what?" she asked, tightening her hold around his chest.

"For being my angel," he began. "For loving me." He pulled back so he could look her in the eye. "For agreeing to be part of our family." He kissed her, slowly and tenderly. "For loving Layla and not letting my short sightedness stop this moment from happening."

Harper smiled up at him, her eyes glistening with tears. "Thank you for coming for me," she whispered. "Thank you for opening my eyes to something more important than working myself into an early grave." She patted his chest. "And thank you for each and every moment that led up to this one. I'll always treasure them."

"Even the bad ones?" he teased.

"Even the bad ones," she confirmed. "Those are the ones in particular that make this moment so sweet."

"Here she is!" Ethan called out, bringing Layla into their little chat. "Here you go, Mommy."

Harper laughed and pulled Layla onto her hip.

"Okay, look this way!" Jayden called. He pushed a few people out of the way until the space was cleared. Then pulled up his camera. "Smile! You too, Princess."

Ethan made faces behind Jayden while his finger flew, snapping pictures from all angles.

Mason felt as if his chest would burst. Who would have thought that he would be standing here, taking pictures with his *family* of all things? The man who had spent years trying to hunt down his sister, whose biological family was breaking apart at the seams, now had a new one. One built on love and respect.

He was grateful Jayden had the foresight to bring his camera because Mason knew he wanted to remember this moment forever. Being an instant father wasn't the plan he'd had in mind, but in the end, he wouldn't trade a bit of it. Layla had opened his eyes and Harper had opened his heart. He couldn't imagine a better gift.

"Alrighty," Harper said, bouncing a whimpering Layla. "I think she's had enough."

Mason nodded. "Sounds good." Putting his hand on her lower back, they began walking to the front door, saying their goodbyes along the way. The night air was cool when they managed to get outside and Harper shivered.

"Ooh, I'm so ready for summer."

"It wasn't long ago you said you were ready for spring." He took Layla and buckled her into her car seat.

"Heat," Harper demanded. "I just want heat, okay?"

"Heard you loud and clear, ma'am," Mason declared. He finished with Layla, then shut the car door. But before reaching for Harper's to let her in, he caged her up against the car. "I have a great way of warming you up," he whispered a hair's breadth from her lips.

"I'll just bet you do," Harper whispered back. Instead of waiting for him to come to her, she leaned in the fraction of an inch and took control.

Mason let her have her way for all of three seconds before he wrapped his arms around her and took over. He planned to spend every moment showing her just how much she meant to him... starting right now.

"We need to put Layla to bed," Harper said, pulling back. She traced his lips, sending a sharp shot of electricity down his chest. "Can we continue this on the couch?"

"Your wish is my command." Mason got her settled, then walked around to the driver's seat. He didn't even try to stop the too-wide smile on his face. He knew life would be difficult at times. They would have to deal with Layla's hearing loss, their relationships with their parents would have to be handled and sometimes life simply had a way of kicking people in the teeth, but right now, right here...everything was perfect. This moment was perfect and Mason planned to have many more moments just like this before his time with Harper was over.

She'd been right. Everything, all the good and the bad, had led up to this evening being what it was. He had been through purgatory and now he was reaping a reward…and it was far sweeter than he could have ever hoped for.

EPILOGUE

Maeve smiled and handed a plate full of cake to the next person coming down the table.

"It was a beautiful wedding, wasn't it?" the older woman said with a smile.

"It was," Maeve agreed. "Absolutely stunning." And it had been. Layla had been the perfect little flower girl, Harper had been a stunning bride and Mason, the big teddy bear, had been a handsome and doting groom. The event was everything fairy tales were made of.

She sighed, pushed up her glasses and continued to pass out cake. Maeve absolutely did not want to admit that she was jealous…but she was jealous. She had felt the same way at Aspen's reception.

Maeve knew she was excellent at hiding it, but she was lonely. She spent her time behind a calculator and a set of glasses she didn't really need, trying to convince herself that they were all the company she needed, but each night when she went to sleep…the heavy need for more crushed her chest like a two ton weight.

"Oh my gosh, did you see him?"

Maeve frowned at her sister. "Who?"

Estelle sidled closer and dropped her voice. "Mason's brother… Crew." She shook her head slowly. "I think that might be the most handsome man I've ever met." She fanned herself playfully. "Too bad he doesn't live here."

Maeve nodded. "Yeah...Cali's a bit of a commute."

Estelle sighed longingly, her eyes still focused across the room. "Guess that just means I should make the most of tonight, right?"

Maeve knocked their shoulders together. "Right. Go get 'em, Tiger."

Estelle scowled before waltzing away.

Maeve deflated when her sister left. If only she had the excuse of a long commute...

Laughter caught her attention and she couldn't help but look. Maeve knew she shouldn't. After all, she knew exactly who was having such a grand time. But as always, the sound of Ethan's voice drew her like a scientist to a boiling beaker.

Ethan was dancing on the small wooden floor that had been placed in the middle of the reception hall for that exact purpose. Layla was in his arms and the little flower girl was leaning back, while he spun them in a circle. Dark curls flew through the air and then Ethan would stop, pull the toddler in and together they would laugh.

Maeve's eyes roamed his face. She could have described it in her sleep. A strong, slightly square jaw that was clean shaven today, though he often left just enough scruff to be attractive. Straight, white teeth that he flashed around all the time, as if his smile wasn't enough to stop traffic. Medium brown hair that he kept just a little too long, which was perfect for showing off the surfing highlights he got every summer. Instead of large, bulky muscles like Mason had, Ethan was lean, but she'd seen him without his shirt on enough times to know there wasn't an ounce of fat on his body.

He was the exact type of man that made women flock to surfing competitions. And his easy-going personality caused those same flocks to stay.

Except when he leaves you.

Maeve jolted when she realized that Ethan had caught her. His hazel eyes were more green than brown today against his suit and when their gazes met, he paused, his smile drooping every so slightly.

Normally, Maeve looked away immediately, but today she felt caught. Like a tractor beam that refused to let go. It wasn't until Ethan's face turned hopeful and he started to walk in her direction that Maeve was able to gain control.

"Would you like some cake?" she asked, forcing a smile at the next person in line. She studiously ignored the hard stare from the most handsome man she'd ever known, no offense to Mason's brother.

It didn't matter that she had known him since he was a young boy. It didn't matter that he ate dinner at their house three times a week. It didn't matter that at one point she had worshiped the ground he walked on. He had lost her trust back when they were teenagers and Maeve didn't have the ability to give it back to him.

His choices that fateful day had nearly cost her her life and Maeve was determined not to let his current choices cost her anything else.

According to her family, Maeve was simply too serious for playful Ethan. She was irritated with his happy-go-lucky attitude and only wanted to spend her time crunching numbers.

Maeve did like numbers. They made sense. She always knew what she was going to get when she added or subtracted or ran formulas. There were never surprises and numbers never left her behind with a laugh or almost killed her.

She pushed up her glasses again. Sometimes they drove her nuts. She didn't need them. Her vision was just fine, but as she'd gotten older and Ethan had refused to leave her alone, she'd adopted wearing them as a way to create a barrier between her and the persistent neighbor.

It hadn't worked as well as she'd hoped, but Maeve was too stubborn to admit it and stop wearing them.

"You should take a break and come dance."

Maeve jumped, nearly dropping the plate she was handing out. "Ethan," she scolded. "You nearly gave me a heart attack."

"So you *do* know my name," he said with a grin, stepping a little closer. He must have passed Layla off to someone else, since his arms were currently empty.

The soft scent of his cologne hit her and Maeve had to forcefully stop herself from leaning closer. Fate must have a daily laugh at her expense, causing Maeve to fall in love with the one man she couldn't trust. It was a cruel, cruel joke and Maeve wanted to be free of it.

If only she knew how.

She'd been fighting her growing feelings for years and somehow, over time, they only became more solidified, despite the incident between them.

"Maeve?"

She blinked, coming out of her thoughts. "I'm busy," she said tersely, turning back to the table.

"I'm pretty sure all these lovely people can pick up their own plate," he whispered in her ear.

There was no stopping or hiding the shiver that ran down her spine from his closeness. She was completely positive that if she simply gave in, all her loneliness would vanish like one of Aspen's cakes.

"Why do you fight it so hard?" he asked, a note of pleading in his voice. "Maeve..."

She straightened and stepped away, his words the reminder she needed to snap back to reality. "I'm working, Ethan. Thank you for the invite, but I'm sure you can find someone else to accompany you."

He sighed and pushed a hand through his hair, messing up the styling job he'd been sporting. "I'll catch you another time," he said, turning away.

Someday he'll get tired of trying, a voice said in the back of her head. *And then where will you be?* "Satisfied," she whispered to herself, but the word rang false. The day Ethan moved on to someone more welcoming would be like a sword through her heart, but Maeve didn't know how to let it go.

She'd almost *died,* and he'd left, breaking her heart and her confidence in him. That wasn't something easily rebuilt and each time Maeve thought of forgiving, she broke out in a cold sweat, memories of her near drowning consuming her.

She wanted to be free, but she simply didn't know how.

KEEP READING!

Keep Reading Maeve's story in

"The Sweetest Neighbor"

Made in United States
Orlando, FL
29 March 2023